MW00616501

NO
SAFE
PLACE

Also in the Michael Gannon series

Stop at Nothing

Run for Cover

Hard to Break

Also by Michael Ledwidge

The Girl in the Vault

Beach Wedding

The Narrowback

Bad Connection

Before the Devil Knows You're Dead

Cowritten with James Patterson

The Quickie

Now You See Her

Zoo

Step on a Crack

Run for Your Life

Worst Case

Tick Tock

I, Michael Bennett

Gone

Burn

Alert

Bullseye

Chase

The Dangerous Days of Daniel X

NO SAFE PLACE

A THRILLER

MICHAEL LEDWIDGE

HANOVER
SQUARE
PRESS

HANOVER
SQUARE
PRESS™

ISBN-13: 978-1-335-00041-5

No Safe Place

Hanover Square Press
22 Adelaide St. West, 41st Floor
Toronto, Ontario M5H 4E3, Canada
HanoverSqPress.com

Printed in U.S.A.

For Andrew and Justyna

PROLOGUE

GIRL GONE

1

The place that everyone at Beckford College just called The House was an off-campus dive bar in some old run-down clapboard structure on Route 4.

It had popped up the year before. It was the track team guys who had found it, they said. One of the sketchy older brothers of a townie cross-country runner was supposedly the owner of it, and more and more people had started coming and now it was THE spot.

The inside of the hundred-plus-year-old house had wide plank pine floors and huge exposed walnut beams that gave it a barnlike feel. But it was a cozy barn that was low lit at night and warm with the bodies of young people buzzing before the music got going.

Girls got dressed up, put on makeup. Guys got fresh haircuts and ironed their preppy shirts. Around eleven, the lights would drop and the DJ's laser light setup would start flashing and there would be an energy to the place, a real glow and electric excitement of healthy nice-looking college kids ready to blow off some steam as they checked each other out across a music-filled barroom.

At eleven this Thursday night, the DJ was starting out with some late 2000s pure nostalgia. Real fun stuff, Flo Rida, Ne-Yo, 3 Doors Down. Standing in the middle of the crowded bar, Olivia Ramos took a sip of her watery rum and Coke as the first jangly strains of Taylor Swift's "Our Song" started up.

Back when Taylor was still country, she thought, shaking her head. *Those were the days.*

"Woo-hoo," she called out as somebody else shrieked out a huge whistle.

Fake IDs, Thursday night bar crawls, Olivia thought as she smiled at herself in the mirror behind the bar. Now she was actually woo-hooing at random.

Olivia stirred her drink and took another sip.

If she kept up this amount of IQ drainage, soon she'd be dancing on the bar like some of the senior girls did every once in a while. Of course, that wasn't the purpose for Olivia coming up to the boonies in Connecticut. On the contrary. When she was offered the Beckford scholarship, she'd told her friends back in New York it was solely the famous writing and journalism program of the nationally top-ranked liberal arts school that had gotten her to accept. Beckford was going to be strictly business, she had said, a necessary way station between either Columbia Journalism School or the Iowa Writers' Workshop.

But now here in her second year, she had to admit she *really* loved Beckford. The school wasn't big but at the core of it was an actual genuine good vibe.

Maybe because it was so isolated up near the western border of Massachusetts or something, but it really did have, corny as it sounded, a school spirit, a sort of primal sense of "we are a family, we are a tribe."

Especially at the basketball games. The men's basketball team, the Redhawks, hadn't missed a bid into the NCAA Tournament in fifteen years and no one blew up a basketball arena like they did. Home or away. Her actual ring tone was the booster club song, "We Are Small but We Are Mighty."

Like me, Olivia thought, taking a bracing sip of her Cuba libre as her roommate and BFF, Naomi, walked into the bar.

2

How the blonde, stick-thin, tall Naomi Dalton, the premed volleyball player, and the petite not-so-stick-thin half Italian, half Puerto Rican, English major Olivia made their friendship work, Olivia wasn't exactly sure.

Was it because they were opposites? she sometimes thought. A mutual sense of the absurd?

Whatever it was, it just worked. Ever since freshman orientation the year before, they'd been finishing each other's sentences like twin sisters and had become as thick as thieves. The entire school was still talking about Halloween last year when they had hilariously shown up to the big track party together as Barbie and Dora the Explorer.

"You're going to kill me," Naomi said now as she huddled in beside her.

"What? Why?" Olivia said.

"They're calling a meeting," she said.

Olivia rolled her eyes. Naomi was rushing the campus's snootiest sorority, Lambda Kappa Delta. Olivia wasn't. She called it the Lamb Duh Society.

"Now? On a Thursday!" Olivia said. "THE hot party here is just getting started and now you have to leave to swallow goldfish or something? You of all people don't need friends, Naomi. Why don't you just drop it?"

"You know why," Naomi said, lifting her vodka and pineapple with a frown.

Olivia actually did know. It was her mother. Naomi's mother was a Beckford alumna and a former Lamb Duh Society debutante herself. She was also a dopey, prying desperate housewife type from Greenwich who liked to run Naomi's life like she was her life-size flesh-and-blood personal Barbie doll instead of her daughter.

"Mommie Dearest strikes again," Olivia said. "Why did you even room with me? You should have just brought mumsy with you. She would have loved that."

"This really sucks," Naomi said. "I hate this. The music is just getting started and we were planning tonight all week and—"

"And it's okay. I'll live," Olivia said. "You can go. I get it. Duty calls."

"Oh, screw you. Duty calls," Naomi said, sticking her tongue out. "And why don't you rush with me already? There's still time. We could still be roomies next year and there's a cook at the sorority house. And as a bonus, there'll be no more easy listening to the pleasant tones of that mysterious guy down the hall who hacks up a lung every morning. It'll be a total win-win!"

"I can't," Olivia said.

"Why not?" Naomi said.

Olivia had put some thought to the very same question and the answer was twofold.

The first part was obvious. She was intimidated. Some rich kids like Naomi couldn't be cooler, but she was the exception not the rule. Most of the sorority kids were pretty snotty toward scholarship kids who had only learned to eat with the one fork and didn't really know how to treat the help as they actually had to clean up after themselves.

And the second answer was, what was the motivation? A social connection for a better job after graduation? Olivia didn't want to kiss ass. No way. Or even need to. Not her. She had talent.

She'd rather just do what she'd always done. Put her nose to the grindstone and outwork and outdo the rest.

"Well, well. How do you like that?" Naomi finally said. "Olivia Ramos is at a loss for words. A first. Maybe that's because there is no real reason. Please just think about it, okay? Some of the girls are really cool."

"I will," Olivia lied as she hugged her roomie bestie and then waved goodbye.

3

Naomi had been gone for about a quarter of an hour when Olivia noticed that none other than Dylan Rimmer had come in with a bunch of his bros.

One of them was wearing a traffic cone on his head like a witch's hat and the rest of them were cracking up.

Dylan, a fellow sophomore, was in Olivia's honors creative writing class and was known as kind of a stoner. But a pretty gorgeous one, she thought as she looked at him grinning at something his friend was telling him. Fair-haired and scruffy, he looked a bit like Bradley Cooper.

And wait a second, Olivia thought, watching Dylan as he knocked his buddy's orange witch hat cone off his head and put him in a fake headlock.

Isn't his current girlfriend, Kimberly Peck, the Lamb Duh Society chapter co-president?

She watched Dylan belly up to the bar a moment later. Why was she watching him? she thought. She wasn't even into him.

Or was she?

When he was done ordering his drink, he turned and then suddenly smiled as their eyes met.

"Hey, Olivia, what's up?" he said as he came over. "I was working on a William Carlos Williams–style poem this afternoon. You ready? It goes, 'I'm so very terribly sorry I drank all the beer you were hiding in the back of your grandmother's old hippie van. I was thirsty and well, I really, really wanted to get drunk.'"

Olivia laughed politely.

"Needs work," she said, mimicking their droll writing teacher, Professor Riboni.

Dylan laughed back at that. He played the trumpet in the school band and did really stupid and funny dance moves with it at the basketball games during time-outs. Some good-looking guys could be jerky jackasses but he was fun. And he was a good writer actually.

"I didn't know you came here, too," Dylan said. "Wow, you look, ummm…"

She gave him an innocent, fake puzzled look. She knew how she looked. During the day, she wore her glasses and was all business but Thursday nights, the contacts were put in as she went all out.

"You look pretty ummm yourself," she found herself saying over the music before she could stop herself.

His big blue eyes went wide. They both looked over at the DJ booth as the Black Eyed Peas standard "I Gotta Feeling" started up.

"What are you drinking there, Olivia? You're looking a little low," he said as the bartender came over.

The crash of glass—a dropped bottle of beer or something down the bar—made them both turn.

Now to make my hasty retreat, Olivia thought.

"I, um, have to take this," she said, quickly lifting up her phone and heading for the door.

Take that, Kimberly Peckerhead, Olivia thought, smiling to herself in the cold of the empty parking lot outside. *While you're busy being a jerk to my friend, I'm just going to have to go ahead and, uh, flirt with your hottie boyfriend a little, okay? Yeah. Thanks.*

Guess who I'm talking to? she texted Naomi.

Waiting for a reply, she turned as she actually heard the soft click of the traffic light on Route 4 a couple of hundred feet to her left. She smiled at the red light as she thought about what Professor Riboni had said that very day about writing skills being so much about being a good observer.

She turned and looked off in the dark. The first structure her eyes hit on was a closed gas station down the street. The one light of its rain shed revealed a small, squared off, lonely building with a glass door. With the dark slabs of its pumps and its worn strip of concrete, it looked...boring.

The next business down the road on the right was a coffee shop and in the parking lot light, you could see flowers along the path in front of it. They were black-eyed Susans that had died in the autumn night cold, she noticed.

In the cold of the autumn night, the dead black-eyed Susans looked... Olivia thought.

Like a swarm of spiders? she thought squinting. *Or no...flying spiders?* No, shit, that really sucked.

"Needs work," she mumbled.

It happened as she was still standing there waiting to hear back from Naomi. When Olivia glanced over at the traffic light again, she saw there was a car stopped underneath it. Not a car actually. An SUV. A huge one. Was it a Cadillac Escalade?

Then her mouth dropped open when she saw the shining silver hood ornament and looked down and saw the New York plates.

Watching the huge Rolls-Royce make the left turn into the

college onto Lawton Road where all the top faculty lived, Olivia suddenly remembered something with a click, like the click of the traffic light.

"Wait," she said as she watched the lights of the SUV disappear up Lawton.

"Wait just one tiny little second," she said.

4

It was 11:24 on the dashboard clock of the armored Rolls-Royce Cullinan when it made the final turn into the college.

Burrowed down deep in the handsewn Italian Saffiano leather of the second row of the $350,000 SUV, Frank Stone sat stiffly, staring at nothing as he slowly tapped the edge of his iPhone against his knee with a metronome regularity.

A soft jolt in the upslope of the road made him glance forward at his two bodyguards in the front seat. They were very large men and they were sitting as stiffly as he was. Completely silent in their dark suits, they could have been pallbearers driving a coffin to a graveyard.

It wasn't supposed to be this way, Frank thought as he crossed his spit-shined Prada Derbys on the Rolls' jewel-box velvet floor mat. Everything had been going great.

He'd been with his new wife at the Flatiron Building in Manhattan attending a UNICEF charity gala event she'd been going nuts about for a month. It was a fashion thing with so many celebrities he'd lost count. That Cajun "bam" chef guy was actually catering it, and the Savannah lady from morning TV was the MC.

And there they were in their element, he and his knockout of a bride among all the beautiful New York people, schmoozing to beat the band. He had little interest in the sub-billionaire-level fashion or celebrities, but his wife was on cloud nine, and the champagne was incredible and most of the women were like his wife, young and hot and hardly wearing anything at all.

Of course, that was when the word had to come down. They had to bail immediately, and his wife was so pissed she couldn't speak. Not a word on the hour-and-a-half-hour ride back to Pound Ridge in Westchester County where he'd just dropped her off back at the estate. Not one.

Her sparkling Cinderella night had been squashed like a rotting pumpkin and they both knew who was getting all the blame. And it wasn't her Chihuahua, Brad.

She wouldn't be talking to him for how long? Frank wondered. *A week? Two?*

"Victoria's Secret models," he mumbled to himself as he shook his head.

"We're coming up on it here on the right now, sir," said Shaw from the seat in front of him.

Frank sat up as the Cullinan crested the hill. Beckford College's elaborate sports fields began to pass by on the left, and on the right were small neat houses. It really was a catalog picture-perfect-looking school, wasn't it? No wonder so many of the überwealthy sent their kids here. *Well, the dumber ones, anyway*, he thought.

Ahead at the end of the lane of houses, he could see a pair of wrought iron gates already swinging inward.

"Where do you want us after we drop you off, sir?" Shaw said from behind the wheel as they swung in. "Out here on the street?"

Frank wiped his sweating palms on the legs of his Dolce &
Gabbana tuxedo slacks as he glanced at the intense eyes staring
back at him in the rearview mirror.

He was glad he'd called for Shaw for the New York trip at
the last minute.

Large and in charge, Shaw was a former Green Beret with
a Special Forces résumé of combat experience that was simply
jaw-dropping.

But of course, it was. Vance Holdings, the firm Frank's hedge
fund contracted with for security, was a private mercenary firm
as well as an executive protection shop and he had been told
Shaw worked both sides of that aisle.

Though the fee Frank was paying Shaw for one night's work
was astonishing, the dude was worth it. Not just for his bone-
crushing skills but also for his handsome chiseled hard-eyed
good looks.

For a big profile event, Shaw was exactly who you wanted
parting the crowd in front of you to project invincibility and
power. Frank's everyday bodyguard, Kenny, sitting beside Shaw
was excellent—a real beast—but matinee-idol looks weren't exactly Kenny's strong suit.

When the paparazzi flashbulbs started popping and you
wanted people to think you were the wolf of Wall Street, you
wanted a Leo beside you, Frank thought. While Kenny was
more of a Jonah Hill.

And Shaw had some mad driving skills. He'd floored them up
here from Manhattan in record time without batting an eyelash.
Kenny, on the other hand, despite a trip to chauffeur school, was
nervous behind the wheel and often drove like a grandmother.
Especially in Manhattan traffic. It was good to have someone
solid with you in a pinch.

"Park on the street, sir?" Shaw asked again.

"No," Frank said. "Park inside the gate. Also, listen up. When
I go in, I don't want you in this vehicle snoozing. You under-

stand me? I want you out of the car keeping your eyes open. Just because we're not in the city anymore doesn't mean you're off duty. I'm paying you for protection, not for you to fall asleep."

"Roger that, sir," Shaw said.

"The both of you," Frank said, looking at the back of Kenny's head.

"Of course, um, sir," Kenny said with a tepid enthusiasm.

5

Founded by nineteenth-century industrialist robber baron-turned-transcendentalist, Horace V. Beckford, Beckford College's campus in Beckford, Connecticut, was laid out in two huge blocks.

At the corner of the most northern block at the end of Lawton Road was the Beckford College president's residence and grounds. Surrounded by an antique wrought iron fence, the gothic two-story mansion constructed of red brick and clapboard was on the National Register of Historic Places and was the actual former home of Horace V. Beckford himself.

And tonight, on the other side of its wrought iron gates, parked before its historic wraparound porch, for some strange reason was a gazillion-dollar Rolls-Royce SUV from New York.

"I knew it," whispered Olivia from where she was crouched in the dark of the women's softball field across Lawton Road.

Olivia looked up and down Lawton. She was surprised that campus security dork Travers wasn't around. If it involved anyone important, Travers was there with bells on. His brown nose was like a heat-seeking missile.

Coast still clear, Olivia took out her phone to take a picture of the luxury vehicle that was very curiously visiting the president's house in the middle of the night when she realized how fruitless the move would be since she couldn't see the license plate from where she was. If she didn't get a shot of the New York plate, what would be the dang point? She considered hopping the field's short chain-link fence and crossing Lawton, getting closer maybe.

But no, she thought as she surveyed the thick hedges along the house's wrought iron fencing on both sides. The hedges were in the way. There was no way she'd be able to get an angle.

Oh, well. At least she'd made a stab at it.

She was past the softball field coming up the stairs for the soccer field, heading back to her dorm, when she suddenly remembered something.

Or maybe the night actually isn't over after all, she thought as she started jogging, and then flat out running, across the field to get back to her room.

6

At first, the slight crickle-crackle sound that began to cut in and out of the cold crisp air beneath the covered porch was so faint Shaw wasn't really sure if it was an outside sound at all. The white noise of silence playing tricks on his mind maybe, he thought as he cocked his head at the dark. Or perhaps just the cold wind vibrating off the drum of his ear.

When the faint suggestion of a sound suddenly became a louder crackling, Shaw took a few steps forward from where he'd been standing to the left of the elaborate front door of the college president's house.

"You hear that?" he said, peering into the dark.

"Hear what?" the meathead muscle-bound Kenny said behind him, not bothering to look up from where he was leaning against the clapboard playing with his phone.

And the key word was *playing*, Shaw noted. He'd gotten a glance at the big dummy's phone screen and he had some kid's game on it. Some Tetris thing with fruit instead of Lego blocks falling down and exploding.

Maybe Frank Stone could do no wrong making money on Wall Street, Shaw thought. But his judgment when it came to personal security was hard to understand. Kenny, a former defensive end for the Miami Dolphins, had some size and strength on him for sure, but he was about as observant and vigilant as a goldfish and had about the same attention span.

"There it is again," Shaw said as he heard the crackling again. It definitely seemed to be coming from the house's side yard on the right.

"What are you talking about?" Kenny said, still playing his game like a preschooler.

Maybe you could hear better if I broke your phone off your bone head, Shaw felt like saying to him. *But I doubt it.*

Instead, Shaw stepped off the porch and moved to his right across the manicured property's flat front lawn. A weeping willow tree commanded the corner of the old house and he skirted past it quickly into a gravel driveway.

It sure was one creepy-looking old place, wasn't it? Shaw thought, looking down the drive where a covered dark wooden catwalk-like structure connected the second story of the house to a separate two-story garage.

Shaw was almost under this porte cochere, slowly scanning the row of pine trees along the left side of the driveway, when he suddenly stopped in his tracks.

From his inside jacket pocket, he removed a black plastic cylinder the size of a bicycle grip. It was an AGM micro thermal imaging monocular and he thumbed it on as he placed it up to his right eye.

He squinted as he pointed the night vision through the bars of the wrought iron fencing.

Then both of Shaw's eyes shot open wide as he realized what it was.

"What in the hell are you doing?" Kenny said as Shaw returned to the porch at speed, flying past him to push open the front door.

Inside the foyer, the college security guy they'd been briefly introduced to was sitting on a folding chair fast asleep with his head back, snoring softly. Another invincible guard dog, Shaw thought with a roll of his eyes.

Shaw ignored him as he pulled open the inner door.

The large front hall inside was even more Bates Motel creepy than the outside of the place, if that were possible. The orange-tinged light from a sole sconce in a corner revealed dark deeply recessed wood paneling and a coffered ceiling and a massive fireplace framed with antique tiles. To the right of the fireplace, light was spilling through a crack of a slightly open door.

As he stood there in the pitch-black hallway of the Gothic residence, all the events of the strange night—the tenseness in the car, the urgent order to drive up here to central Connecticut with no explanation, and now the freaky dark interior of the old house—suddenly gave Shaw an uneasy feeling.

For a moment, Shaw thought if he pushed into the inner room of the strange house, he might see his boss, Frank, in some sort of...compromised position. In some occult getup, velvet robes maybe, and wearing a mask or something like in that batshit crazy Stanley Kubrick movie.

Dark internet rumors flashed through his head as he continued to just stand there. He pictured remote islands with weird owl statues on top of temples. Secret rituals with famous rich people dressed like Druids burning effigies in California forest groves. He'd seen the undercover internet videos and knew, like pretty much everybody on the planet, about that pedophile pimp for the elite who really didn't kill himself.

But with no other option Shaw could think of, due to his penchant for taking orders maybe, he suddenly held his breath and knocked and then pushed slowly at the door.

Shaw let out his breath as he spotted Frank. He was still wearing his tux, standing by a lit fireplace in what looked like a large library. Before him, two men were sitting on a couch facing the fireplace. Shaw couldn't see their faces. Backlit by the fire, the figures were just dark silhouettes.

Frank quickly stepped over as he spotted him. He pushed Shaw back into the front hall, pulling the door firmly shut behind him, his expression furious.

"Shaw, are you out of your mind? What is it?" Frank said.

"Sir, I saw something outside."

"What? Saw something?" Frank said, his fury morphing instantly to a look of shock. "What did you see?"

"Beside the house in the cornstalks is a person with a long lens camera," Shaw said.

"You have to be absolutely kidding me! Are you sure?"

"I'm positive," Shaw said.

"You and Kenny find who the hell it is," Frank said. "And I mean immediately. Scoop up whoever it is and get the camera, okay? Get everything and put them into custody with college security and then you come back here and tell me what the hell is going on. You got me? Find them now."

7

In the part of the Beckford town community garden that abutted the president's property there was an enormous cornfield. And in the corn row three rows back from the black iron fence, a small bluish light suddenly glowed.

"Shit," Olivia said as she looked down and saw the Battery Low notification on her Nikon SLR.

No! Not now! she thought. *This can't be happening.*

A minute earlier, she had been all systems go, about to take a picture of the SUV's New York plates on the sly when a dude—a big dude in a suit—had shown up unexpectedly from around the house's corner.

That was not a happy surprise at all. She couldn't tell if the guy had seen her. But she had noticed that he'd headed back toward the front of the house quite quickly.

Now here she was, kneeling in the dark and cold, unsure of what the hell to do. Should she run? Get closer? Try one more time?

Up in the dark of the path in the direction of the president's house came a sharp metal clang followed by the rusty creak of a gate.

"Okay, then. Run it is," she whispered as she got up.

How damn stupid could she have been to do all this? she thought as she pulled her hoodie over her head and immediately started hurrying west away from the house back down the dirt path.

The first thing she did as she hurried along was to take off the SLR camera strapped around her neck and hide it behind some cornstalks. It wasn't technically hers, of course, just one of the perks from her job as an editor for the school newspaper. Another thing to worry about but whatever. She'd have to come back for it later.

She definitely didn't need it on her in case she was busted. She could say she was out for a stroll or something. Made little sense but what did the politicians call it? Plausible deniability? Yeah, she'd take some of that now, thanks.

She was halfway back to the parking lot where she had come in when she suddenly heard a car engine out by the road.

"What now?" she mumbled as she halted and crouched and stared down a row of the community garden corn toward the street.

There was a sudden gust of wind and as she watched, the individual human-sized corn plants all around her began swaying back and forth in a dance-like rhythm. She swallowed as she listened to the dry blades of them rustling together over the slight whine of the wind.

Of course, the community garden had to have cornstalks, she thought, shaking her head at them. Because being near the president's Dracula castle–like house in the middle of the night just wasn't Stephen King creepy enough, was it?

Then as she watched, through the slowly rocking corn rows came a campus security truck out on Indian Way with its lights off.

"Double shit," Olivia whispered as she heard it turn into the community garden parking lot where she had come in.

They were surrounding her, she realized. Someone was coming up behind her on the path from the president's house and
now there was someone in front. They were boxing her in.

Staring back at the road, she wondered if she went out through
the center of the cornfield that she could somehow get up in the
suburban neighborhood to the west of the school.

But no. The stalks were too dry. The guard on foot coming up
from the house would definitely hear her. Plus, there were lights
along the road that could be seen from the garden's parking lot.

That was when she turned all the way around and looked
across the path at the dark Farmington River running past.

Could she? she thought. How wide was its stream? Not that
bad. There was the current to deal with, but it didn't seem *that*
bad. Maybe the river wasn't even that deep. Maybe she could
actually walk across it.

Wait. What was she thinking? Was she nuts? That would be
a new level of freaking crazy. The water would be freezing cold
and then she'd be soaking wet *and* freezing cold when she got
to the other side. That was, like, highly dangerous.

That's when she pictured it.

The crushed look on her father's face as he was told she'd
been kicked out of school.

She took out her phone again.

"Freaking crazy, here we come," Olivia whispered.

Naomi, she texted.

There was no bubble reply.

Naomi! she texted again.

Still no bubbles. Dammit.

Meet me where we had lunch last Friday not kidding URGENT!!!

Olivia hit Send and turned and got a running start and
chucked her phone hard and high across the water. She listened
and then heard it land in some brush on the other side.

No splash. *So far so good*, she thought.

"Now for the fun part," Olivia whispered grimly as she clambered down the embankment toward the water.

As she got to the bottom and her sneakers filled with cold water, she hesitated for a moment. But as she pictured the look on her dad's face again, she realized there was no going back now.

Then with her next step, Olivia slipped off a slick underwater river stone and was suddenly in the river up to her chin with her breath taken, frantically doggy paddling against the strong current for the opposite shore.

PART ONE

GONE FISHING

8

One year later

The river glittered in the sunny, breezy, cool October morning and out from the rolling countryside hills, autumn leaves were pouring down like golden rain.

Jogging across the deck of an old bridge, I stopped in my tracks midspan to watch the glowing red and orange and yellow leaves twinkle as they twisted and spun and flip-flopped into the shimmering bend of the water. Then I bounded the rest of the way across the bridge into a little wooded neighborhood of nineteenth-century clapboard houses that ran alongside the river, picking up my pace.

Looking up at the windswept baby blue sky over the water as I ran, I suddenly remembered the first and only poem I had ever written. It was for an in-class assignment when I was in sixth grade and it was called, "What a Day."

What a day to be alive
What a day to wish
What a day to cast a line
What a day to fish

Mrs. Lynch had loved it so much she had read it out to the rest of the class, completely mortifying me. But in the decades since, I had actually come to be proud of it.

Well, a little at least.

Write what you know, I thought, smiling out at the river.

It was called the Farmington and its headwaters originated from the base of the Berkshire Mountains in Massachusetts before it flowed on a fifty-mile meandering journey over the border into Connecticut and then through Litchfield and Hartford Counties into the Connecticut River.

The sparsely populated area around it was mostly known for a huge pine forested state park and a small ski resort and a minor Ivy League college.

But I wasn't here for the peace and quiet or to hit the books.

The Farmington just happened to be one of the greatest trout fishing rivers on planet Earth.

How I had missed the existence of it until now was a mystery to me. It was my son, Declan, who had discovered it. Declan had been in an antique store in Montana with his now fiancée, Stephanie Barber, when he had seen an old coffee table book from the 1960s entitled, *The Farmington: Fishing the Greatest Trout Stream in New England.*

Knowing how nuts I am about fly-fishing, my favorite (and only) son had immediately picked up the book for me. And exactly one week after I had turned the last page of this amazing book, I was headed east with my rubber waders and fly rod.

It was definitely an impulsive fishing vacation move of the highest order, but the book had said that the fall was the best time to experience the Farmington in all its glory, so I didn't want to miss out or wait another year.

It was a good thing, too, because the book hadn't been lying one bit. I'd thought since the book was published in 1963 that by now the river might be lined with condos or something, but the great Bob Ross himself couldn't have painted a more bucolic landscape.

And not only were there *Field & Stream* cover shots in every direction you looked, the trout that the river was stocked with were even more fabulous than the book had described.

There were browns and rainbows and beautiful red-bellied brooks, which were my all-time favorite. I hadn't caught anything truly trophy-sized yet in the two weeks I'd been here, but the day before I'd netted a rainbow that was about twenty inches and ten pounds of dripping speckled gleaming awesomeness. And I still had one more day of fishing to go.

"So many trout. So little time. What can I doo-ooo," I sang to myself as I ran alongside the peacefully flowing waters.

I slowed again about a mile and a half from where I entered the path. To my left a majestic, man-made, sheer thirty-foot waterfall bisected the wide river. That would have been delightful enough but on the stone lip of the falls facing the flow of the water were several large dark birds with long necks and beaks.

There were three of them this morning. They were standing with their wings spread out at their sides, their hooked beaks down as they stared into the flow of the water. They were cormorants, a species of aquatic bird that knew how to fish so well that samurai warlords of ancient Japan would actually train them to fish for them.

"Hey, guys, not fair!" I called out to them with a laugh. "Save some for the rest of us!"

I smiled as I looked at the birds, at the flowing parade of glittering water along the banks, at the morning sun lighting up the tops of the happy little trees in the distance.

Beyond the cormorants on the opposite bank, I saw there was an abandoned mill from the 1800s maybe and on its faded brick the words LOVE LIFE had been spray-painted in six-foot-high white-and-blue letters by some local teens perhaps.

Oh, believe me, I thought. *I'm all over it.*

"I'm coming, fish," I said as I started running again, picking up my pace under the red, yellow and orange boughs of the New England autumn trees.

"Don't worry, my pretties," I said. "Right after his coffee, Papa Gannon will be among you very, very soon."

9

I was staying in an Airbnb in a town called Beckford and for two weeks now my morning routine was a five-mile, crack-of-dawn run on the bike path along the Farmington River to a Starbucks near the college.

And keeping closely with this ritual, it was about an hour from when I'd tightened my sneaker laces that I was pushing out of the Starbucks door with my back.

At the corner of the brick coffee shop was a white painted metal outdoor table where I set down the Venti Blonde in my left hand. In my right hand was the warm brown bag of the sausage, egg and cheese that I'd already scored from the bagel place beside the Starbucks and I set that down as well before I screeched out the metal chair and sat.

After making short work of my breakfast, I put my feet up on another of the chairs and leaned back with my coffee. The sky was almost full light now and it was very pleasant to just sit and chill and take in the autumnal action. The buckshot barrages of passing birds heading south; the morning light pushing away the shadows from the undersides of the slowly passing string of clouds; the fox-red leaves from an old maple tree beside the coffee shop doing summersaults into the parking lot.

What was also great to watch were all the young college kids coming in and out of the coffee shop. Sleepy-eyed, some wearing pajamas and bunny slippers with their Beckford College sweatshirts, they reminded me of my son, Declan.

Speaking of which, I thought as I took out my phone.

"Hey, there," I said to Declan, who appeared on the FaceTime screen.

"Dad. Hey," he said with a yawn. "What's up?"

"Nothing much. Weather here is awesome. I'm going to fish myself silly today."

"Are you? Get out of here. Shocker," Declan said, laughing.

"Did you see that rainbow trout pic I sent you yesterday?" I said.

"Oh, yeah, Dad. Really nice," he said with a yawn.

"The pink lateral stripe on her? Wasn't it the most beautiful thing you've ever seen?"

"Simply stunning, Dad," he said as he closed his eyes. "I'm having it framed."

"How's things with you out there, son? How's Stephanie?"

"She's great. What time is it, Dad?" Declan said.

"Oh, I don't know. Eight or something."

"Uh, Dad, you have heard of the time zones, right? It's two hours earlier here in Utah. Little early to shoot the breeze, don't you think?"

"Up and at 'em, son," I said. "You're a ranch hand now. You should be thanking me for the wake-up. You'll be late for work."

"Dad, I love you, so don't take this wrong, but I'm hanging up the phone now."

"Dec, wait. Before you go," I said.

"What, Dad?"

"Show me the watch."

From his bedside table, Declan lifted up the stainless-steel Rolex I had recently bequeathed him for his twenty-first birthday.

"That's a fine timepiece, son."

"Sure is, Dad."

"Remember, since it's an automatic watch, you have to wear it to keep it wound."

"I remember, Dad."

"Also remember to keep the crown screwed down tight otherwise the waterproof hermetic seal will be broken."

"Got it, Dad. I'll call you later when the sun is up."

Then the screen went black for some reason.

"Weird," I said as I put my phone down onto the table.

I went back to my coffee. There was a road called Route 4 on my left with a bridge over the Farmington River, and as I sipped, I looked out at the cars coming over it. Inside of them were mostly tired and grim-faced folks in medical scrubs and business attire heading out to work at the nearby UConn Health complex and the Connecticut state capital of Hartford some twenty miles to the southeast.

As the busy bee drivers periodically stopped at the light and glanced down zombielike at their phones, a part of me wanted to walk over and knock on their windows and point out the fly-fishing mecca of the Farmington River right there beside them that they were totally missing out on.

"Or then again," I said, quietly nodding to myself as I blew on the coffee cup lid.

"Maybe it's just best for all concerned to keep the most beautiful trout river on Earth to me and the cormorants today after all."

Still basking in the zen of the New England fall, I was thinking about taking out my burner phone to get an Uber back to town to get another storybook day of my American fishing odyssey underway when I glanced over at a woman getting out of a car in the coffee shop's parking lot.

Some people from your past you could be sitting next to in a subway car or a plane cabin and look right through one another.

But with other ones, the slightest glance of eyes on eyes clicks things back in time instantly, and five or ten or even twenty years suddenly disappear like they'd never even happened at all.

"Mike?" Colleen Doherty said as she stepped over.

"Michael Gannon?"

10

"Colleen?" I said, smiling in shock, almost spilling my coffee as I leaped up.

Colleen Doherty was from about as far back in my past as it went. One of the first girls I had ever had a real crush on, she was the older sister of my Bronx Catholic grammar school good buddy, Connor.

And back when I was, what, ten years old, I used to sleep over at Connor's house. On Friday nights as we sat and watched *The A-Team* and *Miami Vice* or snuck the remote over to MTV when Mr. or Mrs. Doherty left the room, I would have butterflies in my stomach as I snuck glances at Colleen across the coffee table.

She'd completely ignore me, of course, but like every other boy in the neighborhood who had eyesight, I had been smitten from the first moment I saw the tall black-haired looker.

Because it was not just Colleen's long blue-black hair that turned heads. It was her eyes. She had these icy gray eyes that were bright, almost glowing. They had taken my ten-year-old breath away, that was for sure. Even before I knew anything about anything, I couldn't take my eyes off her. I thought she was like an angel or something.

Talk about getting the blood pumping, I thought as I watched those angel eyes fix on my own again after all these years.

"It really is you," Colleen said. "The shape you're in. Wow! You look twenty."

"You don't look so bad yourself," I said, beaming back at her. "You cut your hair."

"Oh, yeah," she said, touching it. "Years ago. How many has it been?"

My smile suddenly broke as the ancient memories abruptly came to an end.

A dead end.

"Too many," I said quietly.

"Oh, right," Colleen said, suddenly not smiling anymore either as she, too, remembered where we'd seen each other last.

At the funeral of her brother, Connor, a firefighter in the FDNY, two weeks after 9/11.

Like the badass, wild Irish maniac he'd always been, my best friend, Connor, had been running *up* the stairs of the burning North Tower to save people when the scumbags knocked several hundreds of thousands of tons of steel girders down on top of him.

What really made it so much worse was that their dad, Mr. Doherty, was an ironworker who had worked putting up the Towers back in the seventies.

Like everyone in the NYPD back then, I did my time in the pit of Ground Zero. I had actually met Mr. Doherty down there and worked with him. The whole time in that burnt-metal-stinking landfill mess, I prayed to God that I would find some sign of Connor for his family.

That it didn't happen was disappointing though not surprising.

Like a lot of New Yorkers, God was pretty busy that fall.

"I was going to get a coffee," Colleen said after a beat. "I can come back out if you're staying."

"No, you're not getting a coffee," I said, pulling out a chair for her. "I am. Stay right there, Colleen. Don't move another muscle. What are you having? My treat."

"Please, Mike. Don't be silly," Colleen said, laughing now.

"Colleen, I insist. You must understand," I said, smiling as I pulled open the door. "Fate doesn't play games like this more than once. This may be my last and only chance."

"Only chance for what?" she said.

"Are you kidding me?" I said with a wink. "A date with Colleen Doherty has only been on my bucket list my whole life."

11

"Hey, how's your dad? Still living in the old neighborhood?" I said as I came back out with her Venti Americano.

"Of course," she said. "I begged him to head for Florida, but he has this old lady, Mrs. Paulmann, for a tenant upstairs who he shovels the snow for, so he's not leaving. He liked you a lot, Mike. He never could understand why you joined the navy SEALs when he offered to get you into the steelworkers union."

"Go up on the high steel with your crazy old man?" I said as I sat. "I chose the SEALs because it was safer!"

I watched her laugh. It was something to watch.

What a day to be alive, I thought again.

"So, what brings you all the way up here from the Boogie Down Bronx, Colleen?" I said. "Let me guess. You ran out of Pepperidge Farm cookies?"

"Bite your tongue," Colleen said with a laugh. "I'm an Irish Catholic West Bronx girl to the bone, Mike. You actually think I'd ever step out on Stella d'Oro?"

I laughed myself at that. The Stella d'Oro Italian cookie factory was located next to the Major Deegan Expressway, a stone's throw from our Bronx block. Playing outside, you could always smell when the cookie ovens were firing. Even all these years later, the scent of Swiss fudge and anisette gave me Gen X childhood flashbacks.

"I'm up here in Connecticut for work actually," Colleen said, blowing on her coffee. "I'm an investigator now."

"No! You're a cop?" I said. "I thought you were a nurse and your husband—what was his name? Bill? I thought he was the cop, a transit cop, wasn't it?"

"My *ex*-husband's name is Ryan," Colleen said, laughing again, "and yes, he was a transit cop and maybe still is. I wouldn't know because I don't talk to him anymore. After the divorce, I got sick of being a nurse and so I went back to school and now I work as an investigator for a law firm in Manhattan. It's been seven years now."

"Is that right?" I said. "A law firm investigator. But if it's a law firm in Manhattan, what are you working on way up here?"

"Wait, you're not still a cop, are you, Mike?" she said, sipping her coffee.

"Nope. Happily retired, thank goodness," I lied.

I was retired. But happily? Not even a little. That was another story. One that Colleen, or anyone really, didn't need to know about.

"I heard you left the city," she said. "Florida, was it?"

"Yep, first Florida then the Bahamas," I said. "I lived down there for a bit but I, um… I live out West now. I'm actually back East here for a New England fishing vacation my son set up for me. The Farmington River behind the coffee shop here is actually world-famous. See, it's got this special water that comes out of these aquifers up in the Berkshires that give it this not too hot, not too cold temperature that's perfect all year round for the fish. And what fish! You have to see these trout."

"You still with the fishing," Colleen said, smiling as she shook her head. "Some things never change. I remember you with your dad out along the train tracks at the lake in Van Cortlandt Park. You had to be five years old. You were the cutest thing, you and Connor, in your red plaid ties and freckles."

"I think we both know, out of the two of us, who the cutest thing in the neighborhood was," I said.

"Mike Gannon," she said, shaking her head as she looked at me with those pale angel eyes.

"So, what are you working on up here?" I said.

Colleen gestured across the street with her coffee.

"The death of a student at Beckford College. A girl from the city, Olivia Ramos. She was a scholarship kid. She died from a drug overdose last year. Twenty years old and an only child. I'm here to look into it."

"No! Those damn opioids," I said.

"You said it," Colleen said. "Every year they kill more young people than Vietnam ever did. Makes you sick more isn't being done."

"Sure does," I said, sipping my own coffee. "So, you're here on an insurance thing? The parents are suing the school?"

"Kind of," Colleen said, looking across the road again. "Or who knows. Maybe. We're not there yet. Beckford College is small, but it's a minor Ivy with a giant Final Four basketball program and has deep pockets. They have an endowment of thirty-four billion dollars so they actually settled really quickly for a million-plus to keep it out of the news."

"So, where do you fit in?"

Colleen sat up and placed her coffee cup down onto the garden table.

"The girl's parents were divorced and the father was in prison when the mother signed off on it. The dad was released last year and wants us to look into it for him to see what it was all about."

"He win the lottery or something?" I said. "That sounds like it would cost plenty."

"No, not at all," Colleen said. "The opposite. It's a pro bono thing. The father was actually wrongfully convicted for a robbery in Times Square and one of the firm's senior partners was his lawyer at the time. He blew it, so he's trying to make amends. You have to see this poor guy. He doesn't even seem to care that he's been exonerated. He just wants me to see what happened to his daughter."

"Wow. You get thrown in prison for something you didn't do, then your twenty-year-old kid ODs while you're inside. That's about as rough as it gets," I said.

Colleen nodded, looking down at the table.

She suddenly raised her coffee cup.

"To Irish reunions," she said with a sigh.

12

Colleen Doherty arrived at the Beckford College guard booth at eight forty-five and followed the guard's directions to the administration building. She parked and went inside and down a set of stairs.

The campus security office was just to the right of the lower-level door she pulled open, and inside of it the bright fluorescent light gleamed off a high metal-and-glass check-in desk and the white subway tiled walls. A half dozen flat screens hung from the dropped ceiling showing security camera feeds.

Very high-tech, Colleen noted. It was some setup for such a small school, she thought. She'd seen police precincts that were less elaborate.

Behind the Star Trek console of a desk was an alert-looking young Hispanic woman in khakis and a red campus safety polo shirt. She smiled as she clicked the pen in her hand.

"Can I help you?" she said.

"Good morning," Colleen said, finally smiling back as she

took her notebook from her bag. "I'm here to see Campus Security Director Roy Travers. Is he here?"

The young woman paused, blinked as if wondering if she should admit it.

"One moment please," the guard said, lifting a phone. "Your name?"

"Colleen Doherty from Alston Brantwood," Colleen said, placing her law firm's card on the desktop.

"Do you have an appointment?" the guard said, glancing at it.

"I don't," Colleen said as the guard turned and mumbled into the phone.

"If you will have a seat," the guard said as she hung up the phone, "Director Travers will see you in a moment."

Sitting in the hard plastic chair opposite the console, Colleen felt a little like a bad schoolgirl sent to the principal's bench. Especially after several minutes had gone past and no sign of the director.

But she had to expect some pushback, she knew. This had to be a real puzzler for them, thinking that the incident had been put to bed. Which was the point of driving all the way up here. To use the element of surprise and confront them without warning. Get them back on their heels. See how they reacted. See how much they would scramble.

Director Travers arrived at the other side of the console desk a long five minutes later. He was short and wiry with a clean-shaven, tight muscular face. It looked like his cheeks were doing a push-up as he smiled.

"Hi. Colleen, is it? I'm Roy," he said as they shook. "Please come back into my office."

Through the heavy door he closed behind her, his inner office was dimmer than the precinct desk area. The sole light besides the little lamp on Travers's desk came from an eyebrow window along the top of the painted cinderblock wall.

"So, you're all the way up from Alston Brantwood in New

York City?" Travers said as he slowly sat down behind his desk. "Did you drive up this morning? Must have left early."

"Crack of dawn," Colleen said, taking out her notebook. "I'm here concerning the death of Olivia Ramos. I saw from my records you live in the next town over, Director Travers. What time did they call you in that night? Or were you already here?"

The door suddenly opened then and a tall, thin middle-aged woman entered the room. Her wire-rimmed glasses and dry auburn hair screamed cat lady to Colleen, yet she was smartly dressed in an elegant, expensive-looking navy pinstriped jacket.

"This is Dean of Students Elizabeth Darwell," Travers said as the woman shut the door and pulled over a chair to sit beside Colleen.

"I thought I'd sit in on the meeting," Dean Darwell said, smiling as she offered a gaunt hand. "If you don't mind."

"Certainly," Colleen said, smiling weakly back as she shook.

"So, this is about poor Olivia," Dean Darwell said, squinting sympathetically.

"Yes," Colleen said. "I'm here on behalf of Olivia's father, Emilio Ramos, who as you can imagine is interested in finding out the details of his daughter's death."

13

"Are you aware," Dean Darwell asked as she tilted her head at Colleen condescendingly, "of the nondisclosure agreement that Olivia's mother, Dana D'Ambrose, signed concerning the death? By that *legally binding* agreement and *generous settlement*, the tragic matter, I believe, was firmly resolved. Olivia sadly died of a drug overdose in her dorm. Regrettable as it is, and as sympathetic to Mr. Ramos as we truly are, that's really all there is to it."

"Not only am I aware of the agreement," Colleen said calmly, "I've actually read it over several times. But let me repeat in order to be perfectly clear, I'm not representing Olivia's *mother* but rather Emilio Ramos, Olivia's *father*. He signed no such contract and wishes to learn more details about what exactly transpired with his child's death."

Dean Darwell pursed her lips as she considered Colleen's statement. She sat up even more stiffly in her seat if that were possible.

"I see," she said. "I believe Mr. Ramos also was offered a similar agreement with a generous sum of money attached to it. I hate to speak in such frank terms concerning the loss of a young life, but would your presence here perhaps be in relation to a negotiating tactic of some sort on Mr. Ramos's part, perhaps an attempt by Mr. Ramos to receive a larger sum? Again, I don't mean to be insulting or callous in any way. I am merely trying to get a feel for everyone's concerns and interests."

"Mr. Ramos seeks one thing, Dean Darwell," Colleen said, staring at the woman steadily with her serene gray eyes. "Merely the truth. That's why I would really appreciate it if you would share with us all incident reports of the night in question and all follow-up reports as well. Also, I would formally like to request at this time permission to conduct interviews with all security and staff involved. And as I see out there that you have an elaborate security camera system, I would like to formally ask for an opportunity to view video from the night of October 11 of last year from any and all campus-wide security cameras."

"That security array out there is brand-new," Director Travers said calmly.

Colleen turned to him.

He stared back at her steadily, not blinking.

In fact, he hadn't moved a muscle since the meeting began, had he?

Quite a cool one, Colleen thought.

"From the old system, then," Colleen finally said. "The one that was in use at the time of Olivia's death would be perfectly fine."

"But those tapes are—" Director Travers began.

"Ms. Doherty!" Dean Darwell said loudly.

Colleen turned to her. She could see the woman's eyes were wide and even a little bit wild behind her glasses now.

She'd gone full cat lady, Colleen thought. She seemed scared. Sort of terrified, in fact.

My, my, Colleen thought.

What the hell had happened to Olivia that night?

"Yes?" Colleen finally said.

"Ms. Doherty, if you…if you could formally put all of your requests in writing, I will speak to the college's legal counsel to ensure that the best course of action is taken. Is that fair?"

It was Colleen's turn to cock her own head at the dean now.

"Fair to stonewall and lawyer up on a father who's merely trying to find out what happened to his deceased twenty-year-old daughter?" Colleen said as if she were considering it. "His only child whose safety and well-being he very unwisely put under your care?"

She lifted her bag and stood.

"No," she said. "That's not fair. Not even a little. I'm going to be up here for a few days talking to several other people about this matter. During that time, if you feel like—what is the term the police use? Oh, yes. Getting out ahead of this—I left my card and number at the desk. Good morning."

14

If the office of Beckford College president, Martin Cushing, looked like one of those elegant moneyed chambers that most people might only see featured in the glossy pages of *Architectural Digest*, it was because it actually had been in *AD*'s September edition a year before in an article entitled, "Mixing Modern and Classic Styles."

With a floor-to-ceiling bay window that overlooked the campus's beautifully cultivated grounds, it had a varnished behemoth of an antique burled walnut desk, an Industry West sofa and love seat, a Henn&Hart coffee table. The table rode atop a Persian rug on the polished oak floor and along the fine wood recessed paneling was a copper sideboard by Arhaus.

Above the sideboard was Cushing's favorite piece in the room, an oil painting from the college's vast art collection, a Brevoort seascape of an inlet framed by a rocky cliff. As Cushing had told the magazine people, he loved Hudson River School seascapes not just for their Sturm und Drang drama but because they always reminded him of the beach beside his family's ancestral place in Martha's Vineyard.

Referred in the *AD* piece as "dapper and energetic," President Cushing liked to think that he himself was a stylish mix of the modern and classic as well. That was why to keep up appearances this morning, he was wearing a beautifully tailored seasonally appropriate midweight gray wool suit that hung from his frame with a drape that was almost arrogant in its meticulous exactitude.

At a little before ten that morning, Cushing was center stage of his magnificent office sitting on his eight-thousand-dollar sofa. There was a yellow legal tablet in his lap and a MacBook Air laptop on the plush cushion beside him. A board of trustees meeting was upcoming and he was doing some last-minute polishing of his quarterly report.

President Cushing, Marty to his friends, was a big man. Six foot two, 275 pounds, most of it soft. Though with good tailoring, and he had that, it was well hidden. And with his nice blue eyes and razor part in his graying executive hair and his pleasantly bemused, slightly haughty standing expression, he looked solid and aristocratic like an expensive college president should.

What was the word his obnoxious, Wall Street trading, college buddy Frank used to describe him last time they played golf?

Prosperous.

The bastard, Cushing thought. Frank had the gall to keep telling him how prosperous he looked now. Once with a double pat to his midsection after he missed a putt!

But he was prosperous, wasn't he? Cushing thought as he paused looking over his office.

Frank had been right on the money about that.

He was a millionaire now. An actual millionaire and it wasn't like he even had to spend any of it with the way things were set up. The house was free, his meals, even his first-class vacations, granted he attached some silly college business to them.

Not bad for a boy from the badlands, he thought as he leaned back and grinned. *Not bad at all.*

The badlands in his case were Fort Mohave, Arizona, and they were bad all right. Dad was a copper miner, mother was a night cleaner at a hospital, the house a double wide that was once part of some kind of hippie commune oasis resort off Route 66. It was a shack really. It didn't even have an indoor bathroom.

Fortunately for him, what this incredibly embarrassing home did contain was three doting older sisters and a mother who was the black sheep hippie daughter of a distinguished family back East. Mother had homeschooled young Martin like a little prince, hadn't she? Taught him how to speak properly, how to always be neat and mannerly. She and his sisters showered constant attention on him and when his hillbilly dad's height and good looks kicked in around age fourteen, he became pretty much the mayor of the little desert town especially when he went out for football.

But Mother had even bigger plans for him than small-town hero. She had squirreled away money to send him back East to school at the University of Virginia where one of her brothers had gone.

There at UVA, well-groomed and with a line of malarkey as slick as buttered sausage, as his father used to say, he had hit the ground running on a quest in one direction. Upward.

If there had been one roadblock in this quest, it was that Cushing was no scholar. He had struggled through as a C student even after conning several female classmates to do most of his work. Fortunately, what he was good at, with his shoeshine and a smile, was student government. He was even vice president one year, which made him enough connections to squeak into UVA's famous law school despite his grades.

That's where he had met his roommate Frank Stone, another working-class fish out of water looking to put some polish on his blue-collar ambition at the upper crust UVA.

Almost a decade after law school graduation, Cushing was married and still scrambling, working at a no-name Maryland insurance company when his old roommate Frank had called.

Frank, unlike himself, had taken off like a rocket into Wall Street success at some hedge fund. They'd kept in touch, Cushing had made sure of that, and when Frank had called, it was with an opportunity that he thought Cushing would be just perfect for.

Frank, newly on the board of an expensive minor Ivy League college in Connecticut, said they needed a new president and would Cushing be interested.

"You're the greatest bullshitter I know, Marty," Frank had said. "You already look the part. Just do the Southern-loving voice you used to get us laid and these New England Yankees up here will be eating out of your hand."

Cushing couldn't believe it. Finally, some luck.

Now a decade since that phone call, he had gone from faking it to actually making it, hadn't he? He was rich now. And not just rich. He had power. The basketball program gave him national recognition and the entire campus was more like his kingdom than a school. He even had knights, in the form of the campus police.

Cushing smiled as Puccini's *Suor Angelica* started up from the iPhone Bluetooth speaker on his desk. He loved all of Puccini, of course, but something about *Suor Angelica* pierced his soul. As the de capo aria shifted into the B-episode key, Cushing laid the legal pad down, a smile playing on his lips.

He knew all about expensive cultured things now. Fine wine, opera, art. He'd actually seen the opera in person performed at the Teatro Real in Madrid two Christmases ago headlined by the incomparable soprano, Ermonela Jaho.

Lost in this reverie, his half-lidded eyes drifted to the wall beside the seascape where his favorite quote hung in a gilt frame.

"A man should
hear a little music,
read a little poetry,
and see a fine picture
every day of his life,
in order that
worldly cares may not obliterate
the sense of the beautiful
which God has implanted
in the human soul."

—Johann Wolfgang von Goethe

His old fellow defensive linemen back at Fort Mohave were doing what around now? he wondered. Backing an 18-wheeler into a loading dock? Meth? Five to ten?

Cushing laughed.

"Suckers," he said.

He was still sitting there transfixed when from his half-open office door came a soft tap. Opening his eyes, Cushing turned to see the frizzy-haired Dean Darwell staring in at him.

Well, that kills it, Cushing thought as he thumbed off the music.

What now? he thought, reluctantly waving her in. It was nothing good. Poker-faced, Elizabeth was not, and there was a look on her face that was uncharacteristically ill at ease.

Worldly cares, here I come, he thought.

"President Cushing," she said as she slipped in and closed the door behind her.

"Yes, Elizabeth?" he said.

Out with it. What is it? he thought.

"I think we have a problem," she said.

15

On her way to the town police department in her black Toyota RAV4 rental, Colleen passed a white steepled church, a library with painted pumpkins scattered about the grass in front of it, a fancy all-girls boarding school that had tennis courts and horse barns across from its redbrick dorms. All of it draped perfectly with just-so piles of autumn leaves and hay bales as if the Beckford Town Pumpkin Spice Beautification Committee had just struck again.

Had the town of Beckford been laid out by Norman Rockwell himself? she wondered as she crested a softly rolling hill.

No, she thought as she made a left into the police department and parked and got out and followed a leafy path to an actual covered footbridge that spanned a gently bubbling brook.

The Bronx County Courthouse beside Yankee Stadium, this was not.

Used to working in and around the very worst of NYC's falling-apart courts and hellhole lockups, all the happy bird chirping, free parking, peace and quiet and not even one half-naked junkie to step over was almost disorienting.

Almost, Colleen thought as she passed—what couldn't be but actually really was—a little brown bunny innocently nibbling away in the grass beside the flagstone path.

The police department building was a long low antique that looked like it was made out of hand-cut brownstone blocks. Inside the entrance, she lifted a phone off the wall beside the glass-walled reception partition.

A pretty, young, female uniformed cop appeared on the other side of the glass after a few buzzes. She was scrub-faced, maybe twenty-five, with her dark blonde hair up in a bun. M. DAVIS, it said on her name tag.

Remembering the bunny, Colleen smiled.

She was surprised it didn't say B. POTTER.

"Can I help you?" she said.

"Hi, my name is Colleen Doherty. I called a few days ago. Sergeant Tyler has a package for me in his mailbox, he said."

Coming by to pick up Olivia Ramos's full police report from the night of her death while she was up here was a no-brainer. Colleen had called two days before to get ahold of it and was told it would be waiting.

"Sure. Let me check," said Officer Davis with a smile.

As she disappeared, Colleen looked around the little alcove. There were photographs on the wall. The Beckford Redhawks winning a basketball game. A policeman talking to a classroom of first graders. A town Memorial Day parade. The biggest one was of a middle-aged white-haired Chief Phillip R. Garner, smiling stiffly under his very elaborate and official-looking full-dress chief's hat.

As she came back, Colleen could tell by the fallen look on Officer Davis's innocent face that something was not right.

"Sorry. There's no package," Officer Davis said. "But Sergeant Tyler left you this."

She passed a folded note under the partition.

"No report. That can't be right," Colleen said half to herself as she lifted the note.

She knew that by law, police reports were available to the public after the case was closed. They had to hand it over. They didn't have a choice.

She opened the paper.

Sorry, the handwritten note said. *Can't release the report due to the State Prosecutor's office reopening the case.*

Colleen stood there stunned.

That was...crazy, Colleen thought, staring at the note with a perplexed look. She'd checked the state website two days ago. The case had been closed for six months.

They were playing games, Colleen realized.

After she had left the meeting with campus security, someone from the college must have called the state prosecutor and had them reopen the case solely in order to block her access to the report. The only way she could see it now was if Olivia's father decided to sue and they handed it over during discovery.

This had all happened in the last ten minutes. Colleen imagined the kind of juice that it would take to make the state prosecutor jump and immediately reopen a closed death investigation with a phone call. She thought of cat lady Dean Darwell. She was more of a bobcat lady apparently.

Whatever they were hiding, wow, was it a doozy.

She eyed Officer Davis.

"Is Sergeant Tyler around?" Colleen said.

"I think he might be, but he's, eh, really busy," Officer Davis said.

Colleen slowly looked around the deserted alcove. Then turned and looked out at the deserted parking lot out through the glass of the door. The bunny was still out there, she saw, working on a dandelion now.

Yeah, you look really jammed up here, she wanted to say as she turned back.

But she bit her tongue. Her last performance report at the firm had labeled her "inflexible."

Don't be inflexible, Colleen thought.

Think happy thoughts. Think happy flexible thoughts.

Colleen grasped the phone tighter, leaned forward, and dug in.

"Actually, I came all the way up from New York City for this," she said pleasantly. "I could wait if Sergeant Tyler is busy. All day really. I have nothing else to do. And it really won't take but a moment. I just have one question to ask him. Just one, I promise."

"I'll, um, I'll see," Officer Davis said, scurrying away from the booth.

"Yes? Hi. What is it? I'm actually in the middle of something," Sergeant Tyler said sheepishly as he appeared behind the glass.

Sergeant Tyler was frumpy and middle-aged. With his un-shaved cheeks and thick glasses, he looked much more like a back-office mailman than a cop.

He was also having trouble looking Colleen in the eye. But she remembered her nice conversation with him. He seemed like a good guy.

"Thanks so much for your time, Sergeant. Just one question. When did the state prosecutor's office— No, wait, let me re-phrase that. When did you learn the state prosecutor reopened the case?"

The sergeant stared at her.

"It was within the last half an hour, right?" Colleen said pleadingly.

He stared some more.

"I don't recall," he finally said as he nodded very slightly at the same time.

And then he gave Colleen a wink.

She winked back with a grateful smile.

Games it was, then, Colleen thought, and her smile disap-peared as she hung up the phone.

70

16

President Cushing's stepdaughter's house was a charming refurbished Victorian, all the way at the other end of Beckford from the college.

Just after noon, Cushing came up on it fast, too fast. He cursed as the tires of his speeding Volvo XC90 made a slight barking sound as he hard braked his brand-new eighty-five-thousand-dollar SUV off the street into the U-shaped driveway.

Rush, rush, rush, he thought as he came to stop and threw it in Park and leaped out.

He'd been at a lunch meeting with the social justice club, just done with soup, when he was interrupted by a text from his stepdaughter, Ashley.

With her husband, Jake, away on business, Ashley had gone to visit a friend in Boston with his stepgrandson, Carter, overnight. But they had hit traffic or something and couldn't get back in time to feed her dog, Lady, and give it its medicine and let it out to do its business.

"If it's not one thing, it's another," he said as he took the porch steps two by two.

He heard the dog whining even before he finally figured out the lock.

"Hold on, hold on," Cushing called out, irritated, as he flung open the heavy wood-and-glass Queen Anne–style door.

His wife, Jodi, was the dog whisperer in the family, but she was out of contact for some reason so his stepdaughter had called him.

Jodi had gone shopping apparently. Again. His wife was doing a lot of shopping lately, wasn't she? Even worse, these days Jodi was always forgetting to have any dinner on the table when he came home. Wasn't like she had to lift a finger as he more than once said they ought to have a live-in maid.

But she wouldn't have it. Said a live-in was akin to slavery. Boy, did that drive him nuts when she rolled out her Christian act.

No, things weren't doing so hot on the Cushing family home front these days and as he was approaching his dreaded fiftieth birthday, he had been doing some deep dive thinking about it.

He had thought that Jodi, a fellow UVA Law School alum, was going to be a stepping stone on Cushing's upward ambitious climb. Jodi was attractive and liked to have fun. But most importantly, her family were old money Virginia rich who owned an industrial manufacturing company that specialized in plastic packaging that was on the stock exchange and cleared thirty million a year.

But after the wedding came the bad news. No family job offer was forthcoming. Jodi's aristocratic father, who from the moment they met had looked at Cushing like he was something nasty he had stepped in on his horse farm, broke it to him at the reception.

So, what are your plans? he had said.

This was a disappointing question. Cushing had been pretty

much banking on a cushy do-nothing-for-a-big-check job offer from Daddy as a wedding present. It was why he had popped the question to Jodi in the first place. Plus, Jodi already had a kid, a daughter by her first husband, a West Point grad. Now he was going to have to raise some other man's kid at an actual real job?

Jodi was supposed to get him to the next level, he thought with an eye roll as he unlocked the dog crate. But these days she was more like an anchor, wasn't she? Holding him back, sucking him down.

He'd put his time in. Twenty years. Murderers received less.

No, it was time to leave Jodi and Ashley, Cushing thought. Maybe drive them back down to Virginia where he'd found them. Leave them at the door of her father's bluegrass estate with a note. *Sorry, Daddy. Change of plans.*

When the dog, a labradoodle, whined again by the back door that he apparently wasn't opening fast enough, Cushing gave it a helpful shove out into the backyard.

"Get moving, you," he said.

He watched it take off for the tree line. He was probably supposed to clean up after it as well, but that wasn't happening.

He had his limits, he thought as his phone rang.

He saw that it was Security Director Travers.

"What?" Cushing said.

"She's at the coroner's now. She's in there talking to them."

"I see," Cushing said.

"She" was the female investigator from New York. The one who was unburying what needed to stay buried.

"This woman is relentless all right," Travers said.

"But she was told at the police department that the case was reopened, correct?" Cushing said. "Chief Garner told me as much himself. Why wouldn't that appease her? Why won't she just leave and go back to New York?"

"I don't know, boss. You want me to stay on her?"

"Yes, of course," Cushing said. "Stay on her until I tell you to stop."

Hanging up, Cushing turned to the living room window at a metal shrieking sound. Across the street from his stepdaughter's house, a yellow school bus was dropping off children, little kindergarteners with backpacks almost as big as they were.

As the bus left, his eyes locked on a picture on the living room mantel. It was of him on a petting zoo visit with his stepgrandson, Carter, the one bright spot in all of this. He couldn't help but smile at his towheaded little buddy. He'd be heading off to kindergarten himself soon enough. It would be hard to leave him behind.

Then Cushing's smile vanished as he remembered the night with Olivia.

The night that was about to get exposed for all the world to see if he didn't figure this the hell out and pronto.

This damn New York investigator. What was he going to do about her? He looked up and then down, trying to think. He rubbed at the bridge of his nose.

Come on, come on, he urged himself. *What is my play here?*

Then he realized it.

He took out his phone and stepped outside onto the back deck.

It was his other phone, the SAT phone that reached out and touched someone through uplinks to satellites orbiting the Earth instead of regular cell sites. It was supposed to be more secure, but was it really? The satellites were so sophisticated they could orbit the Earth but couldn't record conversations? He doubted it.

But that wasn't his lookout, was it? Even he, the *el presidente*, as Ashley called him, had his own boss, his own orders.

He brought up the only number in the contacts. It was one he did not want to call. But he had no choice.

Some issues you could skirt. This was not one of them. Not anymore. This was getting out of hand.

"Time to call Frank," he mumbled as he pressed the button.

17

Camp Hero Beach in Montauk Point State Park, one of the most easterly beaches on New York's Long Island, was rarely crowded during the offseason.

In fact, it only had two cars in its parking lot when the 600-horsepower shiny black Cadillac CT5 grumbled into it at a little after 3 p.m.

Wheeling Cadillac's answer to the muscle car into the lot's farthest corner, Shaw put it in Park, buttoned off the ignition and pulled up the hood of his Carhartt sweatshirt as he got out of the car.

A lover of privacy, Shaw always liked to be where others weren't, at the beach in the fall and winter, in the warmer months up in the hills.

Shaw's level gaze pivoted left to right over the shiny black hood of his elegant muscle car. Then right to left.

He certainly had his reasons.

With his 6'6" height, short light brown neatly cut hair and a not unhandsome clean-shaven face, to a casual observer Shaw seemed like someone in charge of something, an airline pilot or a basketball coach or business executive perhaps.

But businessmen usually didn't have badly reset broken noses. Or an almost avian, cold watchfulness in their restless eyes.

And although businessmen were sometimes lean, they weren't as lean as Shaw. Nor did they have a jacked-up lift to their broadened out back and shoulders that spoke of the strength training and heavy bag smashing that had taken up multiple hours of Shaw's every waking day since he'd been a fresh marine recruit more than twenty years before.

Now that he'd hit his forties, he worked out even harder than ever. He'd lost a step or two the last time he timed himself in the 100-yard dash. But he was definitely physically stronger and could hit harder than at any time in his life.

Not seeing anyone, Shaw finally walked across the gravel lot to the trail. By the ridge's edge, down at the foot of the bluff toward the famous Montauk Point Lighthouse, the only other soul he spotted was a lady in a floppy hat walking on the beach with a small dog.

No wonder it was less crowded than usual, he thought as he headed east along the ridge. It was unseasonably cold today. Upper forties. Forecast even said there might be snow overnight.

Another two hundred feet up along the bluff, he came around a hedge and stopped before one of his favorite places in the world. In the slanted light, the secluded seaside pasture to his left was like a Renoir landscape, a pastel haze of blue and green with a slash of zinc white in the distance for the beach.

There really was something about the light out here in the Hamptons, he thought as he headed across the meadow. The light was so soft yet had a high-definition clearness brought about by all the water. It gave every vista an extra happy, extra vivid sense of mystery and promise. He'd read that it was the light that had attracted so many famous artists from New York City to stay here. Pollock, de Kooning, Warhol.

Shaw, too, had moved out here because of the light. Or was it the water? Because he was born and raised in flat landlocked Ohio or something? he wondered.

He wasn't sure, but there was something about the endless Atlantic out there—all that water and sky and space—that flat out mesmerized him, pulled at something deep within him he couldn't even begin to name.

He had a place several towns west, a cheap town house in Westhampton, a dump really. But one day he was going to pick up one of the twenty-million-dollar Montauk beach cottages nearby, one of the ones with private beach access and a heated pool where he'd just lie out all day, all week. Hell, he could stare out at all that incredible water forever.

Just a matter of time.

And money, of course.

He arrived at the end of the meadow. There was a stand of trees at the far edge and beyond it was a cleared section of tall grass where he stopped. He took a breath. Took it all in. Montauk in the fall. The smell of hay, the sound of birds, the soft rush of the surf. The Atlantic out there on the horizon like a dream of endless time.

On the ground thirty feet to his right lay two uprooted young white birches about fifteen feet in length. They'd probably been knocked over in a nor'easter the year before. They looked kind of like a couple, he thought. A sad tragic one, star-crossed lovers fallen in a suicide pact.

The gun Shaw took out from under his hoodie was a beautiful stainless-steel Springfield Garrison .45 with thin line, checkered walnut grips. There was a silencer on it, a matte black steel one from a company called Federal Nitro Firearms that he wanted to field test. The silencer was almost the same length as the gun barrel.

MICHAEL LEDWIDGE

Back and forth went the oiled slide over the forged frame, snicking a .45 into the chamber with perfect precision.

He raised and fired. Twice in quick succession. So quick it almost sounded like one sound. With the excellent silencer and the subsonic rounds, there had been no telltale firecracker bang. No echo.

You couldn't help the barrel noise from where the casings were ejected but other than that, the two shots had just been short discreet metallic snaps no louder than a car door being unlocked with an electronic key fob.

Not bad at all, he thought, nodding to himself as he checked the empty chamber and tucked the gun away and scooped his brass. He never scrimped on silencers, and the ones being made today were amazing. He'd add it to his toolbox.

He took a Leatherman from his pocket as he walked forward and knelt at the stump. He snapped its knife open and dug first one then the other spent .45 slugs free from the soft white wood.

What was the Boy Scout expression? he thought, pocketing the smashed lead. Take only snapshots, leave only footprints? Sounded good to him.

When he arrived back at the parking lot, he saw his was the only car remaining now. He'd left his phone in a faraday pouch in the CT5's glove box and when he sat and took it out and checked it, he saw there was a job for him.

He read the details. It was a red ball job. A job in the city that needed doing right this very minute. He smiled. Red ball jobs paid the most.

In every large city in the world, there was a man just like Shaw. A man on call there at all times ready to be summoned to action by those in the know. For the last two years, he had been the top go-to in the Northeast for the jobs that needed doing pronto.

The message said they were powering on a chopper out at the airport as he sat there. As usual, the details of who, what, where on the target in Manhattan would be waiting for him.

That wasn't surprising. He'd done several rush jobs in Manhattan before.

His last one three months before had been on the subway. His first push job. It was on some middle-aged lady who hadn't had the time to utter a single word as Shaw had hip bumped her off the Canal Street platform under the wheels of an arriving Q train.

Easiest six figures he had ever scored.

He smiled at the red ball deets on his phone screen.

Now here came another.

This would help the beach house fund, Shaw thought with a glance out at the water.

Then he started the Cadillac with a 6.2 liter fuel injected grumble and spun back and out of the Camp Hero Beach's gravel lot with a V8 roar.

18

As usual, Olivia's father, Emilio Ramos, left the Bronx Hunts Point Terminal food market facility where he worked at four on the dot.

And just as usual, across Food Center Drive, he saw that the bus stop was already crowded with a dozen of his fellow day shift truck loaders waiting on the BX #6.

Yeah, he was one of the dirty dozen all right, he thought, as he trotted across the 18-wheeler-lined industrial street. Or to be more specific, make that one of the dirty *frozen* dozen as they all actually worked in a windowless refrigerated warehouse humping sixty-pound boxes of frozen chicken parts by hand and hand truck and forklift for eight hours straight.

"*Como se cuelgan?*" said his buddy Victor, who was one of the forklift mechanics.

Victor offered him a cigarette from a pack of Marlboros he took out of his pocket.

"Nah, man. I quit," Emilio said as he accepted one with a wink and a smile.

Finding a window seat in the far back of the bus that uncharacteristically arrived two minutes later, Emilio cursed under his breath for forgetting to bring his headphones again.

Because the diesel engine roar would have been bad enough, he thought from where he hunkered down in one of the bus's plastic rear seats, but it was actually nothing compared to the loose window in the back.

The clattering rattle of the window as they blasted over the south Bronx's countless potholes sounded, not just a little but almost exactly, like an M240 belt-fed machine gun laying down suppressing fire.

He knew this from personal experience. Oh, yeah, knew *all* about that sound. He had made it himself often enough from atop the LAV-25 armored reconnaissance vehicle he'd rode in Iraq II with the marines.

To add to this commuting pleasure, the bus couldn't get over twenty-five miles an hour before it had to stop at the next stop and you got a good healthy blast of the nails-on-chalkboard shriek of its rusty-sounding brakes.

Injured in an Accident? he read off a cheap lawyer billboard as they rattled past the Bruckner Expressway overpass.

Emilio shook his head.

Does hearing loss count? he wondered.

"*Conduccion dura,*" said Victor, shaking his head as the window went off again.

"Hard riding," Emilio mumbled to himself as the window started to rattle again. He thought about his time in the war again.

"Story of my life," he said.

Emilio had just gloriously zoned out when a new sound started. It was a light drumming, sporadic little clicks. He looked out through the dust- and fingerprint-streaked plexiglass into the dark gray afternoon.

Freezing rain was falling now onto the death-pallor gray concrete universe of the Bronx.

Perfect, Emilio thought.

Then he remembered something at least a little hopeful. Today was the day the investigator, Colleen, was going up to Connecticut to find out what had happened to his daughter, Olivia.

He checked his phone but there was nothing.

Oh, well. Maybe later or tomorrow, he thought.

As he put the phone away, something caught his attention. Outside the window of the opposite side of the bus, a guy on a motorcycle, a loud Japanese bike, zipped up and stayed along one side of the bus, keeping pace with it.

The biker was a big dude, made the bike look like a toy. He was wearing a full helmet with a black visor and as he rode along, he seemed to peer into the bus windows. Like he was looking for someone up near the front.

Then he slowed and came around the other side of the bus and looked in at Emilio and Victor next to him.

"*Joder es esso?*" the old man said as the biker suddenly tore away.

"Beats me," Emilio said.

Forty minutes later at just after five, Emilio was back in his fifth-floor apartment on 188th Street and Audubon Avenue in Washington Heights.

His favorite chair was a used leather La-Z-Boy he'd bought on eBay, and he was fully stretched out on it, watching the beginning of a Netflix movie about a hot-looking Pam Anderson–like city slicker lady who inherits an Alaskan gold mine when it happened.

Behind him, he very distinctly heard the front door of his apartment open.

"What the?" he said, putting down his fork in the chicken salad he'd put together for himself.

Was it the super? Emilio thought as he laid down the bowl on the floor. He'd do things like that. Open your door with his passkey, wouldn't even knock sometimes. Dude was an enforcer for the landlord, wasn't he? he thought as he stood up. He treated all the renters like garbage.

"What's up, Angel? You ever hear of knocking? What the hell, man?" Emilio said as he came into the hall.

But no one was there. He could see the front door at the end of the hall and it was closed and seemed locked.

Did Angel open it and then close it? Emilio thought, peering at the front of his apartment. *Was he hearing things?*

He walked over and looked down at the lock. It was fine. Then he tried the knob. It was definitely locked.

Then he turned around and looked at the doorway to his kitchen and saw that he hadn't been hearing things after all.

Because standing there was a large man wearing a balaclava.

19

Shaw swung before the target could blink. He caught him flush in the side of the throat just below his left ear with a full inside forearm and the sudden club-like blow smashed perfectly into Emilio's carotid artery, immediately stunning him.

Stepping forward Shaw seized his left wrist in a steel grip and spun him around. As he did this, he slipped his other arm in under Emilio's chin and when his elbow was snug against his throat, Shaw hauled back with everything he had.

Emilio shrieked and tried to throw him as the crushing vise of muscle and bone cut off his oxygen. But Shaw cinched down harder and swung them both around in a nimble pirouette, bashing Emilio's face off the back of the front door.

That had calmed him down some, Shaw thought, as he saw twin rivers of blood begin to stream copiously from Emilio's nostrils. Shaw dug down and squeezed even harder on his windpipe. A second later, he felt Emilio's knees begin to buckle even more.

"That's it. Don't fight it, buddy. It's so much better when you just go along," he urged in a calm, soothing voice in Emilio's ear.

It took three minutes in all for Emilio to go deadweight on him, but Shaw kept up two minutes more on his carotid to make sure.

He gently laid the dead man down on his front hall floor and went into the kitchen. He peeled free some paper towels by the sink and mopped at the sweat on his face and came back out.

The bag of weed he took from the inside pocket of his motorcycle jacket was several ounces. He tore it open and sprinkled some of the rank-smelling stuff in the hall toward the living room and some in the kitchen. He remembered that in the kitchen by the sink was a butcher's knife and he went in and took it off the sticky plastic cutting board.

He went back into the hall and tossed the knife by the door. Then he knelt and pressed Emilio's fingerprints on the plastic of the weed bag before he tucked it underneath him. He didn't bother pressing his fingers on the knife handle since they were already on there.

The play was a botched robbery.

Emilio's record included some drug busts when he was in his teens. So presumably, Emilio was selling some weed and things got out of hand. Maybe pulled a knife and someone got the best of him and then ran panicked away. Happened all the time. Especially in a neighborhood like this one.

What was perfect was the lack of security cameras in the shitbox building, Shaw thought. Cops wouldn't have a clue. As if they ever did.

Anything else? Shaw thought, tapping at his ski-masked chin with a leather-gloved finger as he surveyed his work.

Shaw went into the living room where the TV was playing. On the screen some blonde was getting onto a bush plane.

Netflix and chill, he thought. Emilio would be chilling all right. To room temperature.

He found Emilio's phone on the arm of the recliner and pocketed it. That would stump the cops even further. Make them think the killer was known to Emilio so they took his phone.

Arriving back at the front door, he looked down at Emilio again. What the simple enough, seemingly knockaround dude had done to warrant a high-dollar death sentence, he wasn't sure. They already had a thick jacket on him from multiple hours of previous surveillance which was why he knew to pick him up from his job at Hunts Point.

It must have been something though. For a red ball, Shaw earned two hundred K.

He was really proud of his first contact, he thought as he stared down at the body some more. No thought, straight to grip through instinct through flow. It had been easy. Almost no effort, no exertion. He had just placed himself in the right space, had understood without thought how to get his body there and it was over.

There was an inevitability to it, Shaw thought with a nod. Emilio had felt it, too, just given himself over.

Shaw rolled his neck to get the kinks out.

What separated the good from the great like him was simple really.

"Practice, practice, practice," Shaw mumbled as he finally reached for the doorknob to get the hell out of there.

PART TWO

THIRD WHEEL

20

I got back late from fishing after dark at almost six, and it was almost six thirty when I was in the shower, head down under its raging stream, trying to let its heat loosen the stiff muscles at my neck and back.

My last day of fishing had been basically a bust. I'd tried a new spot six miles upstream from the Beckford Reservoir west of town. But I hadn't gotten a bite all day.

Yet even with the lack of success, it had been a grand day, hadn't it? I thought as I reluctantly squealed off the hot water. Fish or no fish, just being out all day on the wide, sunny, sparkling river watching it slide around me with that pure river smell in my nostrils and the wind for a soundtrack was about as refreshing a day as possible. At least in my fishing-addicted book.

After scrubbing myself raw with a towel, I came out of the bathroom in my robe and headed straight for the tiny kitchen. The fridge was one of those '50s-style vintage ones and when I cracked open the door of it, I smiled.

On the way back from the river I'd hit the village's sole package store, and I took out the icy six-pack of Stella Artois I'd purchased there and ceremoniously placed it on the counter next to an old New England Patriots bottle opener I'd found in a drawer.

After I opened a beer, I carefully placed the cap of it between the thumb and middle fingers of my right hand. The cap shot across the room like a mini turbo Frisbee when I snapped my fingers. I groaned as I watched it ricochet off the wall, barely missing the garbage pail left.

Oh, well. *Can't win them all*, I thought as I took a long incredibly satisfying pull of my beer.

The Airbnb I was renting in Beckford was on the top floor of an old four-story building. Even for a studio apartment, it was pretty small which made me think that it had maybe once been a unit in a rooming house. What I liked most about it was its tall windows and beautiful wide-plank yellow pine wood floors that I crossed in my bare wet feet to the window.

I took another hit of my Stella as I looked down on the quaint village. On my right was the package store roof and across the road from it, there was a canoe rental place that abutted the river. Dead ahead before me was the town's tiny post office and beyond that next to a bridge over the river was a little restaurant called The Forge that I had eaten at almost every night in the two weeks I'd been here.

The reason I couldn't get enough of this place wasn't just because it was in walking distance to my rental but also because of The Forge's famous hot wings. The wings were fried and sauced twice with a special hot sauce that was so ridiculously good they actually sold it in separate bottles. Being a true sucker for a good hot wing, I had become hopelessly addicted to these bad boys at first bite and since then I'd basically eaten my weight in them.

Behind The Forge restaurant and actually jutting out into the bend in the river was an extremely large brick building that looked like an antiquated industrial complex.

A running path plaque I had read explained that the curious structure was the remains of the Beckford Tool Factory which had been a sort of nineteenth-century version of Black and Decker. The company and town founder, an industrialist and inventor named Horace V. Beckford, had diverted the river through an ingenious array of man-made waterfalls, canals and sluices to power water turbine paddles that spun the factory's lathes.

Beckford axes and machetes had helped settle the West, the plaque said, and when the Civil War came, it made weapons for the Union Army. The vast wartime wealth old Horace had accumulated had prompted him to found the fussy liberal arts college down the river that bore his name to this very day.

The old mostly abandoned factory structure was now an antiques shop, I knew. I was actually planning on sticking my head in it before leaving tomorrow. I wasn't big into antiques, of course, but who knew. Maybe like my son, Declan, I thought I might discover another wonderful fishing book about another secret hidden gem of a trout river out there somewhere. Then I could just keep going from magic fishing hole to magic fishing hole across America, catching fish and eating award-winning hot wings and drinking beer forever and ever and ever.

"A man can dream, can't he?" I said, smiling out at the darkening New England town as my phone rang.

That was funny, I thought. I hadn't even given Declan my newest burner phone's number. *Was it a spam call or something?*

Then I suddenly smiled as I saw the name on the caller ID.

"Colleen!" I said, picking it up.

"Mike," she said. "Sorry for calling so late. I'm still up here for work running around like a nut. Is your dinner offer still on?"

"Are you kidding me?" I said. "Of course, Colleen. Bucket list stuff stays on there until you get to check it off or you die. Where are you staying? Can I come pick you up?"

"No need," Colleen said. "I'll meet you. Where do I go?"

"How about the place by me here in Beckford?" I said as I looked at it out the window. "It's just pub grub stuff, but the food is actually quite good. And there's a great microbeer menu. That sound up your alley?"

"Perfect," she said. "Especially the microbeer part. I've had a long one. What's the name of it?"

"It's called The Forge."

"Got it. The Forge, Beckford. Say eight?" Colleen said.

"Eight it is," I said.

After I hung up, I stood there, staring at my phone.

I thought about life. How crazy it really was.

When I was a teenager, I had been in love with this girl. I mean, I had yearned for her. Coming back from the bars, I'd always walk past her house and stare up at her window, hoping the fates would somehow align.

Then life had happened. War. Marriage and fatherhood.

Now here we were again out of the blue.

A date with an angel, I thought as I stared down at the floor in wonder.

"Wow," I said.

21

The business travelers hotel where Colleen was staying out by the interstate was a squat, ugly, modern building of beige brick and tinted glass that looked more like a cheap office building than a hotel.

Pretty drab and depressing, Colleen thought as she stood in a bathrobe with a towel wrapped around her just washed hair.

She tossed her phone onto the bed and pulled her rolling suitcase out from the open closet.

Which actually made sense though, didn't it? she thought as she unzipped the case. It had been one pretty drab and depressing day.

As she attempted to cobble together an outfit, she went over the epic runaround she was currently on the receiving end of. The suddenly unavailable police report had just been the beginning of it. Heading to a county coroner meeting she had scheduled, she suddenly received a call from its office that curtly informed her that it was now unscheduled.

And then as she redirected and went in person into the prosecutor's office in Hartford to talk to someone about the miraculous reopening of Olivia Ramos's case, she'd hit another dead end. When she'd arrived, she was told the prosecuting attorney involved had just left for the day, sorry.

It was a sorry day all right, she thought as she took out her makeup bag.

Which was why she had called Mike.

Mike had been a hero in the old neighborhood even before he had become an official one with the navy SEALs. Fistfights in the Irish Bronx were not uncommon and Mike—who many had nicknamed Hulk in high school because of his stocky stature and football workouts—had participated in more than one or two or three or four of them.

Then after high school, not only had he become a genuine SEAL, he had also been a detective in the NYPD.

A heavy hitter, too, it seemed from the way her fireman brother and cop ex-husband had always gushed about him. They told her stories about how he had been involved in the bomb squad and NYPD SWAT Emergency Service Unit and how he had been a detective in one of the hairiest precincts in Brooklyn. He was retired now but only recently.

And you don't make detective without really knowing your stuff, right? Colleen thought.

Because she was going to need some serious investigative help here to figure this one out, that was for sure. These people at the college and now the town police and prosecutor's office were seemingly engaging in some major cover-up. No way was she used to something this crazy.

Maybe she could ask Mike about the best way to go forward, see if maybe he had ever come across something like this. Maybe he could help her think of something she was missing to get around this corrupt version of a New England stone wall.

The last thing she wanted to do was come all the way up

here and mess this up and somehow face Olivia's father, Emilio, empty-handed.

Life had screwed this poor guy over so horribly. That was why Colleen was determined to get to the bottom of this poor girl's death. Emilio needed a win.

That was also why she was really glad when Mike had picked up. The highlight of her day without a doubt. She just needed to download all of this stuff.

Was that all though? Colleen thought to herself, remembering how Mike looked this morning. *Downloading? That's it?*

No, that wasn't all, she decided as she fished out her concealer. All day long she kept thinking how handsome Mike still was despite all the time that had passed.

She remembered Mike once from a high school football game crushing some bigger guy coming up the gut on a goal line play. This big guy halted like a car had hit him as Mike—off his feet, flying through the air like Superman—hit him in the chest. The ball popping loose as well as the guy's helmet as Mike drilled him into the ground. The crowd going bananas as everyone chanted, Hulk, Hulk, Hulk.

He was just a more seasoned Hulk now, wasn't he? she thought, smiling. Or was *hunk* the word?

And the look on his face when their eyes met in front of the coffee shop. Well, that brought back memories, didn't it?

Tendrils of her dark hair fell on Colleen's cheeks as she pulled off the towel. She blew a wet wisp out of her eyes as she turned and peered and then smiled even more widely at herself in the mirror above the desk.

"Who knows, Colleen?" she said, squinting at herself. "Maybe, just maybe, you still got it after all."

She had just finished blow-drying her hair twenty minutes later when there was a sudden thumping directly above where she was sitting at the desk.

Looking up at the popcorn ceiling, she heard the sound of

children laughing followed by the bark of a dog. A moment later there was some loud rap music. Then the music stopped and there was a yell and she heard a baby crying.

She smiled, thinking about her own childhood and the happy chaos of their home.

She was pooching through her makeup for her mascara when she heard it again.

There was another thump and then another.

But as she looked up, she realized it wasn't coming from the ceiling.

Colleen turned as another knock sounded against her hotel room door.

22

By seven thirty that night, Beckford's Houzelle Gymnasium in the center of campus had the music pumping and all its lights blazing out against the night. Though the men's basketball season didn't start until the first week of November, every year at the end of October, they held a pep rally where they pulled out all the stops.

Pushing in through the arena's front doors, President Cushing's eyes went wide at the increase in volume, the sound of it like something physical as it blasted out from the inner arena into the outer corridor.

And *corridor* didn't really do the space justice, did it? he thought as he crossed through it. Concourse of champions was more like it. At its center was a massive museum-quality cabinet of glass encasing the team's history. There were *Sports Illustrated* covers, gleaming silver engraved trophy cups. Signed game basketballs and cut down nets. All placed upon pedestals as if they were crown jewels.

And just beyond this dazzling display in the center of the

walkway was a kiosk with a high-def screen showing all the greatest moments in Redhawks history. Twist and turn windmill dunks from the high post, behind the back alley-oops, three-pointers at the buzzer. All put on eternal repeat and slo-mo as if they were moments in history and human progress as critical as the raising of the flag at Iwo Jima or the moon landing.

Across from this epic installation was a Dick's Sporting Goods–like gift shop with window dressing that reverently displayed the famous jerseys and sneakers of players who went on to play in the NBA. Along with these holy sweat-stained relics were plenty of glossy color photos of the legends themselves. And beside those were black-and-white photos from the Victorian days of basketball when it had been invented in nearby Springfield, Massachusetts. In these vintage images, old-timey white males wearing turtlenecks and what looked like football pants were frozen in time, forever jumping for a ball with laces on it.

Beyond the gift shop, Coach Houzelle who had led the Redhawks to their two Final Four berths of the national championship in the '80s had been cast in a bronze bust by the arena's front entryway door. The tradition was to pat his bald head for good luck as you went in, and Cushing, knowing one could always use some luck, dutifully tapped the coach for some.

Beyond this idol the half-filled twenty-thousand-person-capacity arena that he headed into could have been mistaken for Madison Square Garden. There were championship banners strung from the ceiling above the bright red seats and on the waxed shimmering hardwood, what looked like a pagan ritual was in full swing.

There were a bunch of guys with tubas along one baseline while on the other side were drummers led by a bass drum guy who had neon lights on his mallets that went off every time they struck. Between this orchestra, cheerleaders flew, spinning through the air, as two sets of dancers—male and female—battled each other theatrically beneath the jumbotron.

As the band stopped, the students in the half-filled stands did a sudden en masse freeze frame. And then some rap song started blasting and they all started yelling and suddenly hopping up and down in the stands with a sound like thunder.

My, my, my, they were really pumping up that jam tonight, weren't they? Cushing thought, wishing he had some noise-canceling earbuds as he made his way up the stairs to the top row of the midcourt VIP seats. *If only the old jam could be pumped down a little for once.*

Waving back politely at faculty and students as he sat, Cushing noticed how the VIP area was mostly empty still, with the most glaring absence being that of his wife, Jodi. That his wife wasn't already here was strange, he thought. She'd sent a text around five that she was done shopping but needed to stop by their daughter's with some clothes for Carter.

Would she have stayed this late though? Cushing wondered. Jodi loved this. Not just all the major ass-kissing they received from the usual grovelers but the actual game itself.

He was up and heading to find himself a drink from the portable bar that was in the corridor behind the VIP seats when his phone rang.

His wife? he thought. Then he looked at the screen and saw it was Director Travers, who was still out watching the New York investigator, who at last report had gone back to her hotel.

He immediately put a finger in his ear and picked up.

"What now, Travers?"

"This…this isn't good, boss."

"What isn't good?"

"I'm at the hotel," Travers said.

"Yes?"

"Well, I just saw someone go in and talk to our, um, target. I thought I recognized them, but I…I wasn't sure so I went out and checked the parking lot. They are still in there right now with the investigator, sir, and this isn't good at all. Not at all."

"What are you talking about? Who went there? Who's talking to the investigator?"

"It's—"

"Who?" Cushing cried.

"It's Jodi, sir," Travers said.

"J-J-Jodi!" Cushing stammered.

"Yes, sir," Travers said. "It's your wife."

23

Colleen's surprise visitor was tallish and blonde and around fifty. Her salon-textured bob had platinum highlights and her middle-aged pear-like shape was expertly hidden in a well-tailored captain's blazer, silk blouse and linen pants. Even without the designer crocodile shoulder bag, everything about her—her hair, her natural yet glowed up makeup, her nails, the self-assured yet serene expression on her face—exuded wealth.

"Okay," Colleen said to her where she had sat her at the desk. "Go over it again a little slower this time, Ms. Cushing."

"Please call me Jodi," she said.

"Okay, Jodi, so you're the wife of the Beckford College president, Martin Cushing?"

"Yes," she said. "And you're here to find out about Olivia, right?"

"Yes, I am," Colleen said.

"And you work for the law firm Alston Brantwood?"

"That's right."

"They're good," Jodi Cushing said as if to herself. "National tier one. I looked them up. I need you to get me a meeting with your top people. Because I'm going to need help, a lot of legal help. Maybe a safe house. I will definitely need security."

Colleen felt the hair on the back of her neck go up.

"Whoa, slow down, Jodi. Why would you need security?"

Jodi's self-assured expression suddenly vanished. Her face went white as she stared down at the carpet. A moment later she lifted the shoulder bag into her lap and snapped open the Yves Saint Laurent logo clasp and produced an iPhone. When she handed it over, Colleen could see that a video was queued up on the screen. It was a grainy black-and-white video. The image showed the driveway of a house. The date line in the top right corner Colleen noticed immediately was October 11, the night of Olivia's death.

"That's the exterior of my house," she said. "Press Play."

Colleen watched as out from the front door came some people. There were four men walking with Olivia Ramos. Two of them seemed to be holding her up. Olivia was covering her face with her hands. Blood was dripping out from between her fingers, dripping off her chin.

"Wait. That's—"

"The director of campus security, Roy Travers. And with him is the Beckford Town police chief, Phillip Garner. The other two men are bodyguards."

"Bodyguards?" Colleen said as she looked on wide-eyed and gobsmacked as the four men put the injured Olivia into an enormous SUV.

"Oh, my goodness," Coleen whispered as she played the video a second time.

The college incident report as well as the local news stories covering the death said that Olivia had spent some time that night at a local college bar and then at around 11 p.m. had gone back to her dorm where she OD'd on fentanyl.

Colleen couldn't stop shaking her head.

No wonder they were giving her the runaround! No wonder!

"Olivia was at your *house* the night she died?" Colleen said.

Jodi's eyes were just as wide as she stared back at Colleen and nodded.

"Why? Why was she there?"

"I'm not positive," Jodi said. "I was staying over at my daughter's house, babysitting that night. But I know one thing. It has something to do with my husband's friend, Frank Stone. Those men are his bodyguards and that Rolls-Royce is Frank Stone's car. He's the one who got my husband the job here at the college ten years ago. They were roommates in college, at the University of Virginia Law School. They're very close friends."

"Frank Stone?" Colleen said. "He's a billionaire, right? The Wall Street guy?"

Jodi nodded.

"Yes, he's one of the richest men in Connecticut if not the world. He's the founder of a Greenwich hedge fund that is connected with the big defense firms and the intelligence services. He's incredibly connected. A very powerful and dangerous man. He scares the hell out of me. Always has."

"What involvement did Olivia have with him?"

Jodi shook her head.

"I've been trying to figure that out. The only connection I can come up with was the incident with Olivia and the article in the school paper."

"What happened?" Colleen said.

"A year ago, there was a scandal," Jodi said. "My husband Martin attended a fundraiser down in Greenwich for a charity that Frank runs. The country club where it was held historically didn't allow in minorities, and Olivia had gotten hold of a picture of my husband giving a speech there and published it in the school paper. A bunch of the students wanted to get my husband fired then. But it didn't happen. My husband made an apology and denounced the club and it blew over."

"Why would a prominent businessman be concerned with a story written by a college kid in a school newspaper?" Colleen said.

Jodi shrugged. She pointed to her phone. At the SUV behind the van.

"All I know is *that* is Frank Stone's car and those are his bodyguards putting Olivia into it the night she died."

"This is unbelievable," Colleen said. "This video is from your home security system?"

"No, it's from an outside nanny cam that I set up on my own. No one else knows about this."

"A nanny cam?" Colleen said.

"Yes. I thought my husband was cheating on me. I've been considering a divorce for a while so I wanted to gather evidence of his infidelity. I got this instead."

"Is there any footage that shows Olivia entering the house?" Colleen said.

"No. She must have been brought in from the back or something. It shows Frank Stone arrive with his bodyguards and then just shows her coming out."

Colleen shook her head, trying to process what she was looking at. It wasn't working.

"This is beyond…" Colleen said.

"I know," Jodi said. "From the moment I saw this after I heard about Olivia's overdose, I've been tortured as to what to do. I mean obviously I would have immediately come forward but look at this. That's the town police chief! You don't understand how powerful Frank Stone is. If he had something to do with killing Olivia, then he can certainly kill me for blowing the whistle on him.

"But when I heard you were here in Beckford today, I couldn't sit on this anymore. I've been praying on it and I knew you were the sign I was waiting for. I knew I had to come forward.

Something needs to be done here. What really happened to Olivia?" Jodi said.

She was getting very emotional now, Colleen saw. She reached out and held Jodi's hand.

"You're doing the right thing, Jodi. I know how difficult this must be."

"And my husband," Jodi said as she started to cry. "He was in there the whole time. I mean, how can he be involved in this? A girl is dead. He's been the only father my daughter knows. And when this comes out! My family, our whole life here, everything will be over."

Colleen watched as Jodi took a deep breath.

"I can't allow this to go on anymore. That's why I'm here. I need your help, Colleen. They might be following me or you right now. If they know I'm talking to you... Please. Do you have a car?"

"They?" Colleen said.

"Director Travers from the video is the head of campus security. My husband has him and some of the other campus security creeps follow me sometimes. And as you just saw, Garner, the town's chief of police, is in this as well. Please. It's not safe here. For either of us. We need to get out of here."

Colleen looked at her, at her frightened eyes. She looked down at the video in her hand. Then she turned and zipped up her rolling case.

"Okay, Jodi. My car's in the parking lot. Let's go."

24

His thoughts whirling, mainlining panic, Martin Cushing hurried down the back stairs of the raucous whoop-there-it-is, rocking college-hoops stands. Across from where the stairs let out at the court level, there was a door beside the restrooms that he entered at a near run.

At the end of the main basement corridor was the janitors' locker room and Cushing almost took its door off its hinges as he swung it open. Without turning on its lights, he locked the door of the deserted room behind him before he collapsed onto a bench.

He sat in the dark between the rows of lockers, breathing rapidly. The air of the room was scented with the astringent reek of chlorine from the nearby indoor pool and as he sat there, its sharp smell suddenly brought his thoughts clearly into focus.

Jodi knew about Olivia. He didn't know how Jodi knew. But she knew.

He bent over and cupped his head in his hands.

And she was going to tell *all* of it.

Holy shit, Cushing thought.

Why had he told her so much about Frank? Why couldn't he keep a secret? Why had he done this to himself?

He knew why. It was his ego. He was bragging, he knew. Trying to impress her with his connections, his secret life, his pull.

It was also to shock her. To dominate her and spice things up in the sack. Ever since they'd met, she would comply to him. It seemed somewhat reluctantly; she never seemed to completely submit. She always held something back. Probably the memory of her first love, Mr. West Point. He wanted to erase that memory. Play the bad boy.

There was only one thing to do now, he knew.

Cushing smoothed out the imaginary wrinkles of his sports jacket as he thumbed the SAT phone on. He went into the janitor's bathroom and got up on the toilet lid and rotated open the eyebrow window to get a signal.

As the phone rang, he looked up at the starry sky and thought about the office on Frank's new yacht. The pale champagne-colored fabric walls and chrome euro chairs around a zinc glass coffee table. A desk of the same zinc glass with a flat-screen computer on it.

He pictured Frank heading to it, his tan-to-the-point-of-sun-damaged face, his long rusty hair swept back into a man bun, the crafty merry look in his intelligent gray-blue eyes. His trainer kept him in tip-top shape so when on his boat, he always wore shorts and a white linen shirt open to the waist to show off the ridiculous superhero definition of his six-pack. All this with his Day-Glo euro sneakers and gold Rolex prominently displayed, of course.

Frank's fifty-going-on-sixteen look made Cushing think of Peter Pan.

That is, Peter Pan with the heart of Captain Hook, Cushing thought. Or was it the crocodile?

And you didn't want to mess with his Lost Boys, he thought.

"Marty," Frank finally said as he got on the line. "Sorry to keep you waiting. I was night parasailing. My latest addiction. They had to hoist me down to take the call. So it took some time."

Cushing thought about how rich Frank was. No telling. How deep was the ocean? *Parasailing-off-your-hundred-million-dollar-yacht-after-dinner rich*, Cushing thought.

"We have a problem, Frank," Cushing said.

"I don't like those," he said.

"I'll just say it," Cushing said. "There's been some issues between me and Jodi and she's, well, there's no other way to say it, she's left me."

"Oh?" Frank said. "I'm sorry to hear that."

"Just now. Which I wouldn't even have bothered you about except…she's left with the investigator from Alston Brantwood."

"Right now?" Frank said.

"Yes."

"I see," Frank said. "Tell me. How much does she know, Marty?"

Cushing looked down at the toilet he was standing on.

"A little. Nothing major. She's just pissed off at me," Cushing tried.

"Now, now, Marty. Don't equivocate. She knows enough to head to that law firm investigator."

Cushing looked up at the stars again, wishing one would fall on him. An asteroid impact at this point would be quite welcome, just what the doctor ordered.

"She's just pissed," he said, grasping at straws. "You know women."

"I do know women, Marty. She's obviously out to hurt us. Are your security people on them?"

"Yes."

"Good. Here's the play. Have your locals detain the both of them. The investigator and Jodi. Discreetly put them somewhere quiet until my people get there. This has gone far enough. We need to clip this clean before things get even worse."

Cushing swallowed as he thought about what *clip this clean* meant.

"I can talk to Jodi, Frank," Cushing said quickly. "I'll get her back in line, I promise."

There was a pause on the line.

Cushing eyed the stars again. He made a wish, pictured a satellite slamming into another cutting him off from this.

It didn't happen.

"We'll see what rolls out, Marty," Frank finally said. "First things first. Get them contained."

25

Coming out through the side exit of the hotel, Colleen noticed the vehicle right away.

At the far end of the outdoor lot, there was some kind of light blue car, a Nissan sedan, off by itself pointing right at them.

"There it is," Jodi said panicking. "That's Travers. I told you they were following me. That's my husband's campus police squad."

"I'm the black SUV on the right here. C'mon," Colleen said.

As Colleen turned the RAV4 rental over, she saw the Nissan already start to move.

When she pulled out and looked in the rearview, she immediately felt her heart start beating faster.

Because the Nissan was right behind them and it really was Travers behind the wheel wearing sunglasses and a baseball hat.

"He's following us," Jodi said.

"I know. Don't worry about it. It's going to be okay," Colleen said with a calm she was *not* feeling.

Coming down the lot apron for Route 4, Colleen scanned

up ahead. On the left across the road, there was a Subway just before a traffic light.

As she pulled out, she immediately hit her left clicker, hanging back, pretending she was going to turn into its parking lot.

"What are you doing?" Jodi said.

"Seeing what he's going to do."

Colleen let out a tense breath as the campus security car stopped right behind them.

Looking at Travers in the rearview, she remembered her entire purpose of coming up here. Use the element of surprise to confront them and see if they reacted.

They were reacting all right, she thought swallowing.

What the hell will he do? Just keep following us all the way to New York?

A car slowing behind the Nissan came around in the shoulder. Colleen kept waiting, watching. The green light turned yellow. She suddenly gunned it and just made the light.

"Did he come through after us?" Colleen said, still speeding.

"Yes!" Jodi said.

"Shit," Colleen said.

Sixty seconds later the road began to curve up a rise toward the intersecting overpass of the interstate. As they came closer, Colleen realized the road was about to fork into the northbound and southbound entrances of the interstate itself.

The way south toward NYC was on the right-hand side up a long on-ramp, and just as they were about to get on it, Colleen looked up at the interstate overpass and watched as a car pulled off the highway to wait by the top of the on-ramp.

"Look! It's a trooper car!" Jodi cried out. "You can't go up that way! Travers used to be cop. He must be calling in favors from his cop friends. The local law enforcement around here are deeply connected to this. They helped cover it up. Whatever you do, do not go up there!"

Colleen looked back as she slowed.

The Nissan was coming up behind them fast.

She looked forward at the fork in the road. Even if she didn't get on the southbound ramp, she would have to get on the interstate heading north. Other troopers could just as easily pull them over on that side as well, right?

Glancing to her left, Colleen suddenly invented a third option. She whipped the wheel hard left and the car jostled with a thump as she pulled up onto a grass median.

Jodi shrieked as they bumped over the uneven ground around the base of a traffic sign.

When you come to a fork in the road, take it, came a crazy thought in Colleen's head as they continued to make the world's most illegal U-turn.

Boy, was she being inflexible now, she thought as the RAV4's passenger door suddenly scraped loudly against a concrete jersey barrier.

She didn't give a shit. Not anymore. They needed to get out of here.

She squeezed them onto the interstate exit lane back into town. As they drove back the way they had come, Colleen could see that Travers was pulled over across the median in the shoulder now on his phone.

Before she could stop herself, Colleen honked and gave Travers the finger as they blew past in the opposite direction.

Jodi laughed nervously. "Where to now?" she said.

Colleen lifted her phone.

"Siri, directions. The Forge."

26

It was a quarter to eight when I stepped out of my Airbnb onto the town's flagstone sidewalk for The Forge and my date with Colleen.

Beckford really was one of those hidden gems of a little town, wasn't it? I thought as I stood for a moment in the crisp cool air. It had a town green, a bunch of meticulously renovated Victorian houses, old-fashioned plate glass–fronted stores, a white steepled church. There was a big Halloween parade in the town every year and all the giant windows of the stores were already decorated for it.

It looked like something out of an old *Twilight Zone* episode where someone goes back in time, I thought as I came to the end of its main street and crossed into The Forge's gravel parking lot.

I smiled.

Hell, it felt like a *Twilight Zone* episode, I thought smiling as I thought of spending time with Colleen.

Just inside the restaurant's heavy wood door, there was a wait-to-be-seated area, but since I was early, I just crossed to the dark bar beyond it and slid into one of its booths where I could face the door.

The Forge was a casual place but nicely appointed. The walls above the wainscoting were painted English racing green, and there were equestrian oil portraits everywhere of show horses and fox hunts.

The little history about it on its menu said it had been renovated many times but that main part of the barnlike building had originally been built in 1790 as an inn. Then after the Beckford Tool Factory was built just behind it, it had been converted into the depot for the train line that had come through. But the train was discontinued when the factory closed in the 1960s and sometime in the late '80s, it had been turned by one of the locals into a restaurant.

"Well, aren't we looking spiffy tonight," said a voice behind me as I was checking my watch.

The short, feisty and plump bespectacled sixtysomething waitress I found smiling at me as I turned was named Daisy.

Daisy had "a lot of moxie" as they said in old movies. And being a big fan of moxie, I'd gotten into a routine of bantering with her over the last two weeks I'd eaten there.

"Do you really think so?" I said as I rose in my seat, straining to look at myself in the mirror behind the bar.

Clean-shaven with my hair pasted to one side with a little styling gel, I was wearing a pair of khakis with a button-down blue-checked dress shirt. Trying to look my best, I'd even passed everything through the travel iron. My lace-curtain Irish grandmother would have been impressed with the razor sharpness of the creases I'd put in my pants.

"You're pretty as a picture," Daisy assured me with a wink. "Let me guess. Hot date?"

"Is it that obvious, Daisy?" I said, grinning back.

"I figured with that nervous look on your face, it's either that or you're applying for a job. Corona to start as usual?"

"Yes, please, Daisy, and when the lady gets here, please make sure you keep them coming. You know, for my nerves," I said.

The bar she walked off toward was a big, elaborate, darkly varnished horseshoe-shaped affair with all the booze bottles on an island in the middle of it. The bartender behind it, who was also the owner of The Forge, was a tall, lanky, middle-aged man named Scotty.

Scotty had the look of an aging hippie with his long gray hair and wore aviator-style eyeglasses along with a defeated expression of a guy who seemed suspicious that maybe life had passed him by. In front of him sat about a half a dozen regular Joe six-packs staring up at a big flat screen on the back wall where a hockey pregame for the Carolina Hurricanes versus the Pittsburgh Penguins was underway.

As my eyes drifted into the restaurant's dining room, I saw at its biggest table there were a half dozen rough-and-tumble guys laughing and carrying on. I'd seen this group three or four times before. Daisy had told me they were construction workers who were staying in town for the last month, refurbishing the bridge as well as retrofitting a huge modern hydroelectric generator into one of the old Beckford Tool Factory's brick mills beside it.

"What's up with the dinner party with the rowdies?" I said when Daisy came back with my beer.

"I think one of them is leaving or something so they're having a going-away party."

"Are they done with the project?" I said.

"Getting close it seems," Daisy said, "which is making Scotty more depressed than usual. With the way these roughnecks drink, he was thinking of retiring to Palm Beach."

As the men continued to laugh and make fun of each other, I

found myself smiling over at their masculine chop-busting merriment. Like most former cops and soldiers, having spent most of my life working with other men in tight-knit units, one thing I really did miss in my retirement was the goofing around and camaraderie.

With nothing else to do as I sipped my beer, I found myself imagining that the men at the table and I were all in the same SEAL unit together and I decided to come up with call signs for them.

The one with the most serious face on him who was probably the foreman was a wiry medium-sized man of about fifty with short spiky red hair and a reddish mustache. That was Sonic.

Next to him was a thin, long-faced sort of poetic-looking Hispanic guy with a goatee who was maybe thirty. I noticed he favored plaid shirts so he was Plaid Don Juan.

The oldest of them was a stocky white guy in his midfifties with a buzz cut and glasses and a graying beard. He always sat there with his arms folded, drinking beer and laughing softly at everything. He seemed to exude more intelligence and competence than Sonic so maybe he was an engineer or something? I dubbed him Papa Bear.

The bald thirtyish guy in a neon orange hoodie next to him looked like he worked out a lot and had a loudmouth New York street accent. I dubbed him Brooklyn.

And last but not least was a lanky and gangly, scruffy blue-eyed pothead sort of guy of thirty or so with longish brown hair. He was Shaggy, of course.

The farewell dinner must have been going on for quite a bit because the gang seemed even drunker than the last time I'd seen them. Which was saying something.

I took another hit of my own *cerveza mas fina* then decided to check my watch again.

It was 8:15 now, I saw with a frown.

Colleen was running a little late.

Or had she fallen asleep or something?

That would suck, I thought. Really suck. If she was asleep then that would be it. Tomorrow obviously she would be done with her work up here and be gone.

I looked at my watch again.

Was my bucket list going to go wanting after all?

27

A Mormon temple flashed by outside the window. And then a driving range. A red light ahead made Colleen pause, but then it went green and she hammered it alongside a cornfield, picking up the pace back toward the center of Beckford.

They were in Jodi's car now, a new Mercedes-AMG C 43 sedan. It was Colleen's idea to do the quick switch back at the hotel parking lot as Travers was no doubt putting an APB out on her rental.

Jodi was a nervous wreck so she had insisted that Colleen drive.

She wasn't the only one, Colleen thought as she took the nimble silver Merc up to seventy.

It wasn't just the Connecticut countryside out the window that was a blur. That video. *Holy moly, the video,* Colleen thought.

Everything was coming at a pace almost too fast for her to process.

The next time she had to slow was at a traffic light near a supermarket and a McDonald's about three miles from the interstate. They were two cars back, and off to the left along the intersecting road, there was a small truss bridge over a river.

A sense of dread immediately shot through Colleen as her eyes were drawn toward the bridge. At the top of a rise on the other side of it was a dark blue police car. It came down the slope straight toward them, its roof lights strobing red and blue.

"Those are the Beckford town cops," Jodi said with a groan. "Travers must have found the car in the lot and called the police chief about us. What are we going to do now?"

Colleen quickly glanced down at the map on her phone. Past the light, it was a straight shot down Route 4 to the center of Beckford and The Forge. Two miles tops. Before she had time to stop herself, Colleen made a command decision.

She spun out into the opposite lane and gunned it through the red light.

Horns blared at their back as they whizzed down Route 4. They passed a church, and an old, brick firehouse. Past the firehouse was another small truss bridge and as they arrived on its opposite side, Colleen slammed the accelerator to the floor.

The Merc's AMG engine gave out a little scream as they leaped forward. Then there was nothing but trees on the right and a gray cliff on the left rushing past. As they came through a ridge canyon two fast minutes later, they could see the yellow lights of the town square immediately on the other side of the river over another small bridge.

The Merc shuddered as Colleen braked hard and screeched a ninety-degree right onto the bridge.

The Forge was on the right just on the other side of the bridge but Colleen intentionally blew past it. She'd just swerved past a canoe place on the left and a Civil War memorial cannon on the right when she saw a car dealership dead ahead and she slammed on the brakes and made a hard left at its parking lot.

They were still skidding when they hit its curb very hard. They both let out a yell as they bumped up in their seats almost high enough to hit the roof. But they just made it into the lot, and Colleen drove down the row of cars quickly parking at its end.

"Get down," she said, pulling at Jodi's arm as a blue light of the speeding town police car swept by at top speed.

"Out now," Colleen said, pulling open the door. "We need to leave the car. They're looking for it now."

"But where are we going to go?" Jodi said.

"The Forge. The restaurant there," Colleen said, pointing. "I know someone in there who will help us."

At least I hope so, Colleen thought.

28

Around twenty after eight, I turned toward a bunch of yelling and fist pounding by the bar to see that the Hurricanes had just scored.

"A lot of hockey love in the air tonight, huh," I said to Daisy as she placed down a new beer.

"Oh, yeah. Every time the Hurricanes play, it's a real riot in here."

"For the Carolina Hurricanes? I don't get it. Why?" I said.

"They used to be the Hartford Whalers is why," Scotty said from the bar. "The only damn professional franchise this area ever got its hands on. And then in the late '90s, they let them go south."

I smiled at the long-haired man's constant gloomy take on the world. His pessimism was like a bass tone to Daisy's energy and feistiness.

"Whalers weren't the only thing that started going south around here in the '90s," Daisy said to me under her breath as she tossed a thumb at the bar.

"Scotty's one of those real glass-half-empty types, huh?" I said.

"You're telling me," she said. "True story. One time this high roller comes in after a game at the college, some NBA owner, I forget his name. Guy has one drink at the bar and tosses down a hundred. Says to Scotty, keep the change, and leaves. You know what Scotty says?"

I laughed.

"No, what?"

"He holds up the C-note, turns it this way and that, and says, 'Look how dirty this bill is.'"

I was still laughing as Daisy headed back to the bar and then I looked at the front door and I saw Colleen.

Then I stopped laughing.

I did a double take as I saw the crazed look on her face. There seemed to be another person with her, a middle-aged blonde woman, who was looking pretty frazzled as well.

Colleen bolted straight toward me. She sat down in the booth seat opposite with the woman sliding in next to her.

"Mike, listen," Colleen said, flushed and out of breath.

I looked closely at her face. I didn't like her color. She was too pale. And there was a distant look in her eyes. Like they were losing focus, as if she was on the verge of fainting.

She really did seem discombobulated. Both of them did. As a combat vet, I knew trauma when I saw it. They both seemed to be in a kind of shock.

A car accident? I thought. Something had happened to them.

"YES!" someone yelled behind us as the Hurricanes scored again.

"Colleen," I said as calmly as possible. "Take a breath."

"Mike," Colleen said again.

"No, breathe, Colleen," I said, touching her hand. "Breathe first."

Colleen finally took in a deep breath and loudly let it out.

"Are you guys okay?" I said. "Are you hurt or something? Was there a car accident?"

We all looked up as Daisy arrived.

"What can I get you guys?" she said.

"A shot of Jameson with a beer back. Heineken if you got it," Colleen said, sitting up.

I noticed that the color on her face looked a little better now.

"Me, too," the mystery woman said in a too loud almost crazy voice. "I'm having what she's having."

"Alrightee, then," Daisy said, giving them a puzzled look as she left.

"Okay, Colleen," I said. "What's up?"

"Listen, Mike," Colleen said, staring at me steadily with her wide pale eyes. "I don't really have time to explain but do you have a car? We need a ride out of here. Like, now."

I stared at her. What that meant, I didn't know. Though what I vaguely remembered from what Colleen had told me about her investigation, the search terms "dead college girl" and "thirty-four billion dollars" suddenly leaped to mind.

"Your case? You're in some kind of trouble?" I said.

Colleen nodded vigorously.

"We need a ride out of here now. I can explain in the car."

I counted off three twenties from the roll in my pocket and laid them on the table as I stood.

"I have a black pickup truck, a Ford F-150, two blocks away," I said. "I'll run up and get it and honk when I get to the front door here. Sound good? You'll be okay until then?"

"Yes, Mike. That's perfect," she said. "Just hurry."

"On it," I said, moving.

"See? I told you I knew someone who could help us," I heard Colleen say to the woman as I left.

"You weren't kidding," the mystery woman said at my back.

"Leaving so soon?" Daisy called over to me from the bar as I passed her.

"Change of plans, Daisy," I said, forcing a smile as I hit the door.

29

Campus Security Director Roy Travers parked his Nissan in the street beside Desmond Autos just north of the center of town and got out and threaded his way past the three police cars that were already there.

Jodi Cushing's silver Mercedes was parked in the end of the lot, its passenger door open.

"Hey, Phil," he said as he stepped up.

Chief Garner, sitting in the passenger seat, closed the glove box he'd been rifling through.

"Hey, Roy," Garner said as he gave Travers a knowing here-we-go-again look.

It was a look Travers had seen before, many times. He and Garner had known and worked with each other for over a decade, patching up all the things in a small expensive college town that needed patching. The secret things that were best kept out of the papers. And especially the college's marketing brochures and ESPN.

All the rapes, the ODs, the drunk driving accidents, the suicides. Yeah, they had mopped up some real doozies together all right.

But none of them compared to the night they were both called in to deal with Olivia Ramos a year ago.

And here, just like that, the can of worms had suddenly reopened, hadn't it?

It was going to be one hell of a long night, Travers thought.

"Any sign?" Travers said.

"They're on foot," Garner said, standing. "An old lady across the street heard the brakes and saw them walking away from the car toward the town square."

"Does Cushing's wife have any friends over this way?" Garner said as he stood. "Any family?"

"I asked the boss the same question," Travers said. "He has no idea. He doesn't think so."

"Okay, I'll set up roadblocks. What do we do when we grab them at a checkpoint? Just detain them? Give them the runaround?" Garner said.

"Uh-huh," Travers said. "Just hold them in the town tank. The boss said Shaw is on his way."

"Oh, no. Not that guy again," Garner said, rolling his eyes.

"Don't sweat it, Phil. We just work here, right?"

Garner went to his cruiser and reached in and lifted the radio.

"Listen up, guys. Drop what you're doing," Garner called into it. "I need roadblocks on both sides of the Route 4 bridge ASAP. I repeat. ASAP. Set it up like a drunk driving checkpoint. We are on the lookout for two females."

"What?" cried the sergeant on duty after a crackle of radio static. "Why?"

"We got a BOLO from the feds about detaining two women. I will send you the pics forthwith," Garner lied.

"What did they do? Rob a bank?" the sergeant said.

"Some Homeland Security thing from the Counterterrorism Center. Above my paygrade. Just says that they are definitely in the area and if we find them, take them into custody. The feds are on their way."

"You got it, Chief," the on-duty sergeant said over the radio. "Where do you need me?"

"I'm already set up by the canoe place to the west. You take east on the far side of the bridge and set up back a little in the canyon on the other side of the old package store."

"Roger that."

Travers smiled grimly as he shared another look with Garner.

Middle-aged, barrel-chested and short, Chief Garner played like he was a harmless, goofy, small-town dope but he was sharp. Especially when it came to covering his own ass.

"How are we on containing this?" Travers said. "The boss said we need to try to block any calls."

"I heard. Don't worry. I got the big bubble box right here on already so there is no cell service in or out from the area now. If they're still within a three-mile radius, we're good on that front."

"So, what now?" Travers said.

"I need pictures of them for my guys," Garner said.

Travers with his head down at his phone sent the picture of Colleen Doherty he'd already taken from the campus security footage. Or tried to send it. But it didn't work.

"I can't send. Turn off the bubble box for a second," Travers said.

"Oh, right," Garner said, reaching in and hitting a switch on the electronic box on his seat that was jamming all cell service.

"Okay, good," Garner said as he re-sent the pics along to his men with his own phone.

Then Garner turned the cell site jammer to the on position again.

"Let me get this straight," Garner said, peering at Travers now. "You're telling me Cushing wants us to put his wife, his own wife, in the slammer to wait for that maniac Shaw? Wow."

"Yeah, that is some pretty coldhearted shit right there. Isn't it?" Travers said. "I knew the boss didn't play around, but sheesh."

"I guess what they say is really true," Garner said, shaking his head.

"What's that?" Travers said.

"The rich really aren't like you and me after all."

30

"Mike, Jodi. Jodi, Mike," Colleen said.

Colleen was sitting beside me in my Ford F-150's passenger seat with her mysterious friend now sitting behind her in the crew cab.

In the rearview I looked at Jodi's silk clothes, her fancy handbag. There was a well-bred look about her, a Park Avenue elegance and grandeur. She looked like a model in a Nordstrom catalog.

What in the hell was this about? I thought.

I swung a U-turn around on the street in front of The Forge and stopped at the light for Route 4. When I looked to the right about a quarter mile up, I saw there were a bunch of cop cars.

When I turned to Colleen, I noticed that she was looking in that direction as well. None too calmly.

"Where are we going?" I said.

"We need to head left," Colleen said, turning to me. "Just go left."

"Left. Got it," I said.

When the light turned green, I did go left. But instead of getting on the bridge, I suddenly pulled in alongside a boom crane at the worksite that belonged to the construction guys from the bar.

"What are you doing?" Colleen said as I put the truck in Park. "We need to move it. Come on."

"I will in a second," I said. "After you tell me what's going on and who your friend here is. Those cops up there are for...?"

"They're for Jodi and me," Colleen said, staring at me. "Remember I told you about my case? The dead girl from Beckford College?"

"Yes," I said. "Olivia something."

"Olivia Ramos," Jodi said behind us.

I looked back at her.

"Well," Colleen said, turning to the back seat, "Jodi, hand up the phone."

Colleen tapped the screen of the iPhone Jodi handed her and held it out for me.

It was a video and in it, a girl was being led out of a house by four men, two on either side of her. She was stumbling as if drunk. When she turned back in the direction of the camera, what looked like blood was dripping from her mouth as they put her into an SUV.

"That's Olivia. This is video on the night of her death coming out of the house of the president of Beckford College," Colleen said.

"It's my house," Jodi said.

"Your house? You're the college president?" I said.

"No," Jodi said. "My husband, Martin Cushing, is the president. I'm Martin's wife."

I looked back at Colleen, perplexed.

"In the college incident report," Colleen said, "it said that night Olivia went from a local bar and then back to her dorm where she OD'd on fentanyl. It didn't say anything about Olivia coming out of the college president's house bleeding!"

"Wow," I said. "How do the cops fit in?"

"These two bastards here," Colleen said, pointing at the phone screen. "This is the director of campus security, Travers, and this is the town chief of police, Garner. They're in on it."

"Holy shit. For real?" I said.

"Yes," Collen said. "And as we were leaving my hotel, we spotted Travers in the parking lot. He followed us out toward the interstate. And then suddenly we started seeing state police cars and town police cars everywhere. They were still chasing us as we got here so I dumped Jodi's car up the street there from the restaurant and we walked back to you."

"Okay," I said, looking in the rearview at the police lights. "I'm starting to see. Sort of. Who are these two other guys in the video?"

"Bodyguards for Frank Stone, my husband's close friend. That's his car," Jodi said.

"Frank Stone is a billionaire hedge fund guy who President Cushing went to law school with," Colleen said. "So, you can see why they're going bananas to cover this up, Mike. Jodi's video is extremely damning.

"These guys stonewalled me all day. First the college, then the town police. And they must have been following me. That's why you need to get us out of here, Mike. We need to head back to New York now."

I looked down at the screen of the phone again as I thought about everything I had just been told.

"Okey dokey. Time to go," I said as I immediately put the truck in Drive and pulled out.

We went across the bridge and made the turn onto Route 4 to the left and passed a church and a small convenience store.

That's when we saw the line of cars.

Up ahead a dozen cars were at a standstill where the road cut through a small canyon, and just beyond them, you could see blue and red lights swinging along the rock.

"Oh, no. It's them!" Jodi said in a panic. "Garner has a road block on this side, too. Now we're stuck. We're too late!"

31

The two helicopters were slick six-seater luxury Sikorskis and it was 8:45 p.m. when they landed at something called the Robertson Airport in somewhere called Plainville, Connecticut.

"Beach house, here I come," Shaw mumbled as the wheels touched down.

He'd been at the Manhattan heliport, about to be flown home to Long Island, when the office had told him his night wasn't over yet. They were going to do an actual full-spectrum FBI circus con job up in Connecticut and guess who was to be the ringmaster.

He couldn't believe his luck. The bigger the hit, the higher the price tag. And it looked like the hits were going to keep on coming tonight.

And it was a circus all right. A three-ring one. Even though there were only two other mercs in Shaw's helicopter, you could hardly move it was so packed with all the gear.

The three of them plus the two in the other craft added up

to five and they were all already draped in their FBI Hostage Rescue Team tactical regalia.

He lovingly patted at the famous patch on his khaki plate vest.

Nothing like the old G-man hero cover to snow any of the little people who took a questioning little peek at what was going on.

"Just like old times, boys, huh?" Shaw said, smiling like a movie star at the two men across from him.

If the two short pitted-faced Middle Eastern men smiling back at him looked like they could have been brothers, it was because they were.

Their names were Azar and Shahu and though Shaw wasn't the actual goat herding father of the two young Afghanis, they were his boys nonetheless.

He had raised them himself back in the shit of Afghanistan. Took them out of the translator section and put them through the paces of the sweep and clear program he ran.

That they were brothers was key. He could see that they already worked as a team. Soon they were working as *his* team.

On the in-theater off-the-books jobs that enlisted Americans might not have the stomach for, he needed some good local yokels, and Azar and Shahu had fit that bill and then some. They'd been like his right and left hands.

How many night raids had the three of them been on? Helicopter in like midnight angels of death, blow a door, throw all the military-aged men out into the dirt yard and start popping everyone before anyone knew what hit them.

Night after night after night, they would employ the most relentlessly vicious and brutal tactics possible then get the hell out of there.

Once it got started, anyone likely near a target's cell phone took a dirt nap. As in anyone and everyone. Gender, age or anything else need not apply. The brass up top had said send a message, and so Shaw had followed orders. In village after village, he and his men had sent a nightly news flash that no one would ever forget.

When that war had come to an unfortunate close, of course Shaw had brought the two brothers back with him. He was smart enough to know not to leave that kind of finely honed talent behind. It was he himself who had gotten them their jobs at Vance Holdings, the private merc firm.

His boss Vance had thought they were too green still. But Vance didn't know his ass from his elbow. Shaw had put his foot down that they be brought aboard. He had insisted.

So it was a no-brainer that Shaw include them here on this clambake.

He glanced over at his two little hunting dogs, Azar and Shahu, in the chopper light's yellow-greenish glow.

"You ready to kick some ass, boys?" he said.

"Sir, yes, sir," they replied in unison.

Good dogs, he thought.

Oh, yeah, Shaw thought.

The old tingly feeling was coming back.

This is going to be fun.

32

"Shit, the phones!" Colleen suddenly said as we sat at the end of the stalled line of cars on Route 4. "They turned them off or something. Look! No bars!"

I looked at my burner. She was right. Not a single bar.

"Cops can do that? Block cell phones?" Jodi said.

"They sure can," I said. "In the NYPD we had these things called a wave bubble, a wide bandwidth radio frequency jammer about the size of a pack of cigarettes. We used them all the time. Right before no-knock raids."

I made a sudden command decision then. I crossed the double yellow line and made a left into the small empty parking lot of the convenience store. As we parked in front of it, I could see that the lights were off and there was some empty shelving by the window. It appeared to be closed for renovations or something.

Beside the store was a trail for the ridge that ran alongside Route 4. I leaned over and grabbed a pair of binoculars from my glove box.

"Stay here. Be right back," I said, getting out of the truck.

There was a lightly wooded area directly behind the closed store, and I found a deer trail in it and headed up. As I arrived at the top of the ridge, I saw it was higher than it looked from below. I crouched down with the binoculars.

It was definitely a roadblock. There were two blue town police cars parked sideways across the eastbound lane. There were four cops at it and they were getting the driver of a minivan to open up the side door. As I watched this, a fire truck pulled up and a couple of firemen jumped out of it and started laying down orange cones.

I stood then and glassed the other side of the river.

"Gotta be shitting me," I mumbled as I saw there were even more emergency lights on the other side of Route 4 alongside where Colleen had left the car.

"You're right. It's definitely a checkpoint," I said as I arrived back into the truck.

I leaned over and quickly took out the map of the area I had in my glove box. Though Declan gave me hell for it, like many fuddy-duddy men over a certain age, especially former military ones, I hated relying just on my cell phone to know where I was so I always had physical maps as a backup.

Score one for the fuddy-duddies, I thought as I unfolded the paper map of Connecticut.

As I scanned it, I came to the depressing realization that Route 4 was the only way in or out of the town. Rimmed by ridges with a huge reservoir to the northwest of town, we were boxed in.

"Hmm," I said as I looked over the map again.

"Hmm what?" Colleen said.

I looked at the map some more. Then I snapped my finger.

"Wait," I said, pulling the transmission down into Reverse.

"What now?" Colleen said as I backed us around.

I pulled out on Route 4 west away from the checkpoint but

as I made the bridge, instead turning right onto it and heading back into the town, I kept going.

"There's another way out?" Colleen said.

"There might be," I said, handing Colleen the map. "See this huge hill all along the left here and how all these roads dead end up at the top of it?"

Colleen nodded.

"At the end of this road, there's a reservoir. Though it's not on the map, there's a water company service road that runs along its shore and spillway bridge. Its other end leads out onto Route 202. Maybe they didn't cover that far. If we can get on the water company service road, maybe we can head out that way."

"So, we're home free?" Jodi said hopefully.

"Not exactly," I said. "There's a gate across the access road, but I think if we go off-road a little, we may be able get around it."

"Don't say maybe, Mike," Colleen said, crossing her fingers. "We have to get away from them now."

33

The town of Beckford where all the action was going down was a quick fifteen-minute drive from the rural airport.

Riding on the outside running board in the armored BearCat that picked them up at the tarmac, Shaw grinned in the breeze as they came around the bend and he saw the carnival of police lights.

In the flutter of the blue and red were about a dozen cops and another dozen or so lookie-loos obviously jazzed at all the sudden action.

They weren't the only ones who were amped up, Shaw thought.

All this was at his beck and call?

He'd almost do this for free.

They went around a couple of parked fire trucks, and out in the street a fireman on foot with those glowing signal sticks guided them into the parking lot of a post office.

The lot was filled with about thirty people running around and as Shaw and the others disembarked off the tactical vehicle wearing their FBI HRT crap, all the law enforcement standing there looked at them with an almost religious awe.

The sainted FBI Hostage Rescue Team act was one of his all-time favorites, Shaw thought, stifling a smile.

Gape on, dupes, he thought as he strode past them with the swagger of Caesar crossing the Rubicon.

Little do you know that you, too, can become a member of the FBI HRT. You're just one cheap Walmart navy windbreaker and a yellow iron-on away.

His company SAT tablet inside his plate vest vibrated as he heard a beep in his earpiece. He lifted the tablet out.

"Hey," Control said. "Check out the targets."

"Roger," Shaw said as a picture of a blonde woman filled the tablet screen.

"That's Jodi Cushing target one," Control said, "and here's two."

A pretty, dark-haired younger woman replaced the blonde.

"That's Colleen Doherty," Control said.

"Both ice cream flavors, huh?" Shaw said. "Not a bad body on the dark one. Now send a brunette and we can have all three of Charlie's Angels."

"Who's Charlie?" said Control.

How could you not know what *Charlie's Angels* was? Shaw thought. Then he remembered how young some of the new Control people were.

But just being green wasn't a sufficient excuse though, was it? he thought. Growing up, he and his peers had easily understood the cultural references that the previous older generations used. They had instinctually wanted to know them in order to figure out what was cool and what was going on, so they could grow up and be adults themselves. It was how culture worked, the older and experienced passing down things to the new and inexperienced.

But this wasn't the case now? Shaw thought. How? Was it the

phones? The schools? Or 5G? Was the new generation grown in a lab?

"Skip it," Shaw said.

"Also, the blonde is to be delivered intact," Control said.

"Intact?" Shaw said. "Intact is a pain in my ass. Why?"

"The note says, 'Extract her in one piece. Not a hair on her downy head. Vance.' Got it?"

"Got it. Over and out," Shaw said with disappointment.

Extractions, Shaw thought. He hated extractions. They always turned out to be a real pain in the ass. Even if you brought the target back without a scratch, there was always bitching, always complaints.

Especially extractions of females. They would claim you raped them. They also usually tried to scratch your eyes out. When they weren't trying to kick you in the balls.

"Why couldn't it just be a simple hit?" Shaw mumbled as he slipped the tablet back into his chest rig.

He looked around. Control had already told him the town police chief was wise to everything. Shaw was to deal only with the chief whose name was Garner and some other local, a college campus security guy named Travers.

What Shaw hadn't bothered to explain to Control was that he already knew both the stout small-town chief and the college security guard. Quite well.

34

Shaw finally spotted Garner by the loading dock of the post office.

"Hi. Are you Chief Garner?" Shaw said loudly as he walked up to him, starting the snow job theatrics for the cops who were watching.

"Yes. And you are?" Garner said.

"Special Agent Thompson," Shaw said as he vise-gripped his doughy hand.

They both turned as Travers in a windbreaker came out of the post office and walked over.

"And this is Campus Security Director Travers," Garner said. "Travers, this is Special Agent Thompson."

"Very nice to meet you, Agent Thompson," Travers said stiffly.

Shaw had to force himself not to roll his eyes. Travers had the acting chops of a department store mannequin.

"So, what do we got, fellas?" Shaw said.

"Let me show you," Garner said. "We're setting up a command post in the post office here."

They went up onto the loading dock by a little set of steps and went in through a side door into a tiny hall that smelled like stamp glue. At the end of it, in a brightly lit windowless back room, a half a dozen or more busy beaver cops were clearing desks against the wall, snapping open card tables, putting out folding chairs.

Shaw smiled some more at the elaborate production.

This is what blockbuster directors must feel like when they come on set, he thought.

"Thanks," Shaw said as Garner handed him a water bottle from a case of them sitting on a steel desk.

"This is who we're looking for," the chief said, showing him a photo of the blonde on his phone.

"Yep, I know. I got it right here," Shaw said, patting his electronic tablet.

"And there's a black-haired woman as well."

"Uh-huh. The New York law firm woman. Doherty. Got her pic, too. No sign at your checkpoints yet, huh. Nothing?"

Garner shook his head.

"Not yet."

Shaw cracked the water bottle and took a sip. Then they all turned as Azar and Shahu and the rest of Shaw's boys arrived. With the heavy tool cart on a hand truck and a black-and-silver wheeled shipping case they almost looked like roadies setting up for a concert.

Yeah, baby, Shaw thought as he watched the gear land with a loud clunk into the corner.

The show was about to begin all right.

"What's all that for?" Travers said.

In the boxes were all the toys. AR15s, MP5s with a shit ton of ammo. Breaching charges, ballistic shields, grenade launchers with hundreds of cannisters of tear and incendiary gas. Flash bangs and even fragmentation grenades. They'd brought every bell and whistle.

"Some odds and ends," Shaw said. "Never know what the job

might entail. Good carpenter always brings his whole toolbox along. Do you have a map of the town handy?"

"Someone hit the lights," Garner called out as he turned on the interactive Smart Board/whiteboard he had brought in.

"This here is the Beckford town square, your target area," Garner said, waving a laser pointer at a Google Maps satellite shot of the small town. "Basically a north and south oriented square with the river to the west. As you can see, it's not that complicated. North Street, Main Street, South Street run horizontal and Route 4 and Depot Street and River are your vertical.

"We," the chief continued as he wiggled the red dot of the laser pointer at a structure on the upper left northwestern block, "are here at the post office on North Street.

"And here beside us," he said as he pointed to two Google Map knife and fork markers in the northeastern block to their right, "are two of the village's public establishments that are still open. Cosmic Pizza and The Pinewood, a small and somewhat sketchy bar that is known to law enforcement.

"And here," he said as he pointed two blocks down at the bottom of the map to another restaurant marker, "between the river and Depot Street is the third and largest establishment in the town, a bar and restaurant called The Forge.

"Now, I already called in my contact at Eversource to shut down the juice," the chief said. "After they kill the lights, you go in for the scoop and we'll watch the perimeter at these check-points here, here and here in case our targets make a run for it. Sound good?"

They turned as Shahu lifted out the first submachine gun from the popped open shipping case. They watched as he slapped the bolt carrier forward with a loud clack.

"Sounds outstanding, Chief," Shaw said. "We'll be out of your hair in no time."

35

To the northwest above the town, the Beckford Reservoir was a nine-billion-gallon, two-mile square basin with a hundred-thirty-foot-high spillway dam that emptied out into the Farmington River.

Ten minutes after we left The Forge, we pulled up on the driveway of the reservoir's access road and stopped twenty feet before its rolling fence gate.

Its *padlocked* rolling fence gate.

I got out of the truck. To the right of the fence where the edge of a forest started was a small rise that I scrambled up, and I squatted down in the pine needles and looked around. A towering pine stood close to the edge where the fence ended but the gap between was just about enough to get the truck through.

I thought I could get the truck up the rise without flipping it. At least maybe.

But what would happen then? I thought, tapping my chin as I looked at the lakeside access road beyond the chain link.

The water company had to have security cameras especially by the spillway bridge. I remembered there was a small building there that may have housed equipment. Then there was another bit of access road and a second fence that I wasn't sure we'd be able to drive around.

"Screw it," I mumbled as I came back for the truck. "Have to take the chance."

Colleen hopped out of the cab as I took out the Leatherman tool on my key chain and knelt to unscrew the license plates on my truck.

"We're doing this?"

"Yep," I said as I got off the first screw.

"Mike, I can't begin to thank you for all this. Throwing you in the middle of this out of the blue," she said as she knelt, shining the flashlight of her phone onto the license plate to help.

"Nothing to thank me for yet," I said as I got the tag off and stood and pushed in the side mirrors.

"We're not out of the woods—or even in them—yet," I said.

"Are you sure about this?" Jodi said as Colleen and I got back in.

I swung the headlights and us off the asphalt and onto the piney slope in a skidding lurch.

Not even a little, I thought.

But I was right. I just cleared the fence by a hair and then came down the incline and bumped hard back onto the blacktop on the fence's other side.

"One down, one to go," I said as I gave it some gas.

I switched off the headlights as I gunned it. On our left the beautiful vast reservoir was as still as a pane of smoked glass. The access road arced in a long reverse C around the edge of it with the middle part of it being the spillway bridge itself.

As we came past the little bridge house, I immediately spotted the security camera on it.

We got onto the other side of the spillway and another couple of hundred feet up, I slowed as I saw we had a problem.

"Dammit," I said.

"No," Colleen said as we arrived at the closed gate.

It wasn't just the locked gate. With the stone wall of the ridge on the right and the water on the left, there was no way to drive around this one.

"What if we left the truck and walked out? The road's right there," Colleen said.

"No," I said. "That wouldn't work. We'd get picked up as soon as they found the truck. And they may have already seen it. We passed a camera on the spillway bridge back there."

"C'mon, Mike. We need to do something. Let's leave the truck. We'll hide in the woods or something," Colleen tried again.

I thought about that. If I were on my own, I'd already be on foot, completely in the wind. But with the SEALs, I'd had the privilege of being personally trained by an old man who had founded the notorious LRRP Recondo school in Vietnam. Put to the test, no one would find me with all the bush tricks I'd been taught. Not in this kind of forest cover. Not even Rambo himself.

Well, maybe Rambo. Or Colonel Trautman. But they were about it.

But I wasn't alone, was I?

I looked at Jodi behind me, then back at Colleen.

Call me crazy, but my lady friends didn't look like they'd take to sleeping in the mud and brunching on bark moss and swamp water too well.

"So, what are we going to do now?" Colleen said as I did a backward K-turn.

"We go back to town," I said. "There's still a heck of a lot of haystack for these clowns to find the needle in. The ball's still in our court. Time to go back and be patient and see what they do next."

"What they're going to do next won't be good," Jodi said quietly from the back seat as we passed over the top of the spillway.

I looked at her in the rearview. Then out over the expanse of moonlit water.

"I guess we'll just have to see about that, now won't we," I said.

36

"Back again?" Daisy the waitress said as we piled into The Forge.

Over her head, I saw there were more people here now than when we had left. The dining room was lined on both walls with mostly white-haired pensioner couples and what looked like two teens on a date. The party of construction workers were howling now as Scotty and another younger waitress came out of the kitchen door beside the bar, wheeling a rolling cart with a giant ice cream cake with sparklers on it.

"Yep, Daisy. Back again," I said, smiling as we slid into the same booth from earlier.

That it was more crowded was good, I thought. If the jokers after Jodi and Colleen were still on the fence about actually doing this, this would at least stall them. They didn't want so many witnesses to something like this.

Whatever *this* was, I thought as I watched the dining room and the door.

"So, what can I get you guys?" Daisy said.

"Let's go with the two dozen hot wings to start," I said. "And I'll have the steak sandwich."

"With peppers," Daisy said.

"But of course," I said.

I smiled over at Colleen and Jodi, who looked back as if I were nuts.

"Where are my manners, ladies? Please order," I said.

"Order?" said Jodi, wide-eyed.

"Of course," I said, smiling like an idiot. "We're here to eat, ladies, right? It's dinnertime so you need to order."

Colleen ordered a burger and Jodi got a Caesar salad.

"What the hell are we doing, Mike?" Jodi said when Daisy left. "They're going to come in here in five seconds and—"

"Listen to me," I said quietly. "You're damn right they might come for us. We're going to be looking at—I'm not even sure what—but it could get bad. We just can't let anyone here know we are the target, okay? It's not a good idea. You want to get out of here, we have to hide in the crowd and play as stupid as possible and keep it cool. Just follow my lead."

A sad roar from the bar made all of us look over. Back in normal world, the Penguins had just tied up the game with the Hurricanes.

I suddenly wished I was in the Carolinas. Or hell, even Pittsburgh would be fine at this point.

"I have no idea what you're doing," Jodi said, sitting up. "This doesn't seem like a strategy. This is just crazy to sit here. Suicidal. In fact, this is not acceptable."

I stared at the neatly coiffed Martha Stewart look-alike with a patient smile. Obviously, the lady was very afraid and worked up, forgetting that *she* had come to *me* seeking help. I needed yet another tangle with the authorities like I needed a root canal without Novocain.

But her attitude wasn't exactly growing on me. I wasn't a presidential dining room waiter back at the campus. And if she kept treating me like one, she was going to find a fly in her soup.

"Relax, Jodi. Mike knows what he's doing," Colleen said, picking up on my mood. "He was in the NYPD SWAT and the Special Forces before that. Why do you think I brought us here?"

"Special Forces?" Jodi said, squinting at me.

"He was a SEAL in Iraq, a combat vet. Right, Mike?" Colleen said.

Jodi's face suddenly changed. There was a sudden far-off look in her eyes.

"My first husband died in Iraq," she said.

That was the last thing I expected to hear her say.

"I'm sorry, Jodi. What unit?"

"The 984th MP Company out of Fort Carson. In 2004 in the beginning of the spring fighting, he was in charge of a unit helping with the arrest of some Iraqi army people in Najaf when someone in the protesting crowd shot him. His name was Bill. Lieutenant William Dunne."

"I'm really sorry," I said again.

"Our daughter was born four months later."

I didn't know what to say to that.

Luckily, Colleen came to the rescue.

"Jodi, we're all rattled," she said, patting her on the shoulder. "But we need to pull together here, okay? Mike knows what he's doing. Let's trust him."

"Of course," she said, suddenly rubbing at her forehead. "You're right. I'm sorry. I'm just overwhelmed, I guess. I can't believe this is happening. That my husband would... I'm sorry I roped you into this, the both of you."

"No problem at all, Jodi," I said, tapping her hand. "We're going to get through this. Let's all just stay on the same page."

37

"Okay, quiet down, gentlemen. Listen up, listen up," Chief Garner said.

The post office staging area was filled with cops now and Garner stood at the front of it.

Shaw, with his big arms folded, stood beside him on the left with his men. Their faces were pure stone.

"Special Agent Thompson," the chief said with a nod to Shaw.

Now it was Shaw's turn to speak.

As he stepped up, he stared at the town map and then at all the cops.

To level a shithole Afghani village was one thing, Shaw thought. That he was now being given a small Connecticut town to have his way with was practically making him dizzy.

This is doing wonders for my circulation, he thought.

Better than Viagra.

"Gentlemen," Shaw said in his booming marine voice. "What I am about to reveal to you doesn't leave this room. As you may know, this area of Connecticut has many defense companies. These two women we are looking for worked at one of them and are involved in the theft of something that is so vital to our national security I cannot even disclose what it is."

Shaw looked at the cops, not one set of rolling eyes. They were mesmerized. He had them in the palm of his hand.

Shaw tented his hands together dramatically.

"We have already cut off communication in and out of the area so that the data is contained. Now in a few minutes, an evacuation of this section of town is going to be called. We are going to let it be known to the media that a truck crash of a highly toxic chemical has happened nearby and that everyone must leave.

"At the same time, in order to search for and neutralize our targets, the power will be cut. I and my highly trained team will go in and clear our first primary targets, these three public buildings. And if we do not locate our target there, we will then start doing follow-ons by going door-to-door.

"As we proceed with the mission, no matter what happens, please remember the importance of maintaining secrecy at all times. You cannot disclose what is happening. Not even to your girlfriends or wives."

Shaw took in the cops' faces, rapt, serious-as-cancer, utterly and completely suckered.

38

While we waited for our food to arrive, I slipped out of our booth for a recon of The Forge restaurant. It didn't take that long as there wasn't much to recon.

From above, the restaurant would look like a big rectangle with three smaller rectangles at the back of it. The main rectangle was where the dining room and bar were, and the smaller rectangles at the back of it contained a private banquet room on the left, the kitchen behind the bar, and the two restrooms at the back on the right.

I left through the east-facing front door and made a right to the south and walked the perimeter of the place until I came all the way around. I counted eight windows in all. Four on the front and two on each small side. In addition to the front door, there were two more doors, a back one for the kitchen near where I had parked and an emergency exit door in the north side of the building from the dining room.

I walked back behind the restaurant, where there was a small dumpster and some recycling cans, and stood for a moment on the gravel looking at my truck, thinking about things.

No, I don't need to get that hasty, do I?

"Who am I kidding?" I whispered as I hit the electronic fob in my jacket pocket and pulled open the driver's door.

I exited the truck after a minute with a large, heavy canvas kit bag that I had removed from a special hidden compartment in my truck's custom bed. In the kit bag were a variety of things that I had wished I would never have to use on my road trip.

"If wishes were horses, beggars would ride," I said under my breath.

I stopped for a moment and looked at the old brick factory behind the restaurant and at the door of the antique place.

I came in closer and flashed my key chain penlight at the door's old lock. It looked like a cinch to kick in. There was an alarm on it no doubt, but if things went down enough where we might have to retreat into it, I knew I probably wouldn't have to worry about that.

When I turned back for the restaurant, I noticed that the back kitchen door was open, so I decided to go for it. The chef inside was a midsize, soft-around-the-middle Hispanic guy of around thirty with a long beard and tats. He didn't look too happy to see me as I brushed by the fry station carrying my large canvas bag.

"Whoa, what the hell? You can't come in this way," he said.

"Oh, I'm sorry, man. My bad. Won't happen again," I said, hurrying behind him back into the restaurant.

I walked past the bar and tossed my heavy bag into the booth with a clunk and sat down next to it. None of the old-timers at the bar seemed to have noticed.

Good, I thought, as I began counting bodies.

Two waitresses and the owner and the chef made four plus the five old-timers and five roughnecks was fourteen. Then I counted four other couples. With us three, that made twenty-five.

Twenty-five people on board the *SS Forge*, I thought.

What did airline pilots call the passengers again? I suddenly thought, looking out at everyone. Souls.

Twenty-five souls aboard, I thought.

I looked over at the roughnecks again. The guy I had dubbed Papa Bear laughed at something the Brooklyn guy said and took a sip from a mug of beer.

I liked Papa Bear. He seemed smart and reasonable and he had some size on him. Not only that, he was older, which gave him some gravitas. People would listen to him.

If what I thought was about to happen happened, he would be the first person I would try to partner up with.

I looked up as Daisy arrived with the huge platter of wings.

"Here we are," she said with a smile. "Hope everybody is hungry."

"Starving," I said, smiling back.

Which was the exact moment when all the lights went out.

39

Shaw, wearing a borrowed firefighter coat over his Kevlar vest, waved his flashlight in front of the people departing from the Cosmic Pizza parlor on North Street.

"That's right. This way, folks," he said in his soft yet insistent voice of authority as he herded the idiot sheep back toward the post office.

Azar and Shahu were inside doing the sheep-dogging while the other team, Carpenter and Tejada, were spread out in the shadow across the street behind him hanging back, backing them up.

"That's it. Thank you. Here we go," Shaw said to the oblivious crowd.

"What is this, anyway? Where are we supposed to go?" said a rather rotund woman with green-and-purple hair, clutching at a toddler.

"You will all be relocated to the high school, ma'am. Probably only for a short time. It's for your safety."

"But my daughter has asthma and we left her inhaler back at our apartment," she said, irritated.

Sounds like a personal problem, porky, Shaw resisted saying.

"If you just head on over to the post office, ma'am, they can help you there," he said instead.

"That the last of them in there?" he said to Azar, who suddenly appeared at the pizza place door.

Azar nodded.

"Checked the back? The kitchen?"

He nodded.

"Okay, c'mon. Now we do the bar."

Shaw looked back at Carpenter, who gave him a flicker from his vest light from the shadows before they continued down the street.

Half a block down North Street most of the patrons of the Pinewood were already outside on the sidewalk.

Shaw hit them in the face with his high-beam light, searching quickly.

They were all men. Nine in total. No raven-haired babe, no older blonde.

"Hey, cut that light, buddy," one of them said. "You're blinding us."

"Sorry," Shaw said, pointing it down a little. "Listen up, guys. We got a situation here. A tanker truck of some nasty industrial chemicals hit a power line up Route 4 here. We have to get everybody out of the village as a precaution until we get it cleaned up. Anybody else in there?"

"Yeah, the owner, Big Joe. He's in there," someone said.

"Thanks," Shaw said. "Just head that way toward the post office. School busses will take you to the high school where they're setting up a shelter. We need to get everybody out of here. At least for a few hours."

"But my wife and kids. Shouldn't I get them?" a voice said. "I live just right down the block."

"No worries, friend," Shaw said, patting the idiot on the shoulder. "You let us handle it. We'll get them. You'll all be together in a minute. Just head on out. That's it."

Shaw watched the man immediately follow his instructions to the letter.

These people, Shaw thought. Look at them, at how easy it was to control them. A badge and an authoritative tone of voice literally hypnotized them. Made them completely hand over all higher brain function, their human agency, their freedom. *With ease.*

He could have told the dummy to cartwheel to the post office and he would have done it.

I love my job, Shaw thought as he watched them go.

40

President Cushing was at home in his downstairs office.

He was sitting at his desk, and on his desk in front of him was a thousand-dollar bottle of 1989 Gordon & MacPhail Scotch, considered by some to be the best single malt whiskey in the world.

He usually liked to have a glass at Christmas and on his birthday. He would make a little ritual out of it, using a special, fluted, Scotch-tasting Glencairn glass that Jodi had bought for him a few years before.

But there was no glass tonight.

Cushing winced as he took another slug and went back to staring at the SAT phone.

No, this wasn't Christmas, was it? And this definitely wasn't his birthday. Frank had ordered him to stay by the phone, and he was following orders.

"Because that's what slaves do," Cushing said to the empty room.

He was still staring at the SAT when his regular home phone

rang in the corner by his printer. He took the bottle with him as he stood and answered it.

"Hello?" he said.

"Hi, Dad," his stepdaughter, Ashley, said.

He closed his eyes.

How? he thought. How was any of this possible?

"Thanks for the save with Lady today," she said.

"Don't mention it," he said.

Even he was shocked at the normalcy and calm in his voice.

"How are you?" he continued as if he wasn't going to hell. "How's the new baby coming along? What's the size now? An avocado?"

"Close to a baseball," she said. "Hey, did you hear the news about the evacuation of the center of town?"

Cushing glanced back at the SAT phone on his desk.

"No," he lied. "What's going on?"

"A truck with toxic material or something crashed on Route 4 and they had to evacuate everyone."

The material in question was toxic all right, Cushing thought. *But it wasn't in any truck.*

"Dad? Are you there?"

"Uh-huh," Cushing said after another hit of Gordon & MacPhail.

"Isn't that crazy?" she said.

"Insane," Cushing agreed.

"No one's even allowed near the area. Not even the media," she said.

"Makes sense," Cushing said.

"Dad, I know this sounds crazy, but the reason I'm calling is that someone on Facebook said mother's car was there."

No! Cushing thought, almost dropping the bottle. Dammit. They had the news stations snowed, but in a small town, word traveled at light speed with or without the internet.

"Dad?"

Stall. Say something, he thought.

"That's preposterous. Your mother's asleep upstairs. I'm down in my office working."

"I figured," his daughter said. "I didn't think it made any sense. How do these rumors start?"

"Oh, people just like attention, I guess. How's my little lad, Carter, doing?" Cushing said to change the subject.

"Oh, goofy as usual. Remember he went to the doctor for his shot last week and wasn't real happy?"

"Yes."

"Well, one of his new Lego toys has a doctor in it and he's taken to running the doctor over with Thomas the Tank Engine on his train table."

"That's hilarious. Maw Maw will love that," Cushing said. "I'll be sure to tell her when she wakes up."

"Tell Maw Maw Carter misses her," Ashely said. "And Grampy, too, of course."

Cushing sipped the whiskey.

"Tell Mother to call in the morning, okay?" Ashley said.

"You got it," Cushing said as he lifted the bottle again.

41

The second the power went out inside The Forge, there was a general moan in the sudden darkness.

But people didn't freak out as much as I thought and, in general, were pretty calm and good-natured about it.

Someone called out to the owner, Scotty, about why hadn't he paid the electric bill that month and some people laughed. Out came the phones then, of course. The modern flashlight. In a minute, the mood calmed even more as the inside of the restaurant became illuminated in a silvery bluish glow.

It looked strangely festive, even a little fun, I thought. Like a crowd at a concert just before an encore starts.

Looks could be pretty damn deceiving, couldn't they, I thought, glancing at the front door.

As I saw people begin to get up and head outside, I stood myself and went into my kit bag. The nine-millimeter semi-auto I slipped out and tucked into the back of my khakis was a Smith & Wesson Model 5906.

I really liked the 5906. Not only did it hold fifteen with one in the pipe, there's an added safety feature where if you kick out the magazine during a tussle, it disengages the trigger so it won't fire. It was also the same type of gun I had first carried when I was a beat officer in the NYPD, so maybe I was a little biased.

Why I wanted to bring the gun outside with me at this juncture, I wasn't completely positive. But I must say, just like when I was in the cops, I sure felt better with the familiar weight of it nestled at the small of my back.

"Hang back with Jodi and let me see what's happening out there," I said to Colleen as she stood as well.

"Okay, Mike," Colleen said.

But even in the dimness, I could see that she looked pretty shaken up. *Freaked out* would probably be more accurate.

"This date is going pretty great so far, huh?" I said jokingly to cheer her up.

But I guess I needed to work on my material because she only laughed politely and said nothing more as I got in line behind the construction workers and followed them outside.

42

The Pinewood bar was located in a Victorian house known as a painted lady.

This painted lady needed a date, Shaw thought as he climbed its creaking porch stairs and pushed through the front door.

With a wrecking ball, he thought.

The first thing he got hit with was a strong smell of spilled beer and then he halted as a high beam light suddenly flashed in his eyes.

"Hey, turn down the wattage, please," Shaw said. "Fire department here. We got an evacuation situation."

When the flashlight was lowered, Shaw saw that there were actually two men inside the low-ceilinged space, one in front of the bar and one behind it. On the bar top, a cell phone with the flashlight app on was resting on top of a glass. It looked like a small lantern.

"What's going on?" said the patron who had yet to leave his barstool.

He was a short white-haired old man in a denim jacket wearing one of those Irish tweed caps.

"Hi, fellas," Shaw said. "Hate to break it to you, but the bar is now closed. A tanker truck filled with some poison class B materials just hit the transmission pole up on Route 4. We are clearing out the entire village. You got to go now."

"Poison B you said?" the old man said, putting down the glass of beer he was holding. "What kind? I was a trucker after I got out of the air force. What are we talking here, son?"

"Sodium cyanide, hoss," Shaw said. "A load of it out of Canada was on its way to a rubber factory down in Jersey. It's already gone airborne and if the wind shifts the right way and you suck it in, you're going to be deader than grunge music. We need to get everybody in the village out. For at least a few hours."

"Shit," the old hobbit-like codger said, downing the last of his beer in one shot.

He hopped off his stool.

"Why didn't you say so?" he said as he hurried past Shaw.

"You, too, friend. Time to go," Shaw said to the bartender.

The bartender was bent at the waist, reading something in the cell phone's light. It was a *Sports Illustrated* magazine. As he turned a page, Shaw saw a picture of a smiling NASCAR driver.

"Ah," the bartender said. "Screw that, jack. Be on your way. I'm staying right here."

"What?" Shaw said, looking at him in astonishment. "Are you crazy? Brother, this isn't a joke. This isn't a storm you can ride out. It's an industrial disaster. You don't leave, you're going to die."

The bartender licked a thumb and slowly turned another page of the magazine.

"Yeah, well, that's your opinion, ain't it?" he said without looking up.

"Opinion?" Shaw cried. "The driver of this rig is dead. They got guys in space suits at the crash site not a quarter mile from here. This isn't optional."

The bartender shrugged, still not looking up.

"Gotta die sometime," he said with a yawn. "I ain't leaving my bar. I don't have the keys to the front door to lock up. My wife has 'em and she's down in New Haven. I have about 15K in booze in here."

Shit, Shaw thought. Finally bumped into a civvy with some brain activity. Guess it was true you couldn't fool all of the people all of the time.

"How much is your funeral going to cost?" Shaw said, getting louder. "They called an evacuation. You have to leave. This is mandatory."

The guy stood to full height.

Big Joe really was a tall glass of water, Shaw saw as they stood eye to eye.

"Mandatory?" he said. "What's that fireman speak for? The bar is open? Because last time I read my Constitution which protects my rights to run my own life, there ain't no damn such thing as mandatory in America. Fourteenth Amendment that freed the slaves solved that. It says I own myself. And I own this bar. So, in sum, you can kiss my hairy ass about me doing anything you say. Got it? Now get out of my bar before I throw you out."

No more Mr. Nice Guy, Shaw thought as he drew his FBI creds and silenced .45 at the same time.

He pointed both right between Big Joe's suddenly startled wide eyes.

Bright boy didn't look so bored anymore, did he? Shaw thought with a tight grin. He had finally piqued his interest.

"Surprise. I'm not a fireman, jackass," Shaw said. "I'm FBI. So, you can either leave this bar now peacefully or I kick the living snot out of you and then cuff you and drag—"

Shaw heard it then.

The bathroom door beside him opened with a squeak.

From it, staggered a man. He was redheaded and stocky, maybe twenty. He looked like a college kid.

He stood there about five feet away, squinting at Shaw.

"Robbery!" the drunk kid suddenly yelled and immediately lunged at Shaw's outstretched gun.

Without pausing, Shaw's finely honed instincts took over.

As the kid went for his gun, he pulled it back down out of his reach toward his waist and as if on its own, Shaw's finger pulled the trigger twice.

Blood and brain matter splattered loudly against the cheap wood paneling as two .45 hollow points blew the back of the drunk college kid's red head clean off.

Shaw, rearing back to avoid the kid falling on top of him, glanced up to see that behind the bar, Big Joe was already halfway to the back door.

Shaw leveled and fired. But he missed the shot. A perfect circle appeared on the swinging kitchen door a hair to the left of the running big man's head and then Big Joe disappeared through the doorway.

He tapped his mic.

"We got a runner! Caucasian. Tall. Fit. Dark hair. Out the back! Out the back!" he called.

"Green light?" said Carpenter.

"Yes! Green light. I repeat. Green light. Anyone with a shot take him down!" Shaw yelled as he vaulted the bar.

43

Most of the patrons out in front of The Forge stuck around for a little while, but after ten minutes or so, some came over to Scotty, paying him in cash or telling him they'd square things up later, before heading for their cars.

We would find out later these wise folks who left were the lucky ones.

They were the last ones to get out right under the wire before it would all begin.

After they were gone there were just five of us left standing there: the two construction guys Brooklyn and Papa Bear, and Scotty, Daisy and me.

Even the chef and the young waitress had gone, and we all stood rooted, looking east up the dark of Main Street like the diehard remnants of a crowd waiting for some Fourth of July fireworks to start.

I looked up the deserted length of Main Street. The grease pencil ghosts and headstones on the plate glass of the stores suddenly didn't seem so harmless now, did they?

"What in the hell is this?" said Scotty as we still stood there in the cold out in front of the restaurant.

"Look. The lights are on over the river," Daisy said, pointing away from the town, west of the bridge by the reservoir.

"Must be a black-out just here in town, I guess," Scotty said.

"Duh, you really think so?" said Brooklyn as he raised the bottle of Corona he'd taken outside with him to his lips.

That's when we heard the commotion, and we all turned toward Main Street in front of us.

We watched as down the middle of the dark street came a man, a big man running fast.

"Is that Big Joe?" Scotty said.

We all seemed spellbound for a moment as we watched. He was coming at us at top speed, his lanky arms pumping. Even at a distance you could hear the loud chug of his breath. It was like he was doing the hundred-yard dash at a football tryout.

"Help!" Big Joe suddenly screamed. "Help! They're killing everyone! They're killing everyone."

"What?" Scotty said.

We all saw it then a split second later.

I heard it because I knew the sound. But the others just saw it.

From up the rise of Main Street, came the soft clack-clack-clack of suppressed gunfire and with it, a gush of blood blossomed at Big Joe's throat.

He was still running when another soft clack-clack-clack came and he tottered forward, trying to keep his balance. But he couldn't do it. The big man went down in a headlong face-plant so hard he actually bumped up off the asphalt, before he skidded to a stop in a kind of rag doll tumble against the gutter.

"What, what in the world?" said Scotty in shock.

"Oh, my—" Daisy cried. "He's dead! Big Joe's dead!"

I grabbed Daisy and steered her back for the front door of The Forge.

"Everyone back into the restaurant! Now, now, now!" I said.

44

"What in the hell?" Scotty said in shock as the last of us came inside and I bolted the door.

"You, could you help me with this please?" I said to Brooklyn as I grabbed the reservation podium.

"Name's Mario," he said.

"Mike," I said.

"What the hell is going on?" he said as we dropped the big piece of furniture down sideways. It was heavy, easily a hundred pounds. With it propped against the door, no one was getting in without a fire axe.

"What did we just see?" came another voice.

It was Papa Bear. He had an accent. I was going with Swedish as he was the size of a Viking.

"First go the lights? Now a killing?" he said.

After I made double sure the heavy podium had the front door well barricaded, I went to a front window and flipped a blind.

There was no one out there on Main Street. Just Big Joe. He was still lying there in the gutter in front of the grocery store.

"Can't we help him? Maybe he needs CPR. Does anyone know CPR?" said Daisy, suddenly looking out the window beside me.

"No, Daisy. He's gone," I said. "He was dead before he hit the ground and whoever shot him is still out there."

"You heard what he said, right?" Mario said. "They're killing everyone? Who the hell are *they*?"

I shot a look over at Jodi and Colleen, who were standing beside the booth, telepathically messaging them to keep their mouths shut.

"Any ideas what this could be about?" Scotty chimed in.

"I used to be a cop," I said. "This looks like a hit to me. Maybe a drug hit. The cartels are very sophisticated. They will cut the power, jam the cell sites. Even act like cops. They're all paramilitary now. Very well funded, highly sophisticated and highly trained."

I said this because the script had changed, I knew.

We were on this ride together now. That we all had just witnessed that murder meant that not just Jodi and Colleen, but myself and everyone else in the room were all marked for death as well.

We were also cornered together and if war had taught me anything, cornered people, like cornered rats, will turn on one another.

If I was to play this to save as many people as possible, I would have to keep up morale, to keep people as hopeful as possible for as long as possible.

Even if that meant lying.

I also thought my explanation sounded pretty convincing. I wasn't lying about the paramilitary part. There definitely seemed to be some professionals doing this. Cutting the power and cells was no joke. Nor was popping the big man from a distance. I wasn't a Hollywood sound engineer, but the clacking sounds I heard were from a submachine gun, probably the Heckler & Koch MP5. And those usually only had iron sights.

"Sophisticated? What's so sophisticated about that?" Mario said, pointing out at the body.

"You see or hear the shooter?" I said. "That guy was shot more than once in the head from a distance with a silenced gun. That's called highly trained."

Mario peered at me.

"You used to be a cop?" he finally said. "Then why don't you head out there and start arresting people, huh? Do your job."

"Did you not hear the man, Mario?" Papa Bear said. "Which part of the term 'used to' do you need help with?"

"Screw you," Mario said. "This party was for you. Now we got a damn cartel hit squad here! We can't even call the cops with the damn phones out. *And* there's a blackout! What the hell are we going to do?"

"A cartel hit?" Scotty said. "You think they were after Big Joe? Definitely some drugs going on up at that Pinewood that's for damn sure. But enough for a cartel to do all this? All the way out here in the boondocks?"

"No, that's not right," said Daisy. "Sure, there were drugs in there, but Big Joe had nothing to do with them. He was a real good guy. He was a high school football coach up in South-wick for years. Plus, his brother died of drugs. He never touched them."

"Maybe they came into the bar for whoever was dealing them and he was a witness to the hit," said Papa Bear.

Daisy nodded.

"Yeah, that sounds right," she said. "They didn't want to leave witnesses."

"That's not good," I said, looking out the blinds again.

"Why not?" said Daisy.

"Because now we're witnesses, too," I said.

"He's right," Scotty said. "We saw them kill Big Joe. But at least we didn't see any faces, right? Maybe they're already gone. I mean, you don't think they'd come in here, do you?"

"Let's not find out, Scotty," I said. "Go to the kitchen and lock the back door."

Papa Bear came over next to me to look out the window as Scotty ran off. He offered his hand. "Mathias," he said.

"Mike," I said, shaking his hand.

"Why don't we all just leave? Get out of here?" he said. "I have a truck on the other side of the bridge."

I looked at the big man. They would kill him if he left. Stop him at one of the checkpoints and take him into a custody he wouldn't survive.

He couldn't leave. He just didn't know it.

"No," I said. "I don't think so, Mathias. Stay here or at least don't leave yet. I think that sniper is still out there. I think you should stay right here."

"How do you know the sniper is out there?" Mario said. "Were you a psychic cop?"

"I'm a still alive cop," I said. "And I plan to stay that way. You want to get shot, have at it. I'm staying right here until further notice."

45

"So, what's up?" Garner said as Shaw walked back into the post office parking lot with the others.

Travers was with him. Of course he was, Shaw thought. They came as a unit, a duo. New England's Beavis and Butt-Head.

Too bad Shaw wasn't in the market for comic relief after the nightmare that had just gone down.

Casualties, especially civilian ones, were not encouraged at Vance Holdings. Now out of the gate, they had not one but two.

"So," Garner said again.

Shaw peeled off the fireman's jacket and tossed it on the loading dock as his four men climbed into the BearCat and roared it on.

"The pizza parlor and bar are clear," said Shaw.

Boy, are they clear, thought Shaw as he pictured the kid he'd shot.

"So, we think we have them contained at The Forge, then?" Travers said.

"Roger that," said Shaw with a nod. "That's my hunch."

"What's up with your guys and the cat?" Garner said as his men rumbled the truck out onto North Street.

"Have to check something out near the bar," Shaw lied. "Another quick sneak and peek just to be safe."

The truth was that they had to go into the bar and get the body of the dead drunk kid and then go down Main Street and pick up Big Joe.

Then they had to bury them both in the woods.

And the chief and his college security guard sidekick don't need to know anything about that now, do they?

Shaw needed total cooperation from the locals until the mission was over. Letting them know there were already two casualties wouldn't be real good for morale.

The only positive was that since they had successfully cleared the area, it was only the folks who had been outside in front of The Forge who had witnessed the shooting of Big Joe.

They were fish in a barrel, penned in, no comms and they had nowhere to run with the roadblocks. They were in a container. One that Shaw could open up and reach into anytime he wanted.

And the fact that the group from The Forge hadn't immediately run to their cars but had gone back into the restaurant made him seriously think that the women were in there.

Maybe they already knew there was nowhere to run.

Shaw hopped up on the loading dock and went into the command center. From the Box O' Joe on the card table, he poured himself a paper cup full. As he sipped at it, he lifted a cinnamon doughnut hole that was there and peered at it in disgust.

He had been off seed oils for years. They basically existed to pork up the populace. They literally made it impossible for you to lose weight.

And this fried little sucker was a solid block of canola oil.

Why not just eat rat poison? he thought as he tossed it in the trash.

"We're in the bar," said Carpenter in his earpiece. "One down."

"Roger," Shaw said.

When he turned, Chief Garner was standing there. He had snuck up on him. Interesting. Moved quiet for a pudgster, didn't he? Travers was not there shockingly. Probably had to take a leak.

"What's the next move, Agent?" Garner said. "I got the head of the town council coming in. You need to keep me informed here so I don't look like an idiot."

"Of course, Chief," Shaw lied. "We'll go over the next phase after my guys get back with the latest intel. How's that?"

"Okay," he said. "Another ten, fifteen minutes?"

"Less," he said. "Here, have a cup and relax. And try a dough-nut hole. They're really good."

Poor Garner had no idea of the level of sinister hombres he was in bed with right here, did he? Shaw thought as he poured the chief a cup of coffee.

Killing the investigator and bagging the woman was his mission and priority. How that happened—if it left a smoking cra-ter in place of this town—wasn't his lookout.

Garner thought that they were on the same team. He had no idea that to Shaw, Garner was no different than some local warlords up on top of an Afghani camel mountain.

If it came to it, he'd stack Garner and every member of his entire backwater department like firewood to fulfill his mis-sion with no thought to it whatsoever. And it would be about as effortless and remarkable as clipping a toenail.

46

"Hey, look! There's a truck coming now," said Daisy by the window.

I hurried past the bar to the blinds beside her.

The police vehicle that was driving slowly down Main Street looked like an armored car that had been jacked up for off roading. It was a dark khaki color and the metal plates and bullet-proof glass on the front of it were about as friendly as Darth Vader's mask.

It was called a Lenco BearCat, I knew from my time in the ESU, the NYPD's SWAT unit. We used a different kind of truck in the city, more like a firetruck, but I remembered that in many other rural departments they used this kind.

We silently watched its approach. It pulled in at the curb up in front of the body of Big Joe and stopped.

The military-looking vehicle just sat there half a football field away, its diesel engine chugging. I felt a tightness in my chest as I wondered what would happen next. I knew it could hold ten fully equipped officers if not more. Would they try to come in now? Ram the front door? A full-frontal attack?

"What the hell?" said Mathias. "What are they doing?"

"It says Beckford Police on the side," Scotty said in an upbeat tone. "Maybe they're the cavalry. Maybe the bad guys left."

We all took a collective step back from the window as its back doors shrieked open. Beneath its high clearance, boots appeared on the street. Some kind of commotion started at the back of it then the boots disappeared and there was another shriek and a clunk of the back doors shutting.

We all stood silently as it started backing up. As it entered the middle of the street again in reverse, it revealed that the space at the curb where Big Joe had been was now empty.

"They took Big Joe," Daisy said in a shocked voice. "What on earth? Why would they do that?"

"And why haven't they come over here to see if we're okay?" said Mario. "Or even call out with a bullhorn if there's some kind of situation?"

"Maybe they're too busy dealing with the bad guys up at The Pinewood," Scotty said as the BearCat, still in reverse, disappeared around the corner of North Street.

"Maybe it's police procedure?" Scotty tried.

"They're not the police," I said.

"But it says so on the side," Scotty said. "I saw it."

"It doesn't matter what it says," I said. "If someone is murdered, the police have to process the crime scene. They don't just grab a body like a bag of garbage and drive it away in their cop car."

"He's right," Mathias said. "They didn't even lay down a chalk mark. That was crazy. They are the bad guys. Polish those glasses. Open your eyes."

"No, no, no. You're wrong. It's just a kinetic situation," Scotty said.

I looked over at Scotty. He kept nervously brushing back his long hair with both hands.

The dude was losing it, I thought. Grasping at any straw he could. I looked at the others. The raw fear on their wide-eyed faces.

"Oh, man. This shit is too much. I need a drink," Mario said.

"Me, too," said Daisy.

As she and the others began walking over to the bar, I knew this was my chance.

47

As the others drifted toward the other side of the bar, I faded back toward my booth where my kit bag was.

From it, as quietly as I could, I removed a gray cloth travel bag about the size of a shaving kit. I tucked it into my jacket and then grabbed Colleen and stepped away with her into the smaller part of the restaurant to the left of the front door.

"What's up?" she said.

I led her to the door of the banquet room and stopped.

"Just stay by this door," I said as I cracked it. "And if someone comes over, knock."

"Okay. But why? What's up, Mike?"

"I'll tell you in a sec," I said as I closed the door behind me.

Inside the banquet room, there were four square restaurant tables backed up against the rear wall. One of them was stacked with folded table linens that I placed the gray bag on top of.

The window to the left of it looked out the side of the restaurant into the dark of the gravel parking lot. It stuck fast in its ancient casing about an inch up when I cracked it open, so I had to smack its top rail hard a few times with the heel of my hand to get it open half a foot.

The thin plastic rectangle I took out of the bag was about the size of a paperback book. It had four short segmented arms on its top side and on its bottom there was a little gripper device along with three fish-eye camera lenses in a pyramid array.

As I hit its power button, the little arms of the drone all clicked into the up position and a sound like a tiny Weedwhacker filled the small room.

It was a fishing drone that I had brought along on my road trip. It had a line gripper on the bottom where you clipped in your hooks and bait. With it, you could cast your line basically anywhere, out to unimaginable lengths—five hundred yards or more—and then release everything. It made fishing off the beach especially incredible.

But for my purposes right there and then, I wasn't interested in the fishing accessories.

I quickly slipped my phone into its Nintendo-like thumb controller frame.

The drone had a 4K camera on it with thermal night vision so it was about high time I sent it up to take a look around.

The buzzing thing tickled my palm as I brought it to the open window and I reached out and slowly let it go and watched it hover there like a freed hummingbird. Then I thumbed the controller forward and up, and its blades made a slightly higher pitched sound as it rose out of sight into the night air up above the restaurant and parking lot.

The firmware for it was already downloaded onto my phone as an app. On it I toggled the camera choice to FLIR thermal and then looked down at the screen as an overhead shot of the roof of the restaurant and the parking lot appeared in glowing purple and pink and orange and yellow.

I made the drone ascend higher and saw the Main Street stores appear and then the block where my Airbnb was. As I halted the drone high above the village a moment later, I saw that to the east, the roadblock in the little canyon on Route 4 on the other side of the river was still going strong. To the west, I didn't see the BearCat, but I did see a bunch of vehicles and police officers over by the post office on the other side of my rental building.

I sent the drone a little higher as I zoomed closer to the post office staging area. I saw that they had another roadblock several hundred feet north of the post office on Route 4 by the canoe place.

Then I hovered up high over the post office and thumbed the 32X zoom down at the cops in its parking lot. There had to be over a dozen of them milling around. They must have some kind of war room in the post office itself.

I smiled as I remembered all the drone intel we had gotten in Iraq and Afghanistan. How much had that cost? Hundreds of millions of dollars? Now here I was with my own personal eye in the sky. For what? Five hundred bucks?

"God bless America," I said.

48

I watched some more with the drone. It was chilling that the entire department was there. There was no way they were all corrupt, no way they would all agree to come after a fricking whistleblower for the college.

The chief was no doubt the corrupt scumbag who was feeding the rank and file some super amounts of horseshit.

I also didn't see any real people. Which was weird to me. There would definitely be people from the surrounding houses trying to figure out what was going on, right?

Had they evacuated everyone? I thought. And why no news vans?

This was bad. Had they cleared out the village and told the local cops that we were what? Terrorists or something? They hit the lights and went into the bar with tactical guys on the bullshit evac story looking for us and something went wrong. Big Joe ran and they killed him.

That was no regular SWAT team, I thought. That was a team of professional hired killers.

It sounded crazy that all this would happen at the behest of a college president. But then again this was no regular college. The billionaire Stone was deeply involved in this after all. And what had Colleen said about the college's endowment? Thirty-four billion? That was larger than the GDP of many countries. Countries had armies, right? Why not a college?

This isn't a college town, I realized. *This is a banana republic with its very own dictator.*

I shook my head as I thought of Jodi.

And now, lucky me, I have the dictator's wife, I realized.

I stared at the post office and thought about that, about what I would do if I were in their shoes and mixed up with the suspicious death of a young girl with billions of dollars on the line.

The mercs would be back, I decided. And sooner rather than later as bullshit stories tended to start to stink the longer they stuck around. Especially in the bright light of day.

The town tilted as I banked the drone left and rotated it, looking around for a parking spot. It had to be high up.

To the right was a steeple of the church. Maybe there. Nah, it was too far.

Then I saw it to the left.

"No-brainer," I said as I piloted the drone at the 5G tower that was atop the building where I was staying.

It took me a little maneuvering to land it on the highest movie poster–sized array, but I managed it two minutes later.

After I was done, I smiled. Now with my trusty drone looking down at the post office lot from about fifteen stories up, I could see everything.

As I watched, the BearCat came back. Four guys in SWAT FBI gear got out of it and quickly headed toward the post office.

The varsity squad, I thought.

They were met by another SWAT guy who was very tall, and the athletic panther-like way he moved was oddly familiar.

"Holy shit," I whispered.

It was one of the four men in Olivia's video! The slimmer of the two bodyguards. Had to be.

I nodded. It was all making sense now. Stone had sent his goons to stop Jodi from squealing, and the college security guy and the chief of police were running cover, leaving the mercenaries free to run roughshod.

Staring at all the real cops standing around, I was suddenly pissed.

Not one of them could put it together? How fishy this all was? What the hell was wrong with people today? Even the cops didn't ask questions? *No, I'll just go along to get my pension.* It was as if everyone's brain—or was it their balls—had been surgically removed.

I watched the bodyguard stand there with his hit team.

No telling what they would do if I gave them the chance.

Which I wasn't going to.

Because whatever they did next, we would know it immediately thanks to the drone.

And there was something else in my bag of tricks, I thought. Something they weren't going to see coming by a country mile.

PART THREE

MAKING A STAND

49

Shaw was inside the post office at the head of the staging room. Sitting on a desk with his four men on folding chairs in a loose circle in front of him they looked like hunters around a campfire.

This was a hunting party meetup all right, Shaw thought. Just between him and his fellow top-tier operators from the firm. The sort of meeting that needed a firmly closed door.

Behind Shaw on the Smart Board was a Google Earth view of the restaurant. Alongside that were photos from its website that gave them a feel for the interior layout, and at the bottom were the driver's license photos of Jodi Cushing and Colleen Doherty.

"Okay, gentlemen. I know I went over this briefly but as we are about to go in, I'm going to lay it all down again in detail. We are looking at an extraction of this subject here. Jodi Cushing, fifty, white, blonde female approximately 160 to 170 pounds."

"Health issues?" Tejada said.

Shaw watched as Tejada, a stocky light-skinned Hispanic from Texas who wore a goatee, spat chewing tobacco into a Dunkin'

Donuts cup. A former Green Beret just like Shaw, he had worked with Tejada many times before. He was as solid as possible.

"None," Shaw said. "No health issues, but she isn't going to be winning any triathlons anytime soon like you, Tejada, so a light touch is in order to avoid any heart attacks or other problems."

Tejada nodded and spat.

"Inside the establishment," Shaw continued, "judging by the vehicles left in the parking lot, we estimate at least six but up to as many as twelve other occupants. These people are not hostile per se, but were caught inside when the lights went out. We can assume that they are, on the whole, mostly pretty scared and confused. But scared people can be quite dangerous, so be on your guard at all times."

Shaw scanned faces for any concerns and found none.

"We have to assume," he said, turning with the laser pointer, "that they have fortifications at the front door here and the back kitchen door here. That's why the plan is to come in with the BearCat here on Route 4 and turn their focus to here on the right."

He pointed the laser along the wall of the restaurant's banquet room.

"Then in a flanking move, we breach directly into the structure at this point here. Around the east side in the parking lot, we blast this wall down and it will be a straight line inside."

"What kind of structure? Wood frame?" Carpenter said as he sat idly flicking a Spyderco knife open and closed with his thumb.

"Wood frame and clapboard," Shaw said. "The building is over a hundred years old."

Carpenter nodded. Skinny and clean shaven with glasses, Carpenter, a former Army Ranger, looked studious, almost nerdy.

Looks could be deceiving, Shaw thought as he watched the oiled blade go snicker-snak.

"What kind of room is beyond the breach wall? The kitchen?" Tejada said.

"No, it's a banquet room so it should be empty. The gas line feed is actually on the other side of the building, so you don't have to worry about that."

"You hear that, Carpenter? Gas line?" Tejada said. "You make sure you Goldilocks that charge, four-eyes. As in make it just right. I don't need to wake up in hell tonight."

"On it," Carpenter said, nodding.

"Carpenter and Tejada," Shaw said, pointing at them, "you are the breach team. We are going in stealth so I want noise discipline at all times, radios on lowest setting and no talking. After I drive the BearCat into position at this corner, you are to go on my command."

They nodded.

"Azar, Shahu," Shaw said, turning to them, "you are the entry. Utilizing cover and moving quickly through the breached opening, you will enter in behind your ballistic shields to this door here. After opening it and deploying flash bangs, you will identify yourself loudly as FBI before entering the main area. There you will identify the main target here, Jodi Cushing, and bring her and any and all pocket litter back out the way you came."

"What kind of resistance can we expect?" Shahu said.

"Not much," Shaw said. "Maybe a concealed carry handgun. Two at the most. I spoke to the chief. He said the owner is some sort of anti-gun tree hugger type, so no shotgun under the counter here. Even so, of course we move by the book as usual, maintaining cover and concealment and stay well spaced to avoid any cross fire."

"Any threat from the subject herself?" said Azar.

"Probably not. But never say never, so go by SOP. You know the drill. Get control, pat down, handcuffs, the whole nine."

"Rules of engagement?" said Tejada.

"Besides not harming the target, there are none. You see a threat, neutralize it."

"Contingency plans?"

This came from Carpenter.

"Anything unexpected, you retreat the way you came in. I will be in the BearCat and move to you. If the subject moves or anything changes, I will have eyes on the front and side."

"We are sure this woman is in there?" Tejada said.

"We're sure."

That wasn't completely true, but Shaw was done playing games. It was his call.

"Wouldn't it be better to induce a ruse?" said Carpenter.

He had stabbed the desk with his knife and was cleaning his glasses now.

He was talking about smoking them out, Shaw knew. He wished. If it were up to him, he'd set the whole back of the structure aflame and watch them flee out the front like rats from a burning ship. It wouldn't have been the first time.

"Not in this case," Shaw said almost ruefully. "The risk to the subject is too great."

"When do we go?" asked Shahu, who was the shyer of his two Afghani kill dogs.

"Why, Shahu? You have a hot date or something?" Shaw said.

That made them laugh, loosened them up. Of course, it did. Shaw was a master at this. Some men were born to lead.

"Is this like déjà vu or what?" said Carpenter. "Am I the only one who thinks this feels just like an op back in Afghanistan?"

"Yeah," said Tejada, "except this staging area smells like stamp glue and farts instead of goat shit. I don't know which is worse."

Shaw checked his watch.

"We go in twenty, gentlemen," Shaw said, standing. "So, get your rear in gear."

50

"Scotty, can I have a Corona please," I said as I arrived at the bar.

"Where you been, cop?" Mario asked from where he stood three stools down on my left.

His eyes were glassy. I looked at the three beer bottles in front of him, the two shot glasses.

I looked over at Scotty behind the bar. He shook his head.

"I said where you been?" he said.

"Taking a leak," I said cheerily as Scotty gave me my beer.

"'Taking a leak,' he says," Mario said, sneering at me.

He took another swallow of beer.

"That's typical. Never a cop around when you need one."

I knew this guy was scared. That he was looking for someone to feel superior to so his sad and scary feelings of helplessness would go away. But unfortunately for him, I didn't give a shit about his feelings.

I smiled at him as I stepped over until we were almost nose to nose.

"Can I ask you something I've always wondered about?" I said.

"Yeah, what's that?" he said, rolling his shoulders, squaring up.

"Are the bologna sandwiches at Rikers Island as good as they say?"

"Why you—" he said as Mathias stepped between us.

"Stop acting like a child and antagonizing everyone," he said to Mario as I walked away. "Aren't we in enough trouble?"

I brought my beer back to where Colleen and Jodi and I had retreated out of the booth into the smaller part of the restaurant near the banquet room door.

"Here, eat," I said to Jodi, offering her the plate of cold wings we'd brought with us.

"I'm not hungry, but, um, thank you," she said.

You will be, I thought, shaking my head at this unlikely Helen of Troy.

I looked over at Colleen as I sat. She smiled back as encouragingly as she could but even she had a great deal of fear in those beautiful pale eyes of hers.

As I reached and squeezed her hand over the table, I suddenly wished it was another table, our first table, the coffee table in her family's living room all those years ago.

Just had to have my bucket list date with Colleen, didn't I?

Be careful what you wish for, I thought.

For the next ten minutes, Mathias and Mario continued drinking at the bar. In the glow of the half-light from their phones, they huddled together, speaking quietly.

A brooding look had come over Mathias's face, I realized.

What they were thinking about wasn't too hard to figure out. They were thinking of making a run for it. I didn't blame them. We were all in a pinch here.

I turned my attention to Scotty behind the bar. He was taking glasses out of the dishwasher and just looking at them and putting them back. I noticed that a slowness and sloppiness had come over him, his dress shirt now hanging out of his pants at the back.

Inertia was setting in for Scotty. He was giving up, letting the mounting number of problems start to win. Full-blown unhinged panic wasn't with him yet, but it was on its way.

I watched Daisy at the window beside the front door standing as still and vigilant as a guard on a post. I suddenly noticed there was a lively French print on the wall beside her. It was of a can-canning woman beside a mustachioed waiter. *Moulin Rouge*, it said.

Daisy and Scotty in a previous happier life, came a thought in my head.

Despite the feeling of approaching darkness and gathering doom, I managed to crack a smile.

I was on my seventh cold wing when I saw the construction guys get up and walk toward the door.

I mopped up with a napkin as I headed over to them.

"Hey, guys. What's up?" I said.

"We're going to make a run for my truck. Try to get help," Mathias said.

"Is that right?" I said.

"Yeah, we're sick of this wussy retired-cop-waiting-around shit so sayonara, sucker. Goodbye and good luck," Mario said.

"Can I talk to you alone just for a second?" I said, gesturing Mathias over.

"Sure. What's up?"

"I want to show you something," I said as I led him to the banquet room door.

I took him inside and over to the still-open window. A cold wind blew in as I pointed across the parking lot.

Beyond the lot past the end of the factory, there was the flowing bend of the dark river and on the other side of that, the glow of lights on the canyon wall on its opposite bank were visible.

"Those lights are from a roadblock on Route 4," I said. "Even if you get to the truck on the other side of the bridge without getting killed, they'll just stop you there. So if you decide to go anyway, I recommend you get it up to ramming speed."

"What the hell?" he said, punching a palm. "A roadblock! Why didn't you say so before?"

"I just noticed it myself," I said.

"How the hell do they have a roadblock? Where are the real police? Dead?"

I looked at him.

"Wait. You know more about this than you're letting on, don't you? Don't lie to me. What's really going on?"

I didn't want to spill the beans, but at this point I realized I would need this guy's help, so I had no other choice but to trust him.

He was trapped now, too, so what did it matter?

"Okay, Mathias," I said. "You're right. I do know more. I held off to save everyone from freaking out. We need to work together here or we are screwed. I mean done. Over. Do you understand?"

"What is it? Tell me," he said.

"Here's the story. You know this is a college town, right? Whole area is run by Beckford College."

"Uh-huh. The big money school with the basketball team."

"Well," I said, "the blonde woman with me is the wife of the college president. She's blowing the whistle about a girl who died last year at the college. Her husband, *the college president*, is involved and the local Beckford cops including the chief of police helped cover it up. See, so it's not a drug cartel out there. It's a hundred times worse. It's the real local corrupt cops and because we all saw the murder of Big Joe, they are going to come in here and kill every last one of us if we don't figure something out."

51

Mathias stood mute.

In the silence, you could hear the thrum of the water outside as it came over a fall under the bridge. In the cold, you could smell the water, the metallic edge of it.

I watched his troubled face turn somber.

"That tattoo on your forearm, the anchor," I said. "You were a sailor somewhere?"

He nodded.

"Royal Norwegian Navy," he said.

"You ever been in a dangerous storm out at sea?"

"Yes."

"How did everybody on the ship react? Well?"

"No, there was a lot of panic."

"How did the captain react? Did he panic?"

"No, he was as cool as a cucumber."

"Exactly. That was his job. To lie and say, hey, everyone, everything is A-OK, even though it wasn't. We're in a storm now,

Mathias. A real shitstorm and not everyone is as smart and seasoned or trained as you and me. Add fear, and we're looking at as many problems inside this place as outside.

"You think that Mario is going to be able to handle the truth? He's already falling apart. Instead he will try to kill the messenger, namely me. I've seen it before. We would be at each other's throats instead of against the bad guys. I want us all to get out of this. But you can't save drowning people if they're flipping out and fighting you and not even believing what you're telling them."

"I see," he said. "I get it. You were keeping up morale."

He shook his head sadly as he absorbed what I had told him.

"When I left for this job two months ago," he said, "my little girl was crying. To make her stop, I told her I would bring her back a present. A pink Red Sox cap just like the one her mother has. Her mother is from Boston, you see."

I watched his face, watched it fall. He passed a hand through his hair, gripped at his beard.

"I already bought the cap," he said very quietly. "I was supposed to leave today but I stayed for the party that my guys threw. Now this. Why didn't I just leave?"

I looked at him.

I pulled up my sleeve to show him the tattoo I had on the inside of my left bicep. It was a small one of the skeleton of a frog.

"You ever see this one before?"

His eyes lit up.

"Frogman. The SEALs! You are a SEAL?"

I nodded.

"I thought you said you were a cop."

"I was both," I said.

"So, what do we do, Mike?" he said with a sudden hope.

"Simple," I said as I lowered my sleeve. "Just follow the frogman."

"You have a plan?" he said.

"Just follow my lead, Mathias," I said, giving him a wink as I patted him on his big shoulder. "Start by getting your buddy Mario to listen to you. And when they come for us, just stay out of my way, all right? Let me take the lead. And if I tell you to do something, you do it quick. No questions, no bullshit. You do that—you have my back—your little girl gets her hat. You want that, right?"

"You think you can really get us out of here?"

"It's a done deal," I said brightly. "Especially now that I've got the Iron Swede on my side."

"Iron Norwegian," Mathias said with a smile.

"Aye, aye, Captain Norway," I said. "Batten down the hatches because if what I think they are about to do is coming, this is about to get bumpy."

52

Carpenter swung the BearCat's armored plate back door closed like the door of a Swiss bank safe and then Shaw, all alone now behind the driver's seat, put the transmission into Drive and hit the gas.

The twin turbo diesels purred as he pulled off from the first waypoint. He drove down the block and before the left turn onto Main Street, he pulled the indestructible monster truck in under an old oak.

He needed to wait a bit now, give the boys some time to sneak down to the side of the restaurant.

He rolled his neck as he took a look around at the square. The whole town was like something out of an innocent yesteryear, wasn't it? he thought, surveying the bumpy sidewalks, the wide lawns trimmed with actual picket fences.

The front porch of the hundred-plus-year-old house to his right had a hanging rocking chair swing. In a minute Ma and Pa Ingalls would come out and sit down and sip some fresh lemonade as they read the Bible, wouldn't they? Shaw thought, shaking his head.

"Worthless hayseeds," he mumbled as he fished into his gear bag.

"Ah, there you go," he said brightly as he found his pill bottle of Adderall, dry swallowing three of them. Almost immediately he felt his heart rate begin to kick.

Hitting on the tunes on his phone, he began drumming the steering wheel along to the ominous jungle drumbeat of the opening of Van Halen's "Everybody Wants Some!!"

"Oh, yeah, scratch my back, baby," he called out as Eddie's first screeching chords filled the inside of the cab.

Nothing like a handful of lid poppers and a stadium rock classic to get the old game face on, Shaw thought, doing a little air guitar.

Just like old times indeed.

Juices starting to flow now, he turned off the tunes and adjusted his comm link microphone as he brought up the electronic tablet surveillance screen.

It was all done through the firm's control center, and it was like something out of a computer game. On a maplike background, his four men were closing in on the target on the left. On the right was the real-time street view from each of their body cams in gull-gray-and-white thermal footage.

His merc firm wasn't as good as the guys in the service, Shaw thought. They were better.

A minute later, he watched his men glide smoothly into the parking lot to stop behind a car.

On the screen he could see Carpenter hold up the breaching unit as he brought it out of its satchel.

It consisted of a bundle of Primacord, a kind of flexible plastic tubing filled with PETN, an explosive very similar to nitroglycerin. The shaped charge it was connected to was a plastic explosive called HMX.

All of it was laid out on a large square of double-sided soft and thick almost candy-like adhesive that had a plastic backing that you had to peel off like a Band-Aid once you were ready to stick everything in place.

Once that was done, all you needed was to get safely back, pull the electric detonator and Bob's your uncle, the wall had a hole in it and you were in.

"How we looking?" Shaw said in a low voice.

"Approaching," Carpenter whispered as Shaw watched him head for the side of the restaurant with Tejada, the brothers following right behind in a tight train.

That was Shaw's cue.

Showtime, he thought as he flicked every outside light of the BearCat into the ON position.

Then he put the badass vehicle into Drive and pulled slowly out onto Depot Street and made a left.

It was a real promenade all right. He gunned the turbo diesels loudly as he came down the rise and then, a hundred feet from the restaurant's front door, he stopped.

The armored plate driver door squealed loudly as he muscled it open. He flipped open its circular gun port and rested the barrel of his .45 on it and smiled.

Jesse James robbing a bank hadn't felt this good, Shaw thought, grinning. *Reach for the sky!*

That's it. Eyes on me, suckers, he thought as he saw movement at one of the windows. *Now we play my way.*

"I'm in place. Are you ready?" he called over the comm link.

"Almost. Peeling the tape back," Tejada said, watching Carpenter. "There we go. Placing it on the structure and—"

The pure bright white that suddenly flashed on the screen before Shaw's startled eyes came a split second before the thunderclap explosion.

Even at a hundred feet away, the blast wave shook the truck like a hurricane gust, slamming the door shut and sending Shaw flying back into the cab.

As this happened, the driver's seat smashed into the back of his head like a club. When he half came to in a concussed daze a moment later, outside the windshield where his men had just been was a billow of smoke.

The nine-thousand-pound truck was still rocking off its run-flat tires when Shaw detected the sound. It was the still-falling debris of the side of the shattered restaurant beginning to pitter-patter off the roof of the truck in a shower of toothpick-like wooden rain.

Then a large portion of roofing slammed off the hood filling the windshield with shingles.

He was shell-shocked and dumbstruck, gaping in unhinged terror. His concern for his fallen comrades as well as twenty-five years of military training instantly fled. Shaw with a shaking hand began to mindlessly slap at his seat belt and then finally managed to slip the transmission into Reverse as he pinned the gas.

53

RDX, which stands for research department explosive, is an extremely nifty, highly effective British plastic explosive used in underwater demolition.

In the SEAL units, we used it all the time in training and after I had retired years ago, I had found a bunch of it—twenty kilo blocks of it to be exact—that I had accidentally left in the trunk of my car.

This find came months after my honorable discharge so I had decided it was probably easier to just keep hold of the restricted stuff instead of trying to explain my potentially illegal possession of it.

It turned out to be a good thing that I had decided to bring a couple of bricks of it with me on my trip, didn't it? I thought as I cracked open the door of the banquet room.

Stuff came in pretty handy indeed, I thought, as I saw that the banquet room had now become the parking lot.

The entire side wall of the banquet room and half of its back wall were gone now and the roof was missing. Half of the tables were in splinters and the parking lot was covered in debris.

Among the shattered boards of what was formerly known as the banquet room lay four figures in tactical gear. The blast had sent them back between a dozen to about twenty feet. All seemed to be missing limbs. Few still had shoes on. None of them were moving.

What was that term? I thought, staring at them.

Something around and find out?

They seemed to have found out. That was for sure. They wouldn't make that mistake again.

I'd been waiting for them all right. I'd set my beautiful little eye in the sky onto the BearCat so the second it had moved in the post office parking lot, it had sent me a notification.

Watching on my phone as the men split up by the church, I knew where they were most likely headed, so I hurried to get ready.

Hearing them scurrying around on the other side of the building wall in the banquet room like bad little mice trying to play a trick, I'd decided to place a block of RDX from my bag of tricks on *my* side of the wall.

I placed it down low and then covered it with three of the heavy flipped-over tables to direct the charge only outward. And just before they could blow the wall *in* at us, I decided to conduct a little demonstration on the two-way nature of nasty surprises.

By blowing the wall *out* onto them.

I'd beat them to the punch all right, I thought, looking out at the dead. Fair was fair, right? And all was fair in love and war.

"What in the hell?" Mathias said, suddenly next to me with the others. "What happened?"

I pointed outside the blasted down wall at the dead mercenaries.

"Looks like they tried to blow a hole in the wall to get in and had an accident or something. Must have crossed a wire or something too soon," I said.

"My restaurant!" Scotty said, suddenly next to Mathias. "There's no roof! The whole building is wrecked. They blew up my joint!"

"Is the BearCat truck still out there?" I said to Daisy.

"No, it took off a second after the explosion. What now?"

"We need to retreat," I said.

I pointed out past the dead men and the debris toward the old brick antique place behind the restaurant.

"We need a new hideout now," I said, patting Scotty on the back as I passed him. "This one here is done."

54

Around eleven o'clock Cushing stood in his upstairs bedroom, looking out at the dark waters of the Farmington River that ran behind the house.

The Forge where Jodi was now was north up the river and he looked to his left in that direction.

Then he looked back at the empty bed.

Like all the other rooms in his historic home, his bedroom had all the ingredients of a designer's touch. Neutral tones, soft lighting, statement furniture in the sitting room. The king-size bed was draped in luxe Italian linens and behind it was a creamy, velvet, cushioned custom headboard.

Truly, the whole estate was a masterpiece. A rolling lawn went down to the scenic river and in the southwest corner of the property was a sunken garden, a greenhouse, a fountain.

And the artwork. They had several of the more important impressionist paintings—a Degas, a Monet—as well as several Whistlers, all from the college's vast art collection.

How happy Jodi had been when they first were shown the stunning place, Cushing thought. It was like the Virginia manor house that she had grown up in, only better. He would never forget her happy tears.

But what did all that matter now? Cushing thought.

He looked back at the empty bed again.

The whole place felt worthless now, dead, abandoned.

He lifted the Scotch bottle that was still in his hand. It was two-thirds empty now. Not a big drinker, he should have been drunk by now, he thought.

But there was no way to get drunk enough, was there?

There would be nowhere to hide from what he had done.

He remembered that night. The meeting with Frank interrupted by someone near the house. The bodyguards running out in a search and bringing Olivia in through the back door.

She was soaking wet, terrified. He remembered how her nose was bleeding. How one of the thugs laughed as he admitted he had broken it. He remembered standing there, stammering, not knowing what to do.

That's when Frank smacked him and demanded that he look up her records. Red-faced with his lip bleeding, going to his computer, doing what he was told as the girl sobbed and bled on his hall floor. The shock of all of it like a dream.

Cushing closed his eyes.

He couldn't wait anymore. He couldn't stand this.

He lifted the SAT phone in his other hand and called Frank.

"Hello," said Cheryl, Frank's assistant.

"I know he's busy, Cheryl. Just take a second."

"I'll get you on the front of the line, Mr. Cushing."

"Thank you, Cheryl," Cushing said. "Where are you guys? Already out at sea?"

"No, we're still in Montauk. We set sail tomorrow if the weather holds," Cheryl said.

"Well, bon voyage."

"Thanks, Mr. Cushing," Cheryl said. "Just hold a moment. You're next up."

"Marty," Frank suddenly said. "I have the South Koreans on the phone. We're in the middle of a bond thing. What can I do for you?"

"Just checking in," Cushing said, trying to hide the fear in his voice. "Any word yet?"

"None yet. Like I said, I'll call you."

"Of course, Frank. I was just—"

"Worried. I know," Frank said. "Don't be. The people we have on this are the best in the world. I've already told them to treat Jodi as if she's been kidnapped. They will extract her with white-glove treatment, I promise. Stop worrying. We're going to settle this, I promise. Jodi will be fine. We'll smooth this thing over, Marty."

"Do you really think so?" Cushing said, hope like a sudden lightness in his chest.

"I don't think so, I know so."

"That's...really great, Frank. Thank you so much. Really. I'm—"

"Don't give it another thought. I'll call the second I hear," Frank said.

55

Back at the post office, Garner and Travers helped Shaw out of the truck.

"What happened?" Garner said.

Shaw, still in shock, was only able to make half the stairs on the loading dock before he collapsed in a sprawl on the concrete.

"Water. I need water."

He sat up as Travers handed him a bottle.

"Could you take off the cap?" Shaw said, holding it out, his hands still shaking.

He drained half of it and took a deep breath and let it out slowly.

"What happened?" Garner said again.

Shaw took another long sip and poured the rest over his head and shook it off with a shudder.

What an overconfident ass he had been.

Playing Van Halen, he thought. He should have tried AC/DC instead. Because his ass just got shook all night long.

"It was the breach," Shaw said. "They were about to... I'm not sure. A faulty wire maybe."

He thought of the roof debris that had smashed into the hood like Dorothy's house from *The Wizard of Oz*.

"They must have hit the gas line or something," Garner said. "Because it sounded like a nuke! The side of the damn restaurant collapsed."

Thank goodness for the armored truck, Shaw thought.

"So, we're talking men down here?" Travers said.

"Men down?" Shaw said, gazing at him. "Men gone is more like it. My guys are all gone."

"And the target?" Garner said.

"I have no clue."

"Maybe if you brought me in on what it is you're actually doing, we'd be done by now," Garner said. "This is turning into a freaking disaster! I've got the head of the town council demanding answers and a state senator on her way. So, what do we do now?"

Shaw stared at him, still trying to get his bearings.

"I need to regroup here, Chief. I need more time. Make something up. Tell them the wind is shifting with the tanker spill or something. I can't think right now."

"What if they call the real FBI?"

"We've got people there," Shaw said.

Which was completely true. That was why Vance Holdings was so expensive. They had the juice in the Bureau and the Department of Justice to make the feds look the other way. The juice to get away with just about anything.

Like Shaw wouldn't be up here running amok *without* a Never Go to Jail card in his back pocket? What did he look like, a schmuck?

"This is over. We're running out of time," Garner said.

"It's over when my boss says it's over," Shaw said. "Let me give him a call. In the meantime, do we have eyes on the restaurant still?"

"Of course."

"Monitor what they do," Shaw said, taking out his SAT phone. "We're going to need more SWAT officers. Can you put that together?"

"I'll see what I can do," Garner said as he left.

Shaw told Control to put him through to the big enchilada, Vance.

Vance was the guy who ran the outfit, some rich little shit. Very smart but a shit nonetheless.

Shaw had started in the business working for Vance's father who was a rich shit, too, but at least he had been a marine.

"Four of my guys are down? Four?" was the first thing Vance said.

"Uh-huh. I'm sure you've seen it for yourself by now. All blown to bits but me. Thanks for asking if I'm okay. Your unwavering support and concern is touching as always, boss. I'm actually not okay, by the way. I think I have a serious concussion."

He wasn't even joking about that. The door slamming him against the headrest had rung his bell. He was nauseous and dizzy and his ears were still ringing.

"How is that possible?" Vance said, ignoring him. "All four gone?"

"Carpenter screwed things up and they hit the gas line is how."

"How could he have screwed up that bad?" Vance said. "He was a wizard with that stuff. Those soft hands of his were way too good. That's why we hired him."

Shaw stifled a sigh as he thought of all the men who were better than Carpenter, better than even Shaw himself, who were rotting in graves on foreign soil because some jackass tripped or farted or sneezed at the wrong time.

"I just don't understand," Vance said.

If you were ever in a war you'd know, Shaw thought.

"Whatever," Shaw said. "The game has changed. No more extractions. No more bullshit. You want me to finish this, I can.

But I'm tired of washing my feet with my socks on. Unless this is full bore, I leave now. The natives are getting restless up here after that firecracker. There's too much heat now even for me."

"I get it," Vance said with a sigh.

"You want to call the client and talk about it?"

"Screw that. I don't need to call. Do it. Take the woman out. Wrap this up."

"The wife or the investigator?"

"Both. They said if push comes to shove, by any means necessary, wipe it up. I'll handle any problems."

"How do you like that?" Shaw said in sudden happy surprise.

"Like what?"

"You making a command decision. I didn't think you had it in you. Maybe the apple didn't fall that far from the tree after all. Your old man would be proud."

"Screw you, Shaw."

Shaw smiled.

"That's it. Now you even sound like dear old dad." Shaw stood, feeling the cobwebs start to clear from his head.

"No more screwups, Shaw. Just get this disaster over with."

"Sir, yes, sir," he said, getting his second wind with a deep breath.

56

With its sturdy brick walls and wooden floor, the inside of the two-story factory-turned-antique-shop we had retreated into had the look of an old firehouse.

Having kicked in its front door, I quickly got everyone straight to work barring the entrance. Just inside was an incredibly ancient and heavy weighted dime-store scale and with the help of my new friends, we lifted it up and maneuvered it into place behind two sideboards, a chest of drawers and half a dozen chairs.

When we were done, Mario ran off and came back bearing a massive concrete driveway lion that he had found somewhere. He heaved it up with a yell on top of the sideboards. There was a crash of glass as it slipped off the top and smashed out the little window in the center of the door.

"Try to get through that, you stupid pieces of shit!" Mario yelled.

"That's the spirit, bro," I said, high-fiving him. "I like it!"

Mario grinned at me from ear to ear. He seemed happy that

we were finally doing something. I was, too. He went over to the pile and cupped his hands at the broken window in the door.

"Screw you!" Mario yelled out of it, getting pumped up. "You picked the wrong bar! We're going to make you bastards sorry you woke up this morning. We won't give you an inch!"

"You finished?" Mathias said to Mario. "What now, Mike?"

"Let's go upstairs with the others and take a look at the street and see what they're doing," I said, leading them for the stairs.

Atop the stairs, the second floor of the old factory was open and had high ceilings almost like a school gym.

One that was in the midst of hosting a massive flea market, I thought as we walked for the south of the building through a narrow corridor between the collectibles.

The whole building was remarkably cluttered. To the right and left were a hoarder's dream come true of antiques and bric-a-brac separated by dividers into little room-like sections.

No way was this to fire code, I thought.

Despite the craziness as I walked past these staged rooms piled with old toys and disco balls and chess tables and old suitcases and packed-to-bursting China cabinets, I smiled as I remembered my neatnik deceased wife Anna's zero tolerance policy for clutter.

She wouldn't have set foot in here even with a gun to her head, I thought.

We found the rest of our crew at the south end of the building. Colleen, who was sitting on an old steamer trunk with Jodi, leaped up and hugged me as I came in. I could see she'd been crying.

"Hey, it's okay. We got this," I said as I guided her over to a corner and hugged her back.

"I know, I know," she said. She stared at me. She was shaking.

"C'mon, really. It's going to be okay," I said.

"I'm sorry, Mike," she said, sniffling. "This is just so fricking crazy. I never imagined anything like this when I started this investigation into Olivia's death. Now all of us, especially Jodi, are in real trouble."

I smiled at her. Then found myself giving her a kiss on her forehead.

Why I did that, I wasn't sure.

"Check it out. Our first kiss," I said. "My bucket list checkmarks are piling up now."

I winked as she chuckled at that.

"And if you think these jacks are crazy, ain't nothing crazier than me, Colleen. Remember the old neighborhood? I've only gotten crazier since then."

"Hulk," she said in my ear.

I laughed. I hadn't heard that nickname in…wow. A long time.

"You do remember."

I let her go and looked around.

The seven of us looked pretty shook up but we at least were all still in one piece. And with Mario's new attitude, we were actually in better shape than we had been before the blast.

And it wasn't just the attitude adjustment that was in our favor.

What was also truly looking up was that we were armed now. Armed quite well, in fact, as the fallen tactical guys had all been carrying MP5 submachine guns with four thirty-round magazines apiece. With these came sidearms—three nine-millimeter Glocks, a SIG Sauer, and a .45 Smith & Wesson—as well as several flash-bang grenades and two fragmentation grenades. We even had two ballistic shields.

One negative was that the battery on the drone had died so we had no more eye in the sky. Now we just had to rely on our own eyeballs.

I stepped past Scotty, who was sitting in a rocking chair next to an old slot machine, to take a peek out the window at Route 4.

"Anything?" Mathias said as I turned back.

"No," I said. "All quiet on the Western Front. They're still licking their wounds, I guess."

"Why are there no fire trucks?" Scotty said. "People across the river heard this. The authorities would have been here by now. Why the hell has no one come?"

"Are you kidding me?" Mario said. "You still haven't figured it out? Wake up! Your local cops are corrupt. They let your buddy Big Joe get killed and now, because we witnessed it, it's time for us to get greased. They blew up your restaurant!"

"I can't believe Chief Garner is involved in this," Scotty said. "I've met him. He's eaten at my place with his wife. How can he be out there? How?"

"No one can be this naive," Mario said. "Dude, no one ever lied to you before? You've never heard of a corrupt cop? We're fighting for our lives here, bro. This is the Alamo and you're inside of it. Get a grip."

"Mario, calm down," Mathias said.

"Tell him to wake up," Mario said. "I'm not taking a bullet in my head because this numbskull refuses to put two and two together."

"Fine!" Scotty yelled as he jumped up. "Fine! Chief Garner is a psycho. I got it. Happy now? But so what? How are we going to get out of this, huh? What are we going to do?"

"We hold them off until the morning," I said. "In the light of day when more regular people show up, they're going to have to change their plans."

"Mike's right," Mathias said. "That big bang has rattled some windows across the river. People have to be asking questions."

"Exactly," I said. "This bullshit story has an expiration date. Too many crazy things are happening for them to keep the cover-up going. We're not some goofy religious group in a compound they can lie about. We're a bunch of construction workers and Joe Six-Packs who were in a bar watching a hockey game. Justifying all of this in the light of day isn't going to be difficult for them, it's going to be impossible. We just have to hold these scumbags off until dawn."

57

Shaw, out in front of the post office, waved in the arriving vehicles. There was a diesel engine roar as two more BearCats,
another khaki one and a gleaming black one, pulled up to the
loading dock. As Shaw watched, the back doors of both opened
and about a dozen men in tactical gear piled out.

They were from the next two towns over. Chief Garner had
finally proven quite useful after all. Once Shaw had told him
what he needed, he had gotten on the horn and finagled some
decent replacements.

Normally Shaw hated working with weekend warrior types,
but at this point beggars couldn't be choosers, could they? He
was running out of time to get this done and get gone before
sunrise, so he needed any and every Tom, Dick or Harry he
could find.

"What do we got?" said the large tactical uniformed cop who
had gotten out of the black truck. He was a big black-haired kid
in his late twenties. He was already wearing his tactical goggles.

Shaw waited until the other SWAT chief from the khaki BearCat arrived a moment later. He was older, forty maybe, a thin almost prissy triathlete-type guy with blonde anchorman hair.

"Chief Garner said this is a national security thing?" the kiddie SWAT cop said.

Shaw assessed the young man. He was big all over, wasn't he? Big hands, big bovine face and head. His dark eyes, which were a little too close together, had a determined look. Shaw had played football in high school in Ohio, and this boy reminded him of his teammates, big bull-like farm boys who were not too smart but plenty strong.

Perfect cannon fodder, Shaw thought. His favorite kind of soldier.

"What's your name?" Shaw said as he put his arm around the wide back of the new arrival.

"Minton. Don Minton."

"And you?" he said to the anchorman.

"Doug Needlemeyer."

"I'm Special Agent Thompson," Shaw said as he herded the men toward the loading dock steps. "Leave your men there. Let's go inside, just the three of us. I need to talk to you both in private."

58

There was a bathroom on the first floor by the stairs and I was coming out of it two minutes later when I almost bumped into someone there in the dark by the stairs.

It was Jodi.

"Mike, can I talk to you?" she said.

"Sure. What's up?"

"Mike, listen, I want to turn myself in," she said.

I pointed my cell's flashlight up and looked at her expression. She looked detached, had a thousand-yard stare.

"What is it, Jodi? What's wrong?"

"This has gone too far," she said. "That poor man shot in the street. Now those other policemen are dead in that explosion. I thought I could do the right thing for that girl, for her family. But now all these other people are dead and I want…"

She covered her eyes with a hand.

"I need for all this to stop," she said.

"Jodi, listen to me," I said. "You think you're responsible for this? Think again. You're the opposite. A good person. There is a tiny group of human beings in this world who ever truly stick their necks out for other people. You're among them. That's a real rare thing."

I gently patted her on the shoulder.

"But see, the men out there—the ones who just died—they weren't cops. They were stone-cold killers. Even if you turned yourself in, they would just kill you and then kill us anyway because we know what's going on. That's why we only have one move here. We have to fight them. With everything we've got."

"I don't know," she said, starting to cry. "I just don't know."

"Jodi, no. Shush. Listen to me," I said, holding her by her shoulders now. "We're not just going to fight them, we're going to beat them. I promise, okay? I'm going to get you and all of us out of this."

When she looked up, there was at least a little more life in her eyes.

She snuffled and took a deep breath, wiping at them.

"You remind me of my husband," she suddenly said.

I looked at her.

"No, not Martin," she said. "My first husband. We were high school sweethearts. So happy. My father hated him. Especially when I went to school in New York to be near him at West Point. We eloped the day of his graduation. He...he was... like you. Sweet. Funny. Strong. He played baseball. He was the catcher. Everyone loved him. I never got over him. Even now, I keep thinking it's like a...dream. It's a dream and I'm going to wake up and he's going to hold my hand and our life, the one we never got to live, is going to start."

I didn't know exactly what to say to that.

"Jodi, this isn't as bad as it seems. If we all stick together, this will work out," I finally said.

Even to my ears the platitude fell flat. Jodi started crying then. She collapsed onto the stairs and curled up against the wall sobbing.

As I patted at her back, I thought about the people outside doing this to all of us. Playing with our lives. Terrorizing us. Look at the trauma this poor woman was being put through.

By who? I thought. *Some college president? Some billionaire? For what? Money? Power?*

As I looked down at this sobbing woman, I didn't know what was going to happen next except for one thing.

I wasn't going to stop until all the parties responsible paid for this.

Paid in full.

If the cops out there weren't going to do their jobs, I would.

If the corrupt courts weren't going to prosecute, then fine. I would be the judge, too.

I had after all been trained to do this by the US government. They taught me how to still the fear within me, taught me how to plan, to pick my moment. Taught me how to penetrate into the most impenetrable walls with one single focus, one single mission.

Now that I was retired, did that matter?

Even up here in this beautiful small town in the middle of nowhere, the corruption had come.

There was nowhere to hide, I realized.

There was no safe place.

Not until justice came back.

Right there, as I looked down at Jodi, I decided *I* would be that justice.

I was all in.

59

"Leave us now!" Shaw yelled at a couple of the tech cops in the war room as they entered.

That seemed to impress his new friends, which was the intention.

"Okay, here's the story, men," Shaw said after the geek squad left. "What we have is an officer down situation. Four of my men—my whole team—were lost."

"You have to be shitting me!" Minton cried in shock.

"Four FBI agents died in that explosion?" Anchorman Doug said. "The entire HRT team was killed! No! How?"

It really was crazy that they were all gone, wasn't it? Shaw thought. He had hardly processed it himself, especially Azar and Shahu, who had been like sons to him in a way.

Without even wanting to, he suddenly thought of the raids they'd been in. Room-to-rooms where they had to shoot their way up stairwells so thick with gunsmoke you couldn't see your hand in front of your face.

But that was war, wasn't it? Brothers-in-arms were lost and in the thick of battle you had to bounce past it and reengage, get right back on the bicycle.

"Keep it down, gentlemen. This stays in this room. No one can know."

"Right, of course," Minton said.

"Sorry about your men," Doug added.

"Me, too, brother, but this is a matter of the highest importance to the country. We can grieve later. Two women who worked in a local defense corporation stole highly classified national security information. When we came to do the arrest, they barricaded themselves in this restaurant, The Forge. In trying to defuse this deadly situation, we tried to do a breach, but we hit a gas line."

"Shit," Minton said.

"Gets worse," Shaw continued. "Now the suspects have taken my men's weapons and retreated with them."

Shaw turned and brought up the photo of the antique place on the Smart Board.

"Into this building down the street here."

Shaw tapped the Smart Board hard.

"What I now need from you and your men is help in getting me in there. We need to storm this son of a bitch and fast. What can you do for me, fellas? I need a way in."

Minton took off his goggles and placed them up on his skateboard helmet. Furrow-like wrinkles appeared on his large brow as he pondered the layout. He seemed to be squinting at the roof of it. Doug beside him folded his arms.

Suddenly a flash of something appeared in Minton's eyes: inspiration.

"Good news. I think I can get you in there. These bastards won't know what hit them."

The sudden exuberance and confidence the young man exuded was surprising. Perhaps Shaw had underestimated him.

"How?" Shaw said. "They're armed now and we couldn't breach those brick walls. It would take artillery."

Minton shook his head.

"That's not going to be a problem."

"No?"

"No way," Minton said, rubbing his big farmer's palms together. "We just got in something brand-spanking-new that I think you're really going to like."

60

We were all back upstairs monitoring things from the window and just sitting there waiting to see what would happen next when a muted clank brought Mathias to the window.

Mario had found a telescope from among the antiques and Mathias bent to where it was pointed outside.

He quickly waved at me from where I sat catnapping on a toddler's race car bed.

"Mike, look."

"What?" I said, coming over.

"They're bringing something in."

I went to the window and peered down into the scope. By the post office command center, the cops were shuffling and circling around as a large truck came into the parking lot.

It was a flatbed truck and there was some kind of cherry picker, a hydraulic motorized construction platform on the back of it.

But it wasn't a normal cherry picker, I saw as the skids were dropped and it was backed down.

It was a cherry picker modified with a giant ballistic shield on the front of it for a SWAT team to stand behind.

It took me a second to recover when I saw that.

"What is it? I don't like that look on your face," Mathias said.

"This is not good," I said. "I haven't seen this before. It must be brand-new."

"What are they going to do with it?" said Scotty who had come over and was looking out. "They can't get past the door."

"They won't need to," I said. "They can get in directly to the second floor now. And straight to the roof, too."

"They can get in now," Daisy said, suddenly standing. "We're sitting ducks!"

"The tunnel," Scotty suddenly said.

"Are you feeling okay?" said Daisy.

"The tunnel," Scotty said again as he stood up from the rocking chair. "There's a tunnel in this building in the basement. I grew up a block away and I remember it from when I was a kid."

"A tunnel," I said.

"Yes. It leads to the town museum across the street. It goes under the street directly into the basement of the museum there."

He went to the window and pointed to the right, across the parking lot to an old stone building.

"Before it became the town museum, that was the office building for the factory. This whole town was just for the workers of the Beckford Tool Factory and the owner, Beckford, was apparently a very generous man. He was like the mayor and boss and Santa Claus all rolled into one. In gratitude, the workers all pitched together and built the tunnel for old man Beckford as a surprise one Christmas so that he could visit the factory from his office when it was raining."

"Are you sure it's still there?" I said.

"I'm positive. This building used to be abandoned and in

high school me and my buddies would party in it. We'd walk through the tunnel on Halloween back in the '80s. It was the thing to do, like a haunted house."

"Now he tells us," Mario said, throwing his hands up. "We're sitting here biting our nails when there's a freaking escape hatch."

"The '80s is going back a while," I said. "Isn't it possible that it's gone now?"

"We would've heard about something like that. Not much changes around here. Just look at this place. They've hardly touched it."

"Okay," I said. "I'm convinced. My pickup is parked near the museum building so when we go through the tunnel, I grab my truck and we all pile in and make a run for it.

"I thought we could hold them off here because it's like a castle but that cherry picker is a game changer. Changes the entire terrain, so we need new tactics."

I went to the window as I heard the rumble of the machine again.

"But we have to time it right."

"How so?" said Mathias.

"We have to have them come at us first. They have to think we're still in here hiding. Have to keep them busy here while we skedaddle or it won't work."

61

Shaw, in the war room going over the siege plan with Don and Doug, fished out his SAT phone that was going off.

He blinked at the caller ID.

Shahu, it said.

Shahu?

Shaw quickly took off down the corridor.

Because it wasn't Shahu.

It was the targets who were inside the factory building who had taken Shahu's phone.

"Who is this?" he said.

He walked outside and headed down the loading dock.

"I need to talk to who's in charge," said a woman.

He jogged out to the street to stare at the old brick factory.

"I'm in charge," Shaw said. "My name is Special Agent Thompson of the FBI. Who am I speaking with?"

"Special agent, my ass," the woman said. "Who are you trying to kid? I watched my friend Big Joe get gunned down in cold blood then taken away like a bag of garbage. Cops or FBI agents don't do that."

"Who am I speaking with?"

"Me? You can call me J Lo. What do you want, anyway? Why did you come here?" she said.

"You seem pretty sharp, J Lo. You tell me what we want."

"You're looking for a woman, right? The college president's wife?"

This broad really was sharp.

"Maybe," Shaw said.

"I knew it," J Lo said. "I've been to games at the school, seen ol Jodi, the Martha Stewart clone, with a stick up her ass and her nose in the air waving down from the VIP section like Lady Godiva. She comes in with some broad from New York all upset and they leave and come back and the lights go out. Figured it wasn't a coincidence the way those things added up."

"Keep talking," Shaw said.

"I can also subtract and multiply, too, believe it or not."

"I'm sure you can, J Lo. I'm listening," Shaw said.

"Thought so. You looking for her or do I hang up?"

"We're looking for her. We get her, you get your life back. That's why we're having this conversation, right, J Lo? To get your life back? You don't want to end up like Big Joe, right?"

"I get my life back and..." she said.

Shaw squinted, confused.

"And what?" he said.

"And what does my retirement package look like?" she said.

Shaw almost laughed out loud. This J Lo was playing for all the marbles.

"Whoever is willing to go to these lengths has got the kind of pockets that don't quit. That college's got billions. I want three million dollars in bitcoin delivered where I say and then and only then do you get Jodi on a silver platter."

Three million? Shaw thought wide-eyed. This lady did not lack chutzpah.

"That's a tall order. Where you getting your numbers, lady?"

"Two for me and one for Big Joe's widow is where, you filthy disgusting murderer."

"I'll see what I can do but you have to give me something first. How many people are with you?"

"Go figure your end out, and I call back in five so you can send the coin."

"We can come in in four and take care of things ourselves you know," Shaw said.

"Yeah? We're armed to the teeth in here with all the shit your dead guys left the last time you failed so I doubt that," she said and hung up.

62

Down in the old factory's basement, the barrel-mounted flashlight of the stolen MP5 cut through the darkness.

The circle of its light revealed wire mesh fronted storage bins that contained an amount of stuff that didn't seem possible.

Inside were dartboards, Persian rugs, china, nutcrackers, license plates, comic books, a porcelain Bugs Bunny cookie jar, Mickey Mouse slippers, Barbies, a *Happy Days* lunch box next to a *Charlie's Angels* one, old board games.

Every fossil of Americana from 1970 onward that still existed seemed to have been gathered here to molder, I noticed. It was like a Gen X childhood museum. One bin we passed was filled only with old Cabbage Patch dolls lined up on tables like an army regiment.

"Now, there's something you don't see every day," said Colleen behind me.

Scotty led the way toward the tunnel with me close behind with the MP5 followed by Colleen, Daisy and Jodi.

I was also carrying one of the salvaged ballistic shields. Why not? Whatever the heck happened next, not getting shot seemed like a good idea to me.

I had another curious item that we had stripped off one of the tactical guys. An M67 fragmentation grenade. I say curious in that police SWAT teams didn't tend to go around tossing grenades when civilians were about. These psychos were clearly geared up for a guerilla war. I was almost surprised we hadn't found a flamethrower and some claymore mines.

Sticking with the escape plan we'd cobbled together, once we found the tunnel and made it to the town museum, the ladies could wait there safely. Then Scotty and I would head back and join Mathias and Mario in the old factory.

A successful escape would have to be all about the timing, I knew. We needed the bad guys to start laying siege on the factory. As they came at us, we would let off some rounds in the air to make them think we were truly pinned down. Then as they went through the laborious process of searching room to room, we would boogie down here to the basement, escape through the tunnel in the chaos and be well on our way in my truck before they figured it out.

That was the plan, anyway.

Someone grabbed almost painfully at my back a split second later as there was a clang ahead.

"It's all right. I just kicked over an old paint can," Scotty called back as I turned to see a wide-eyed Colleen behind me.

"Sorry," she said.

"This is the way. I remember now," Scotty said as we came to a short set of descending steps.

At the bottom of them, there was a big metal tank, an old oil tank by the sour smell of it. Beyond it along the wall was of course some more stuff, rusty wheeled hand trucks, a collection of old doors, a legless pool table with a torn felt top.

And what do you know, a Mr. T pinball machine next to a Michael Jackson one followed by a Ms. Pac-Man arcade game.

I looked at Michael in his white suit standing on a dance floor.

Now, if only we could find his sparkly glove, I thought, we could maybe moonwalk the hell out of here.

I almost bumped into Scotty as he suddenly halted.

"There it is. In the wall. See? I told you."

As I stepped closer, I saw the opening. It was tight, about the width of a coffin. From within it, you could hear a slight dripping of water, and I noticed that the air in front of it seemed discernably colder.

As I poked the light in, I saw the walls of the tunnel were made of rough yellowish blocks of rock on the bottom with an arching vault of brick above. The stale smell of damp earth was intense.

"We're supposed to go into that?" Jodi said.

"Wimps," Daisy said, holding her own phone forward as she tried to get past Scotty.

"No, let me go first, Daisy," Scotty said. "I have the flashlight."

Daisy relented and Jodi went next, then me and then Colleen.

Thirty steps in, the walls became rough stone like a mine shaft and after another ten, we came to a part where water was dripping from a crack in the ceiling and down the left-hand wall.

"See? They made an underground storage room off it to the left here," Scotty said, pointing his light into an opening ahead.

I pointed my own light as I got to it and saw a windowless cell with what looked like railroad ties in it. It smelled like mushrooms and dead mice.

Jodi shuddered in front of me. I patted her gently on the shoulder. The last thing we needed now was for someone to get cold feet.

We walked on for another hundred feet or so and then the tunnel seemed to get even narrower. I saw a few leaves along the floor and noticed it was getting colder. Moss appeared along a wall. Small piles of fallen bricks and rock began to pass on both sides.

"We're close now," Scotty said. "Up ahead it turns left and then it's only another hundred feet or so."

A second later, there was a strange scuffling sound.

"I can't take it. It's too tight. Help. I can't breathe," Daisy called out, pushing past Scotty.

"Daisy, wait. We're almost there," Scotty said.

A moment later, there was a loud thump and scuff ahead along with a short cry of pain from Daisy. In the choppy light ahead, I could see she had fallen down.

"Daisy, stop freaking out. It's dangerous," Scotty said.

In the light we watched as she got up and without turning around bolted ahead into the dark of the tunnel.

What the hell? I thought.

"Wait for us, Daisy!" Scotty called out. "Daisy, wait up!"

63

The basement of the Beckford Historical Museum was a surprisingly clean and neat wide-open space with a sandwich board sign in its center that displayed factoids about the factory town's history.

You want some history? Shaw thought as he glanced at the board then down at the SAT phone in his hand. How about some military history? The final decisive battle of Podunk, Connecticut, coming up.

And boy, was it going to be an extremely bloody one, he thought.

It was ambush time now. "J Lo," their contact on the inside, had called twenty minutes before and Shaw had passed along the counter offer of two million dollars in bitcoin from the client.

Half of it was successfully sent into a wallet she had provided while they were still on the phone with the other half to be paid when she delivered up the others.

At that point, she had told Shaw that there were seven people all together. The two women, her boss, two construction

workers and a vacationing fisherman who was apparently a retired New York City cop.

The cop was the pain in the ass. He was now in the lead of
defending the group. After the explosion, it was his idea that
they retreat into the old factory building and to strip his fallen
men of their weapons.

But that didn't matter now.

Because it was all about to be game over and out.

J Lo had told them about the tunnel and their plan to escape
through it and four minutes before as Shaw had arrived at the
museum with the other new SWAT officers, she had texted that
they were in the tunnel right this very minute on their way.

The entry of the underground tunnel to the factory was behind a small door in the brick wall opposite the sandwich board
and now to the left and right of this door, Shaw, along with Don
Minton and three other tactical SWAT officers, stood wearing
ominous black balaclavas, their gloved fingers hovering over the
triggers of their MP5s.

Five, Shaw thought as he stood there staring at the door. *Four.
Three.*

Shaw and the rest of them twitched as if at a small electric shock
when they heard the sudden knock on the closed tunnel door.

"It's me. It's J Lo. Open up quick," said a voice.

Shaw nodded and Minton hit the lights and they all pulled
down their night vision goggles as the officer beside Minton
pulled the door.

The short bespectacled pudgy woman standing there shrieked
in fright and her glasses went flying as Shaw reached out and
seized her.

"Jodi Cushing is in the tunnel?" Shaw whispered in her ear
as he pulled her to the side with a gloved hand over her mouth.

He took away his hand.

"Right behind me," she said after a gasp for breath.

"How many all together?" he whispered.

"Four. Cushing, the New York woman, the cop and my boss."

"They have guns?"

She nodded.

Shaw looked at her face as she said this. Even in the green light of the night vision optics, he could tell that her fear and seriousness were real. She wasn't playing games.

Shaw turned and nodded to Minton. Minton peeked into the opening and then he entered with his men at his back.

Minton's orders were simple.

Shoot everyone on sight.

"Okay, good. Go upstairs," Shaw said, releasing the woman.

"I need my glasses," she said.

Shaw searched the ground and handed them back to her.

"And the rest of my money," she said.

Shaw looked at her again, the conniving eyes behind her glasses. He actually admired her. She knew how to put the bite on when opportunity knocked, didn't she?

"As soon as we're done," Shaw said.

"Which way do I go?" she said.

Shaw flicked on his MP5's undermounted flashlight and pointed its beam across the sandwich board at the stairwell.

"Past the board," he said.

She did as instructed and was coming past the sandwich board when Shaw's silenced gun went click-clack. As the two rounds of 9mm Parabellum hit her in the side of the head just behind her right ear, she toppled forward like a sack of potatoes, her glasses shattering as she face-planted off the concrete.

Sometimes getting the money was the easy part, wasn't it? Shaw thought as he hurried over and grabbed her ankles and dragged her into a broom closet under the stairs.

Staying alive to spend it, Shaw thought as he closed the door and scooped his brass and ran for the mouth of the tunnel.

Now, that was the real bitch.

64

We were coming up on the corner of the tunnel when behind me I heard Colleen kick something. It made a skittering sound beside me a second before I felt it ricochet off my left foot. As I swung the gun's flashlight down, I saw it was a cell phone.

Not just any cell phone but a satellite cell phone, I saw as I knelt and lifted it up by its antenna.

When I realized what it was and that Daisy must have dropped it when she fell, I suddenly knew that what had made her flip out and run wasn't a sudden bout of claustrophobia after all.

"Scotty, no! Come back! Come back!" I yelled at his back in the tunnel ahead.

But I was too late.

The rattle of automatic gunfire that started from around the turn of the tunnel was as deafening as it was sudden. I watched in shock and horror as Scotty's light shook crazily and I heard him scream in pain as he fell.

"Back! Back! Back!" I yelled, trying to dodge around Jodi in front of me in the narrow corridor with the ballistic shield.

But I wasn't fast enough.

Just as I came shoulder to shoulder with Jodi, a bright white blossom of gunfire came from around the tunnel corner ahead. I heard some rounds skip off the stone wall right beside me and some whip past my ear and then I felt a splash of something wet as Jodi suddenly fell into me.

I felt rounds smack into the shield as I finally dove forward and lifted it up in front of me. There was one and then another and then two more. Each made a clunking sound like an axe chopping wood.

When I glanced at the bulletproof aperture, it was just in time to see a gray smudge of lead smack a spiderweb crack across it. Another round hit almost at the same exact spot a split second later, dimpling back the cracked glass.

With my free right hand, I thumbed down the MP5 that I was holding to full auto, put the barrel along the side of the shield and pulled the trigger. Raking it side to side, I let off a long burst down the tunnel and then another and then a third, emptying the mag.

When I turned back, I saw that Colleen had already grabbed Jodi from under her arms and was dragging her backward. As I backed with her, keeping the shield in front of all of us, there was another burst of gunfire and another spray of lead pinged and punched off the shield. Bits of glass almost got in my eyes as it was hit yet again.

This shield was saving our lives at the present but it had its limits, I knew. Every time it was hit, its steel was weakened. Bottom line, we needed to get the hell out of the tunnel or we were going to die.

"Pull her into the side storage room there," I called to Colleen behind me.

Another roar of fire came at us, chipping the brick opening as we all hurried in.

The first thing I did as I got clear of the corridor was replace the magazine of the MP5 and the second thing I did was stick it back into the tunnel without looking and pull the trigger until it stopped firing.

By the time it went click, the gun smoke was so thick and hazy, I couldn't see the other side of the corridor. I put in another fresh mag and slapped down the bolt carrier before I turned to see Colleen giving Jodi CPR.

But it wasn't necessary, I saw a moment later as I crouched forward with the light.

Jodi was dead.

A bullet had hit her high in the forehead and another had gone in right under her left cheekbone.

I shook my head, trying to stay focused.

They killed her. They actually killed her.

I closed my eyes as I thought about what she had said about her husband.

Man, that hurt.

It hurt even worse when I remembered my promise to get her out of this.

What bastards, I thought, looking at the blood on this pretty lady's cheek, in her blonde hair. What total psychopathic scum.

"It's over. Stop. She's gone," I said to Colleen, who was still pumping away.

"No," Colleen cried, continuing to pump.

"Stop, Colleen," I said, pulling her off of Jodi. She was in shock.

"We have to go or we're next," I said as calmly as possible.

I held her by her shoulders and looked right into her eyes.

"As I empty this last magazine, you just turn and run full out back for the factory as fast as possible before they start firing back again, okay? It's our only chance."

She nodded slowly.

"What about you?" she said in a whisper.

"Don't worry about me. I have the shield. Are you ready?"

I helped her up, hoping she would be steady on her feet.

"Okay," I said. "One, two, run!"

I stepped out with the shield and gun and opened up down the hall again as Colleen ran.

When my gun went click for the last time, I was already moving backward as fast as I could. Then I finally reached the end of the tunnel and was back in the factory basement gloriously unshot.

I immediately dropped the shield and ran across the basement and grabbed one of the antique doors, a heavy oak thing, and ran back for the mouth of the tunnel with it.

I laid it across the opening and ran back for another. As I returned with the second door, several rounds suddenly punched through the first one.

Undeterred, I propped the second door against the first and I ran back and grabbed the old hand truck. I jammed the lip of it under the side of the Ms. Pac-Man console and tilted it up and ran, pushing it across the basement floor to slam it hard up against the two doors. The cheap pool table made a screeching sound, or maybe that was my spine, as I carried it on my back to sit it beside the Ms. Pac-Man.

Another round came through the wood and then I remembered something.

I fished out the baseball-shaped frag grenade, pulled its pin and ran up and dunked it hard into the small gap between the top of the doors and the top of the tunnel.

I heard it skitter deep into the tunnel and then I lay flat against the wall as it ba-boomed.

I was already at the stairs when I was rewarded with a thoroughly satisfying scream.

How's it feel, losers? I thought as I started running.

"Come on! Come on! Let's go!" I said to Colleen as I grabbed her hand and pulled her around the old boiler for the stairs.

To where, I had no idea, since our escape hatch was now sealed.

This was bad, I thought.

Bad, bad, bad.

65

As one of the weekend warriors ahead in the tunnel continued his loud bellyaching, Shaw stood in the dank and dark, looking down at the dead hippie, checking out his handiwork.

He'd put a real nice tight burst in the head, neck and chest area of the four-eyed sucker as he came around the bend, hadn't he?

A closed casket job wasn't too shabby at a hundred feet moving in the dark, now was it?

"I still got it," Shaw mumbled as he continued farther into the tunnel.

Up ahead, Minton and his men were cursing a blue streak. They dragged one of their own before him and laid him down at his feet. It was a skinny fair-haired dude of about twenty-five, moaning and crying as he clutched at his bleeding face.

"What's his malfunction?" Shaw said to Minton.

"The bastard threw a grenade," Minton said. "He caught a piece of metal in his cheek."

"Let me see it," Shaw said. "Move his hands out of the way."

They did. The guy screamed as Shaw spread the skin and muscle back. Shaw looked at it. A piece of steel the size of a cornflake was stuck in the cheekbone.

"Give me a break," Shaw said as he took out his Leatherman tool and pulled it free. "Stop being such a baby," he said.

They had just taken him away when Shaw entered the side chamber and found Jodi Cushing's body.

He looked at her dead open eyes, the look of dismayed shock frozen there. She'd probably been pretty hot once, he thought, glancing down at the length of her.

He looked at the rose pink lipstick on her lips.

Maybe not the head cheerleader but on the squad.

All this trouble to take her alive, he thought with a look of disgust on his own face. For what? Stupid. He would have whacked her clean and simple. Just her. Now all these others had to go, too? Patently ridiculous. He should be safe home and dry already.

He checked her pockets, searched around for her bag. Even did an underwear check.

There was nothing.

This wasn't over yet, Shaw thought, shaking his head.

But at least half the mission was over. That was something at least.

Minton appeared in the doorway behind him.

"They blocked the end of the tunnel with something heavy. Won't budge," he said. "What now?"

"What time you got?" Shaw said.

"One a.m.," said Minton.

Shaw nodded and snapped a pic of Jodi Cushing with his phone.

"Stay here so this way out stays blocked," he said, standing.

"Where are you going?"

"I'll let you know. Just stay here and keep this position until I tell you otherwise."

Shaw had just exited the front door of the museum when his phone rang.

He smiled when he looked at the caller ID.

Shahu, it said.

66

"Hey, there," I said into the satellite phone as I heard it stop ringing.

We were in the stairwell of the old factory by the back window. I looked over at Colleen as we waited.

"Who is this?"

I smiled.

"Let's kick it into gear already," I said. "Time for you to throw something new at me, buddy. Think outside the box, would you?"

"Who are you?"

The voice was American. Cold and deep and gravelly, like that of a drill sergeant.

"It's obvious," I said. "I'm the king of the castle which makes you the dirty rascal."

"You think this is a joke, pal? This is the FBI and this is an evacuation situation and I am ordering you to come out with your hands up right now."

"Hands up?" I said as I began to pace in front of the window. "Nah. Feet up is the only way I come out. Which, I take it, is how you're probably taking Daisy out right around now. Gonna bury her in the woods next to Big Joe? And I thought she was smart. Boy, was I wrong about her."

"You're wrong about a lot of things," the drill sergeant said. "That's why you need to give up on this. You're done. The wife is dead. You got no place to go. This game is over."

"Over?" I said, laughing as I continued to pace. "Not only is it not over, I'm still up by at least three. Or maybe four now as I heard one of your guys maybe didn't like it so much when I returned one of the presents you left us.

"Speaking of which, you guys are carrying some real nasty gear. What are you? A Green Beret? You sound like a Green Beret to me. A retired one who didn't really retire because old soldiers never die, do they? You're a mean green professional killing machine, the kind that the big-dough, billionaire, white-shoe types keep in the break-glass-in-case-of-emergency box, am I right?"

"You're the one in a box," the voice said. "A pine box that I'm going to drop the lid on if you don't start cutting a deal here."

"Cutting a deal?" I said, laughing. "Are you not noticing that your guys are starting to stack up like firewood out there? Like those first four suckers you sent. They were all thumbs with the explosives, huh? Not good. Butterfingers cost you plenty in the big bang biz."

"What's your play here?" he said. "The waitress said you were a retired cop. What's up with the hero routine? Trying to re-live the glory days? 'Cause it's going to cost you everything."

"I'm a man with a cause," I said. "You know what my cause is?"

"Being a pain in my ass."

"No, surviving at all costs by any means necessary. So, I'd take a hike right around now if I were you," I said.

"Take a hike? We have you surrounded on every side."

I smiled.

"I know," I said. "You dirty rat bastards can't hide now."

"What's your angle?" said the mercenary. "Nice face that Miss Doherty. A real Irish beauty. You sleeping with her or something?"

"Don't know what you're talking about, Sarge," I said. "*Dateline* is showing a rerun again tonight. That's why I'm here. There was nothing else to do."

"How about this, cop," he said. "Work with me. Jodi Cushing didn't come by to borrow a bowl of sugar from your girlfriend. She must have had something, some evidence. A video maybe? You hand that over, I show it to my boss, you and your girlfriend get a free ride back to the gutter and we call it a night."

"A free one-way ride into the forest is more like it," I said. "With you and a shovel. I'll pass. I figure the longer I hold out, the faster all the people you're suckering with this shit carnival are gonna start smelling the BS."

"You have more faith in the intelligence of people than they deserve," he said. "Honestly, I'm here to help, cop. You come out now, I'll take it easy on you. But if you make this any harder than it has to be, there's going to be consequences for you and especially Miss Doherty. Consequences of a kind you never even heard of."

"Oh, I'm going to make this harder," I said, gritting my teeth. "So much harder that you're going to wake up in the graveyard. Do you think this is the first phone call I made with this satellite phone? See all the hills around here? The hills are going to have eyes real soon, Sarge. You think you're the only one who knows how to play bury-them-in-the-woods?"

"Oh, I'm shaking," he said.

"Fine, you have to make me say this, don't you?"

"Say what?"

"I got a confession to make. That explosion wasn't an accident. That was me."

"Yeah, right," he said.

"It's true. I beat your buddies to the detonator punch. Daisy told you I was a cop, right? Maybe she forgot to mention what kind of cop I used to be."

I paused smiling.

"I was on the bomb squad, dummy. Out of all the walls of all the joints in all the world, your buddies had to try to breach one that had a block of MDX on its other side."

Over the phone line there was silence. He was pondering what I'd just told him. I knew I'd struck a nerve there. Bringing up your opponent's own personal safety tends to do that.

"As a final warning, you stick around, there's a real good chance I put a bullet in your head before you put one in mine. So why not wave the white flag, Sarge? Take a knee. Get out of here. Or don't. Come in here so I can snap your neck.

"One last thing," I said. "Do me a favor and tell your boss that if he has one of those billionaire bunkers somewhere, it's bugout time. Because when I'm done with you, he's up next."

67

"What happened? Where is everyone?" Mathias said as we saw him appear in the stairwell.

"They're gone," I said as I handed Colleen the phone and jogged up the stairs back onto the ground floor.

"No!" Mathias said. "Dead?"

"Yes," I said. "They all got shot in the tunnel. We barely got out alive ourselves. They were waiting for us."

"How?"

I pointed down at Colleen.

"The phone she's talking on, that's a SAT phone. Daisy had it. She must have found it on one of the dead mercenaries when we were taking their guns and tried to cut a deal."

"She betrayed us?"

I nodded.

Mathias interlaced his fingers on top of his head. He blinked rapidly. He was in total shock.

"Now they know about the tunnel?" he said. "They'll come in now. We're boxed in!"

"No," I said. "I blocked the tunnel. No way they can get in. At least not for a while."

"But we have no way out now."

"Not so fast, Mathias. Listen to me. Things are different now. We have a link outside," I said, pointing at where Colleen had just started speaking into the phone.

"Colleen is calling her law firm. They're very heavy hitters with contacts in the media. Once we put some outside pressure on those thugs out there, they're going to have to back off. They'll cut bait and get out of Dodge. Sunlight is the best disinfectant, and now with the SAT phone, we have a flashlight to make the cockroaches run."

Just then, there was a loud diesel rumble from outside. It was followed by a sharp whistle from up the stairs to the second floor behind us.

We looked up as Mario poked his head over the banister.

"Yo! Yo! Yo!" he barked. "They're on the move."

Mathias looked at me.

"But I thought you said things would get better," he said.

"They're just getting desperate," I said reassuringly. "I'm telling you, this is over."

There was another diesel rumble, another whistle.

"Come on," Mario said. "What are you waiting for? Get up here and man your battle stations. They got that freaking cherry picker moving around again."

"We're going to die," Mathias said, rubbing at his brow.

"No," I said, clapping him on the back. "People might die. But it won't be us."

68

Cushing opened his eyes.

The phone was ringing.

The empty bottle in his lap rolled to the floor with a crash as he leaped up from his chair by the bedroom window.

He scooped the phone off the floor.

"Martin, bad news," Frank said. "Jodi didn't make it. She's dead."

"What? No! That can't be right. No," he said.

"You're in shock, Martin. Just breathe. Take a deep breath."

"But I thought you said—"

"There was an accident," Frank said.

The reality of it hit. What he had done to Jodi was like a black void opening up inside of him.

He had done this. He was a murderer. He had murdered his wife.

Why had he called Frank?

Why?

A sound came out of him. A keening.

"That's good, Martin. Cry it out. Cry it out."

He couldn't think straight.

"She and the New York investigator had a cop helping them to get out. There was a shoot-out between him and our people. Jodi got hit in the cross fire. Probably by this cop. There was no pain. She didn't suffer. It was instant."

"No," he moaned. "What am I going to do? Where is she? I need to go there. I—"

"I'll take care of everything, Martin. Take a sleeping pill. Knock yourself out. You need to sleep. When you wake up, I'll call," Frank said and the phone went dead.

69

When Shaw hurried back to the post office staging area, the first thing he did was check in with the surveillance team.

On the Smart Board in the war room, he saw that the brick factory was in focus. It was live footage from a SWAT sniper up on the roof of the grocery store.

"Any movement?" Shaw said to the tech cop at the desk.

He was more chicken nugget–shaped than Chief Garner if that were possible.

"No. No one in or out."

"Not even at the windows?" Shaw said.

"The sniper can't really see anything. Most of those old windows are painted over."

"Leave the sniper where he is, but get all the other men together and tell them to meet me in the parking lot," Shaw said.

"You got it," Officer Seed Oil said.

Shaw went back outside. He was beyond formalities and pretense now. Without asking, he opened the driver door of the nearest police cruiser and reached down to pop the trunk latch.

Along the left-hand portion of the compartment, there was a red plastic gasoline can, bungee corded. Shaw smiled as he lifted the handle and felt its heaviness. He took the full gas can out and shut the trunk.

When he turned, he found several officers standing there, staring at him silently. He smiled at them.

He'd been drunk with anger before, but now mischief glinted in his glassy Adderall-laced eyes.

"Any of you boys smoke?" he said with a grin.

After Shaw received a pack of Marlboro Lights and a Zippo lighter, he lifted the gas can and went up Route 4 to a volunteer firetruck parked across from a canoe rental place.

The axe he took from the side of it was the fireman kind with a carbon steel blade on the front head and a nasty sharp-looking pickax on the back of it. He hefted its well-balanced weight by its light yellow fiberglass handle.

Oh, yes. Sweet. This would do quite fine, he thought.

Coming back into the post office lot with the axe and the gas can, he found Chief Garner and Travers talking to the other tactical officer, the thin blonde guy with the anchorman-type hair, Doug.

Beside them was the cherry picker with the ballistic shield on the front of it and Shaw went to it and laid down the axe and the gas can on its platform.

"What's up, Agent?" Chief Garner said.

Shaw ignored him. He tapped Doug on the shoulder and pointed down the road at the top of the old factory.

"Doug, I need one of your officers to drive this contraption with me."

"What's the play?" Chief Garner wanted to know.

"We have to smoke them out now," Shaw said merrily over Garner's head to the two dozen police who had started to gather.

"Just got word from up top. We're in dire straits so we need to move now, full force. On my call, you will get into a firing position around that factory and get on your weapons. It's take-no-prisoners time, gentlemen. Do you understand? Now go to your vehicles and wait for my command."

As the men headed away, Shaw turned to Doug.

"Doug, you're in charge back here. As I get closer with the platform, on my call, I'm going to need full covering fire into all the windows."

"On it," Doug said, hurrying off. "Give us five."

"Covering fire?" said Garner wide-eyed as the SWAT cop left.

"Yes. In order to get onto the roof, I'm going to need these jerks with their heads down."

"What are you going to do on the roof?" Travers wanted to know.

"Set the structure ablaze, forcing the suspects to exit the premises," Shaw said matter-of-factly.

"Are you out of your freaking mind?" said Garner, leaning in and giving Shaw a hard-edged glare.

"You can't burn down the Beckford Tool Factory. It's a historic landmark!" he yelled.

"He's right," said Travers. "It's the reason this whole area exists. Be like burning down the Empire State Building."

Shaw didn't debate. Didn't even answer. He just shoved Garner and Travers out of his way left and right. Garner flew back so hard against the side of the cherry picker, it knocked his big hat off.

Then Shaw climbed aboard the cherry picker.

"Where is the operator of this thing? Get up here now! Let's go!"

70

Rumbling slowly out of the parking lot at the rail of the elevated boom platform a moment later with the fire axe on his shoulder, Shaw drank in the awed looks from the local cops.

This is glory, Shaw thought. *Actual glory. I am Ben-Hur on his glorious chariot being borne to the battle. Stand aside!*

"Can't this thing go any faster?" Shaw said to the operator, some Hispanic cop who looked like he was still in high school.

"This is it, sir," the kid said from the control console as they turtle crawled, finally turning onto South Street.

Passing the grocery store, he gave a thumbs-up to Doug propped in a sniper's position up on its roof.

Doug wasn't messing around, Shaw noticed. He was pointing the big barrel of a Barrett, an actual fifty-caliber Barrett, at the upper windows of the brick factory.

Shaw smiled. Doug had his orders. They all did.

Shoot to kill, kill, kill.

"Okay, Doug," Shaw called into his mic as they turned onto State Street.

"Get everyone into position now."

"Roger," Doug called.

As Shaw watched, first a half dozen and then ten cop cars screeched down Route 4 and Depot Street to surround the entire north half of the factory. He watched the cops stop and open their doors and crouch down beside them, holding long guns.

"Okay, wait, wait," Shaw called into the mic as they got closer.

The platform finally arrived at the parking lot beside the wrecked restaurant.

"Okay, covering fire. Now, now, now."

First there were a few pops and then Shaw smiled again as they all opened up at once from behind the hoods of the cruisers.

The cops letting it rip was something to see all right. *And hear*, Shaw thought as a full-on symphony of blasting shotguns and rat-a-tat-tatting AR15s filled his ears. Added to this Hollywood blockbuster soundtrack soon came the sound effect of the factory's twenty front-facing windows all simultaneously getting shattered into bits by flying lead.

In fact, the entire front facade seemed to shatter and shudder as windowpanes imploded and bricks were obliterated in puffs of red dust. Bullets ripped off the window headers and exploded the jambs. Under this withering barrage, a waterfall of brick fragments and glass shards and wood splinters began dropping down into the parking lot.

Shaw smiled some more as he thought of the cocky cop inside. He was in there, no doubt sucking the floor, probably pissing himself, as the place got filled with an unrelenting fusillade of lead.

Or had he already taken several bullets to the head? Shaw wondered. He certainly hoped so.

King of the castle? They were tearing a hole into the wall

of this little castle, weren't they? he thought as he watched the glorious destruction.

No way was he going to let this cop win. He was going to put this pesky piece of shit where he belonged. In a body bag.

"That's it, boys. Get some, get some!" he cried into the mic as the moving platform came alongside the factory itself. "Let's take this place down brick by brick."

Coming ever closer, Shaw crouched low as he heard a stray friendly round whip past his ear.

"Cease fire! Cease fire!" he cried. "And stay the hell away from the left. Just at the north of the building, not the south side where I am!"

He slammed the operator on his back hard.

"Move the boom up now. Let's go! Get me on the roof. Move it!"

Shaw already had the platform gate open as they came to the side of the two-story building's roof.

The tar paper under his feet had a springy give when he stepped onto it, but it seemed firm enough. Jogging with the axe and gas can, he arrived to the midpoint of the roof and placed the gas can down and went to work.

The tar paper gave easily under the head of the axe when he whacked at it. He chopped once and then twice. The third time he chopped, he saw plywood and a snarl of wooly insulation and he knelt and touched it. It was yellowed. How many years old? he wondered. A hundred? More.

It was as dry as tinder.

Perfect, he thought.

He stood and turned the axe around and swung again. The long pickax side sank deep. After he wedged it loose, he looked down and smiled. There was now an opening into the building below.

Once he had four such holes into the building two feet apart in a rough square, he paused for a moment, his face a sheen of sweat. He leaned on the shaft of the axe like a farmer resting in a field. Out behind the factory he took in the clear view of the bridge, the flowing river, the lights of the roadblock on the ridge on its other side.

He giggled as he dropped the axe and retrieved the gas can. He proceeded to pour the gasoline hole to hole to hole to hole and back.

The heady sweet masculine reek of the fuel was invigorating. As was the sound of it splattering into the factory floor below. After the can was empty, he tossed it aside and wiped his hands on the thighs of his tactical pants and lit a cigarette. The red cherry on it pulsed as he blew on its tip.

He took in a deep drag and let it out with a few smoke rings. Then he flicked it.

"Nothing but net," he said as it tumbled end over end and disappeared down into the first gasoline drenched hole.

There was a pause and then a ribbon of flame flicked out of the hole like a large tongue out of a mouth. Then there were two tongues, then a trio, then a quartet.

The smoke started to rise and Shaw began to back away from the flames toward the platform, smiling ear to ear.

71

When the shooting finally stopped, I was on the north end of the second story of the old factory building by one of the blasted-out windows.

Eyes closed, flat down on my belly with my cheek pressed to the floor, it took me almost a full minute to brush the glass dust out of my hair and eyes in order to look around.

I should have kept my eyes closed.

The room around me looked like an artillery shell had struck a direct hit on a landfill. Not just the windows had been shot out, but everything that was above waist height in the room. The antique furniture and cabinets and paintings and knickknacks and toys. Everything was broken, cracked, pulverized or in splinters. There were even big hunks missing out of the plaster and brick walls where they had been peppered with countless rounds.

When I had antagonized the mercenary on the SAT phone it was to make him do something emotional, to get him to do something stupid.

But maybe the additional anger I'd drawn out of him, I thought as I helped Colleen crawl out from behind a bullet-riddled chest of drawers, hadn't been the best idea after all.

"Where to now?" she said.

"The middle stairwell. Come on. And stay down. Those windows are exposed now. There might be snipers."

Down on all fours careful to avoid the glass, we crawled away south toward the stairs.

As we reached the next room, I called out.

"Is everyone all right?"

To our left, I saw Mathias and Mario crawling out of the rubble toward us.

"Just swell," Mario said as he dusted shattered glass off his bald head. "This is better than Disneyland."

We all reached the middle stairwell thirty seconds later. Suddenly, Mario pointed to the other side of the factory.

"Fire!" he yelled. "Fire!"

I peeked out. Mario wasn't being sarcastic this time. Down the corridor, the entire ceiling was on fire.

"Down the stairs now!" I yelled as I saw one of the rooms down at the far end blossom up with flame.

We got to the ground floor by the barricaded door and then continued down the stairwell for the basement.

At the landing between the first floor and the basement, I stopped and went to the half-open window.

"Help me open this all the way," I said to Mathias.

Mathias came forward and forced it open hard enough to shatter one of the glass panes.

"Now what?" Colleen said.

"We have to go out the back here and get up to the bridge and cross it to Mathias's truck," I said.

"But it's too open. They'll see us," she said.

"We have to try. What other choice do we have?" I said.

"Wait," Mathias said. "I have another idea."

72

"I'm all ears, Mathias," I said as smoke began to billow down from the floor above.

He pointed out the window but not at the bridge to the right. He pointed down river to the left.

"What if we crossed the river to the south beyond where that roadblock is?"

"But how are we going to get across the river?" I said. "This is the only bridge for miles."

"About a quarter mile from here along the river on this side is a small brick building."

"Next to a waterfall," I said, remembering the running path and the cormorants, which felt like a million years ago.

"Yes," Mathias said, nodding. "We're working there as well on a second hydroelectric generator and one of the company trucks is parked there in a lot on the other side of the river along Route 4."

"But how do we get across the river?" I said. "Swim? The river is deep there and wide. And there's a thirty-foot waterfall."

"We won't need to swim," Mathias said. "There's a phone cable that goes across the river above the waterfall. The telephone pole has rungs on it. We climb up and go hand over hand across the cable to the truck."

I thought about that.

It sounded insane.

"The cable will hold us?"

"Yes. If we go one by one, we should be fine."

"We're going to cross the river on a phone cable above a waterfall? That's the plan?" Colleen said.

Something fell above and more smoke filled the ceiling of the stairwell.

"That's what we're down to now," I said.

"Then it's agreed," Mathias said. "When we leave out this window, you three head south to the utility building. I'll go to the bridge and drop the crane across Route 4 to block them from pursuit. Plus, it will have them looking the other way while you head down river."

"No," Mario said.

"No?" Mathias said.

"I'll block the bridge with the crane," Mario said.

"You?" Mathias said. "Why you?"

"You suck with the crane is why. That's my specialty, remember?" Mario said, smiling.

"But—"

"But nothing," Mario said. "You go with them. I don't have a kid waiting for me at home. And don't worry. You think I'm going to let these jackasses catch me? After I drop that bitch, I'll be coming straight down the river on my boogie board."

"Your boogie board?" I said.

Mario nodded.

"It's in the crane cab," he said.

Mathias rolled his eyes.

"He has a surfing suit and he plays with his boogie board in the river after work," Mathias said. "Sometimes *while* we are working. If you haven't noticed, he is an idiot. Like a child."

"Yeah, well," Mario said, "my boogie board skills are coming in real handy right around now, aren't they? After I drop Big Mama, I'll be coming straight down that river like the *Mississippi Queen*."

A shattering crack came from above followed by another thud.

"C'mon," I said. "Let's do this. We need to get out of here!"

PART FOUR

RUN FOR YOUR LIFE

73

Beside the silver ribbon of the moonlit river, the old brick factory burned.

Up on the grocery store roof now beside Doug and his rifle, Shaw gazed at the fire, at its reflection in the water and at the smoke that was rising steadily into the starry sky.

He'd done a good job of setting the fire. That was for sure. Even before he had fully retreated on the moving platform back to Main Street, the south half of the roof had become an inferno and most of the windows on the second story beneath it had become completely engulfed.

As he continued to survey the dramatic vista, Shaw thought the whole scene of it looked oddly familiar, like something from a history book or a fairy tale.

No, it was a painting, he realized. What was that famous one called with the marble city burning alongside a body of water? People were falling into the water and there were dead bodies everywhere.

For the life of him, he couldn't remember.

As if it mattered, he thought. He was the artist here. And this was his masterpiece.

Shaw glanced down at Doug manning the Barrett, and knelt beside him.

He lifted the man's spotting scope and scanned it over the second-story windows on the north of the factory for movement.

Please stick your head up, cop, he thought as he scanned the upper windows and the front door. *Pretty please.*

Shaw was passing the spotter scope over the second story again when he detected movement to the right of the factory.

It wasn't in the factory itself, he realized, but behind it.

On the other side of factory to the north was the bridge and on the other side of the bridge, there was a construction crane, its arm extended upward to the sky. This boom arm was latticed and yellow and as Shaw watched, it slowly tilted downward as it swiveled toward the front of the bridge.

"Hey, who's working that crane by the bridge?" Shaw called into the mic.

"Not one of us," came the reply from Garner.

Shaw suddenly remembered what the waitress had said about the others in the restaurant.

Construction workers.

"Shit," Shaw said with a gasp.

They had gotten out of the factory somehow, he realized. Gotten out on the back of it on the river side maybe.

The sons of bitches were playing games, Shaw thought. They were making a run for it.

He tracked down the latticed yellow boom for the cab with the spotting scope. But he couldn't see it. The north end of the factory blocked the view.

"Rifle!" he cried at Doug.

"What?"

"RIFLE!" Shaw screamed.

Doug handed up the huge Barrett. Being the length of a bench press bar, Shaw had to hoist it up over his shoulder like a marching soldier in a parade before he was able to turn with it and run.

Behind them to the east was a larger apartment building that butted up against the roof of the grocery store with windows on the level of the grocery store's roof. Shaw smashed in a window with the butt of the Barrett and climbed into the bedroom of an apartment and ran quickly through it and found the front door. In the outer hall, he took the stairs and hammered up to the third floor, then took a fourth flight to the roof.

Out the roof door, back into the cold again, he ran to the west edge of the building facing the bridge. Just as he arrived, he saw the now fully extended yellow crane arm come down across Route 4 with a screeching thud and enormous boom.

Son of a bitch! It was completely blocking the road to the bridge now, making it impossible for them to cross it.

Shaw racked the Barrett's bolt, the metal-on-metal clack of it loud, like two swords clanging together.

Weighing thirty-two pounds and almost five feet long, the Barrett semiautomatic shoulder-fired .50 caliber sniper rifle was the king of the jungle. Each of the ten rounds of .50 BMG 660-grain full metal jackets in its box magazine were the length of a can of Coke and weighed a quarter of a pound.

Powerful enough to take down aircraft and tear open a personnel carrier, what it did to a human body, Shaw knew from experience, was perverse. An unholy act of desecration.

"You wanna dance? Let's go!" Shaw yelled as he laid its bipod down near the edge of the roof and sighted.

The glass windshield of the cab zoomed up huge in the eyepiece of the Schmidt & Bender riflescope.

There was a figure in the cab.

Shaw was a disciplined enough shooter to go instantly reverent and humble. *Slow is fast, slow is fast*, he thought like a mantra as he stilled himself with a deep breath.

Then there was a double explosion in Shaw's ears and a double bucking bronco kick at Shaw's shoulder as he pulled the trigger of the gigantic .50 caliber sniper rifle twice.

He sighted on the cab windshield again. The glass was shattered now, obscuring the view inside. His eyes probed, up and down and side to side. There was no blood on the broken glass.

Shit. Had he gotten the bastard or not? He couldn't tell. And where were the others?

He looked around, passing the crosshairs over the bridge, the water, the trees. Slowly and methodically, he scanned the entire area between the bridge and the burning factory. Then he did it again.

Dammit! He couldn't see anyone.

A sense of terrible dread roared through him. That he was failing. That he already had failed.

Shaw refocused, stilled himself, breathed away the turmoil until he was an object at rest again.

He got off the scope and stood scanning the roof around him. Twenty feet to his right, the fire escape of the building faced out toward Route 4. He shouldered the rifle and began to run.

74

The leaves and tangled underbrush rustled loudly in the dark as we hurried along the steep forested west bank of the river south of the burning factory.

We were following a narrow deer trail in the woods that we had found about a quarter mile from where we had jumped down from the window. Mathias was ahead, leading us with Colleen behind him and me bringing up the rear.

When we heard the tremendous crashing of the crane behind us by the bridge, we were at first elated to hear that Mario had seemed to have accomplished his mission.

Then the loud sound of gunfire that sounded moments later ended that celebration abruptly.

Was Mario dead now? I thought.

I followed Colleen over the trunk of a fallen tree that was half-submerged in the water and then we all started jogging and then full-out running.

It didn't matter. We didn't know anything now and couldn't find out. It was run-for-your-life time now.

The trail started up a steep hill and as we came down on its other side, we suddenly heard the sound of the waterfall. Then a structure of windswept brick, a kind of ruin, appeared on the dark track dead ahead.

It took me a moment to realize it was the old LOVE LIFE graffitied brick building I had seen on my run.

We stood looking at it as we caught our breath. It looked like a miniature version of the castle-like brick factory.

Then we stood looking up at the telephone pole beside it. As Mathias had said, it had little rusted iron climbing rungs stuck on each side of it. I turned to my right, tracking where its black phone cable bellied out across the moonlit river and falls.

The incredibly wide river and falls.

"Okay, then. We're through the woods," I said with a confidence I was hardly feeling. "Now for the over-the-river part."

"There's the truck. See?" Mathias said as he pointed across the river.

We turned and looked through the mostly bare October trees where a white panel truck was parked along Route 4.

"Awesome," I said. "Now all we have to do is get to it. Let's go."

"That's not possible, Mike," Colleen said. "Cross hand over hand on a phone cable over a waterfall like we're monkeys in the circus? Count me out."

"I'll go first," Mathias said. "If it will hold me, Colleen, it will hold you."

"Exactly," I said, hurrying over to the pole. "Step in my hand, Mathias. I'll give you a boost."

75

Shaw arrived at the bridge to see that the crane was still on, its diesel engine steadily rumbling.

He came in closer to the operator's cabin up atop its half-track crawlers, staring up at the shattered windshield.

"Shit," he said when he came close enough to see the door of it was open and no one was inside. He climbed up and looked in for blood splatter but, even up close, there was nothing.

"Shit," he said again. *How did I miss?*

He left the crane running and climbed down and hurried back out to the road. Doug was standing beside the fallen boom with two other SWAT cops, all of them jawing and looking around like tourists at an attraction.

"Get in that cab there and move this boom out of the way," Shaw said. "We also need to start a search on both sides of the river. They're probably already across."

"How do you know?" Doug said.

"Why would they drop the crane across the road? For kicks

and giggles? Stop asking stupid questions. Just get in there and move the crane."

"How? I look like a construction worker to you?" Doug said.

"Improvise is how. Figure it out. Overcome."

Shaw climbed over the steel lattice of the crane onto the bridge. He went to the factory side of the bridge and stood looking at the back of the factory and at the water.

The river current was strong enough to throw up white water in the middle of it. No way had they crossed right here, he thought.

He looked north across the bridge up the river where it was open and then south down the river where the bank was covered in trees.

They had gone south under those trees, he decided.

"Where is the next bridge over the river south? Close?" he called into the mic.

"Not really," Doug told him. "Seven miles."

"I want a search team in the woods south of the factory," Shaw called as he headed back toward the dropped boom.

After he climbed over it again, he hopped over the Route 4 guardrail on his right and went down an embankment to the shore of the river beside the factory.

He walked along the back of the burning brick building and saw the open window where they had come out.

Walking south under the trees, he found a deer trail two minutes later. He was just about to head down it when he looked out over the water. The river had a bend here with a clearer view, and he thought he saw something. A mile away or so, there was a building.

He raised his night vision binoculars.

Then detected movement in the middle of the river.

It was a person on a cable.

Shaw dropped to one knee, raised the Barrett to his shoulder and put his right eye to the scope.

76

"Please, Colleen. It's not as hard as it seems," I said.

"I don't know about this," Colleen said, her arms folded tightly across her chest. "It must be twenty feet to the water. If I don't die hitting the lip of the falls on the way down. And I can hardly even swim."

"I'm telling you, Colleen. It absolutely can be done. You're not going to need to know how to swim," I said. "Just follow me up the pole and I'll show you how to do it just like a SEAL."

Without waiting for an answer, I turned and headed up the pole, happy to hear her scrambling up behind me.

At the top, I grabbed the cable and made my way out on it a few feet.

"Just keep the cable between your legs and bend your right knee. Wrap your right instep around the cable. Let your left leg hang down straight and pull yourself across with your arms like an inchworm."

I looked back at Colleen. She looked petrified.

"You can do this, Colleen. The weight of your left leg hanging down really balances you. This way, if you get tired, you can take a break."

That's when it happened.

There was a boom from up river, and the cable suddenly exploded at my feet and I was falling like a rock.

The cable I'd been hugging moved me out over the river in a Tarzan swing and then disappeared from underneath me.

And then I was headed straight down in a free fall.

I saw the dark raging waterfall beneath me, the shimmer of the moonlight on it and the bubbling white water beneath it rising up.

As I fell in a kind of slow motion, my eyes locked on the waterfall's stone edge.

I was going to hit it, I realized.

Shit, this is going to hurt, I thought as I tried to get my feet below me so I wouldn't hit headfirst.

But I was wrong.

I just missed the lip of the edge of the falls. *By a whisker.* The waterfall passed by the tips of my toes and then the tip of my nose by about a centimeter. I hit the water at the bottom of the falls hard in a kind of pencil dive and then went under, felt the bottom and kicked up.

I broke the surface of the freezing cold water with a gasp of breath.

"Shit!" I cried as I spotted Colleen, half the river away, still at the top of the pole.

I could see that she was yelling something at me but it was fruitless. I couldn't hear a thing over the roar of the waterfall.

Suddenly, there was another booming gunshot and a chunk of the pole next to her exploded.

Get down off the pole, I wanted to scream as I treaded in the ice-cold water.

I watched as she wisely began to scramble down the pole and

I swam toward her side of the river. She reached the edge by the lip of the falls and stopped.

What are you waiting for? I thought, realizing then how panicked she was.

"Jump, Colleen! Jump!" I screamed.

She just stood there, shaking her head. I could see she was crying now.

That's when we heard a new sound.

Dogs were barking furiously in the woods behind the little brick building.

"I'll come back for you!" I yelled.

I couldn't look back at her. I turned and started swimming for the opposite bank, knowing that her only chance at rescue depended on me getting out of this river in one piece.

I promise I'll come for you, I thought.

I swam as hard as I could along the gushing water and then heard a whistle and as I hit the shore, a big hand seized me by my forearm, helping me out.

Mathias pulled me up on my soaking feet, and when I looked up, I was shocked to see that Mario was there. He was drenched, too.

"You made it!" I said.

"Whadya think? Fuhgeddaboudit!" Mario said, hugging me.

"Where's Colleen? Is she in the water?" Mathias said.

I shook my head.

"No. She was still on the pole. I heard dogs as I crossed. We have to assume they've caught her. But we can't worry about that. We're of no help to her unless we get out of here now."

"Come on, then," Mathias said. "Let's get to the truck. Hurry."

We climbed up a steep bank onto the bike path and then ran up toward the Route 4 parking lot. We were in the trees approaching the guardrail about fifty feet away from it when a police SUV blew past us and screeched to a stop behind the truck.

Seeing that there was only one cop in it as it went past, without thinking I leaped over the guardrail and tore across the parking lot and crouched at the back of the SUV just as the driver door opened and a cop stepped out and began turning at the sound of me.

But I was already off my feet.

I knocked the gun clear out of the cop's hand as I slammed into him like a wrecking ball. I heard the back of his head clunk loudly as it bounced off the doorframe as he fell.

We came down in a pile to the asphalt and after I quickly retrieved his gun, I rolled him over and realized that it was a female cop, a surprisingly pretty one with her blonde hair tied up in a bun.

I saw I had knocked her clean out. I had just taken her pulse to confirm she was still alive when I heard Mathias roar on the panel truck.

"Come on!" Mathias called.

77

Shaw, along with Travers and Chief Garner, stood along the side of Route 4 beside the Beckford PD SUV watching an ambulance take away the injured female cop. Chief Garner sighed as its red running lights receded and then disappeared around a distant curve in the empty country road.

As the three of them looked at each other, from somewhere an owl hooted and in the silence that followed, they could hear the humming gush of the nearby falls.

"She has a concussion," Chief Garner said.

Who cared, Shaw thought.

"She's lucky to be alive," Travers said.

Not the only one, thought Shaw as he remembered the roof landing on the BearCat's windshield.

They looked at each other again. There was a feeling in the air like after losing a football game.

And it was Shaw himself who had blown it. He was the one

who'd blown the crucial end zone tackle and let a runner slot through the gap.

They had gotten the Irish beauty, but the cop was nowhere to be seen. He was in the wind.

"Any description of the van they left in before Blondie didn't do her job?" Shaw said.

"None," said Chief Garner with a scowl.

"Where's Doherty?"

"At police headquarters," Garner said.

The cop had cut out on her, Shaw thought. After all that tough talk, too. Typical. Talk was cheap.

Or maybe he had drowned in the water? Shaw thought, suddenly hopeful. A body would wash up in a day or two? He had successfully shot apart the cable and the fall into the river was a doozy.

As if he could be so lucky with this snake bit job, Shaw thought.

"And we're positive she doesn't have a video on her? A phone? Maybe a thumb drive?" Shaw said.

"Positive," Garner said. "I frisked her myself."

Shaw allowed himself a groan. He'd been through the ringer all right. And not just mentally either, he thought as he rubbed his shoulder where the Barrett had kicked it. It felt sore, tender. The skin there, no doubt, was already black and blue. He'd once dislocated an elbow and now he wondered if he'd done the same to his shoulder.

He was exhausted and had the beginning of a splitting headache.

Smooth this job was not.

Shaw looked at Chief Garner, who was staring at him.

"Sorry for getting overheated with you back there, Chief," Shaw said. "You, too, Travers."

Garner gave a sweeping gesture with his hand.

"Forgotten. We're all stressed out. Now what?" he said.

Shaw crossed his arms and held a fist to his chin like *The Thinker.*

Oh, well. They had failed. It happened. He wasn't a miracle worker. Besides, this wasn't over. Just round one of however many rounds it took.

They would have company analysts on the cop now, evaluating any and all possibilities. They had access to all the databases.

Shaw would pay the cop a visit soon enough. Or one of his relatives. It was a matter of when not if. They'd get back the evidence whatever it was. They always did.

"We keep getting calls from Doherty's law firm," Garner said. "They want to know what the hell is going on."

Suddenly, they all looked up as there was a sound. The rotor chop of a helicopter approaching became louder and louder.

"I wouldn't worry about that," Shaw said. "Just stonewall them. Money will change hands. It always does."

"And the press?"

"Same deal. They can use money, too, last time I checked. There's nothing to be nervous about. It's all negotiable. We did our bit. Let the higher-ups do theirs."

"What should we do with her?"

"Doherty?"

"Yes."

"Get rid of her."

They looked at each other. Then back at him.

"My job is getting after the cop," Shaw said. "So, you boys are going to have to do the mop-up yourselves. We all have to pitch in on this one."

They heard the helicopter louder now.

Travers's and Garner's jaws dropped as the Sikorsky Shaw had arrived in landed right in the middle of Route 4.

"That's my ride, boys," Shaw said, giving them a salute. "Pleasure working with you again. See you around."

78

The helicopter had just lifted off when I rolled out from underneath the police SUV where I had been hiding.

In the SEALs, we had learned lots of dirty tricks. And one of the lesser-known ones is to wedge yourself on the underside of a vehicle to sneak into army bases and embassies and such. This is why sharp people involved with embassy and military base security usually have a mirror on a stick to search beneath any incoming vehicles.

Lucky for me, the jackasses I was up against here weren't very sharp.

No, not in the slightest, I thought as I came around the trail side of the police vehicle and stood staring at the backs of the two men.

Five feet away stood Travers and Garner. I recognized the both of them from Jodi's video. They were just standing there oblivious, staring up at the deafening ascending bird.

As I stared at them, a mean rhyme from my childhood popped into my head.

Fat and Skinny had a race
Up and down the pillowcase
Fat fell down and broke his crown
And Skinny won the race

Sounded like a plan, I thought.

Except Skinny was about to lose, too.

I shot the both of them simultaneously with the weapons I'd borrowed from the female cop.

With my right hand, I shot the skinny Travers through the back of his left knee with the Glock 17, blowing out his knee-cap. At the same time with my left hand, I shot the corrupt chief right in his large backside with the officer's Taser.

A moment later, they were both on the ground. As the sound of the rotor wash died down a little, I could hear that Travers kept saying uh-uh-uh and the chief kept saying ah-ah-ah. The way they were doing it at the same time sounded oddly musi-cal, like they were warming up to sing in a barbershop quartet.

"Surprise, fellas," I said as I stepped up.

I saw that Travers was crying like a baby as he clutched at his bloody knee. I patted him down and found a Glock and a pair of handcuffs. I disassembled the Glock and tossed the parts into the trees. After that, I gave the chief a couple of blasts with the Taser to give him something to do. He gave out a yah-yah sound this time and actually flopped over. I guess the backside of him was done.

Then I handcuffed Travers behind his back and dragged him to the far side of the SUV next to the guardrail. I hauled him up and dumped him in the back. When he started howling, I pulled his hair back and rammed the Glock in his mouth.

"Either you're going to shut your piehole or I am," I said.

Then I attended to the chief by giving him a healthy twenty-second press on the fizzling buzz trigger of the Taser.

"Please," he said as I knelt and relieved him of his .38 and his cell phone.

"Shut your mouth," I said as I ratcheted his own handcuffs on his wrists. I hauled him up and dumped him into the passenger seat of the police SUV.

I looked down Route 4. We were still alone for now. I realized I needed them in order to have Colleen released.

"Time to get on the horn, Chief," I said, holding up the radio to his mouth.

79

The cold cinder block cell had a shelf bed beside a stainless steel toilet. Colleen sat on the bed and rubbed at her left wrist that was cuffed to a bolt in the wall. The disgusting toilet had an attached water fountain that, even though she was getting thirstier and thirstier, she refused to drink out of.

She was at the Beckford station house now. She shook her head at the gray painted cinder block. It didn't seem so quaint anymore.

They'd caught her in the woods not two hundred feet from the telephone pole. It was some canine cop and his German shepherd and they about gave her a heart attack as they pounced on her, the dog nipping at her arms and head while the cop laid his knee in her back. His disgusting gloved hands on her, searching her pants all over, going under her shirt.

Then the fat chief showed up and gave her more of the same. She thought they would kill her right there and then.

But they hadn't.

Yet, she thought as she rattled the cold cuff on her wrist.

The door of the holding room opened. It was the dog cop. A square thirtysomething with a beer gut and a blonde copstache, his Beckford PD ball cap pushed back on his head.

He squealed open the cell and came in and undid her cuffs. And re-cuffed her behind her back.

"Let's go," he said.

He led her out of the holding area into a corridor and stopped at a door and opened it and put her in an interview room. He uncuffed her and sat her down behind a table and cuffed her to another wall bolt.

There was a bottle of water on the table. He cracked the cap.

With her free hand, Colleen punched it across the room the second he laid it back down.

Her fear was gone now. She was beyond pissed. Straight-up enraged.

The bastard stood and retrieved the fallen water and capped it. He took off his hat. She looked into his brown eyes. There was something bad in them. Something sneaky and malicious.

He interlaced his fat fingers on top of his square head and leaned back staring at her, smirking.

"Where'd you hide it?" he said.

"Hide what?" Colleen said.

"We know there was a phone. A phone with a video on it. Did you leave it in the woods?"

Colleen looked steadily into his mean eyes.

"The only phone I know about," Colleen said, "is a SAT phone I called my boss on. You're going to jail, you know that. You and every other cop in your department."

"Oh, yeah? For what?"

"Murder, attempted murder, false arrest. That's just off the top of my head."

He clucked his tongue and laughed quietly, smirking some more.

"Sure," he said. "Keep telling yourself that. Now, about that phone. Or should I bring Lacey in here? Lacey hasn't eaten. You want to spend some more time with Lacey?"

That's when his phone rang.

He looked at it, looked at her. Then he got up and left the room.

When he came back two minutes later, he seemed to be in a hurry. He unlocked the cuff from the wall and re-cuffed her behind her back.

"What now?" she said as they headed down the corridor for the front door.

"Shut up," he said.

There was a hint of light in the dark of the sky when they walked outside.

The terror came back now. The cop, his dog, the SUV.

Was this it? she thought.

"Where are we going?" she said as he put her into the car and they roared out of the lot.

"I told you to shut up."

They headed down Route 4 and a few minutes later, they passed the dealership where she'd buried Jodi's car.

When they turned into the town square, she saw the fire-trucks. The fire in the old brick factory seemed to be out, but there was still some smoke as they continued to hose down the building.

As they came into the parking lot beside the ruined restaurant, she looked over at the bridge and saw the crane still blocking the road. The cop pulled in next to Mike's pickup near the museum. He got out first and then let her out and uncuffed her. Then he handed her his phone.

"What's this?" she said.

"It's for you," he said, rolling his eyes as he got back into the SUV and took off.

"Colleen? Are you there?" said a voice from the phone.

"Mike!" Colleen cried. "How...?"

"No, questions. I'll explain later. Are you at my truck?"

317

"Yes."

"My extra fob is on a magnet under the left panel."

"Got it," she said as she pulled it out and opened the door.

"Okay. Remember where we met yesterday?" Mike said as she pushed the ignition button.

At the coffee shop, Colleen thought.

"Yes," she said.

"I'm in the parking lot waiting for you," he said.

80

Cushing woke from a deep sleep to find his cell phone on the nightstand ringing.

Still groggy, he wondered if the ringing would wake Jodi beside him.

It took a moment to remember Jodi would never be beside him again.

The ID screen said TRAVERS.

"Yes?" Cushing said.

"Can I come over and talk?" said Travers.

"Now? Why? What's happened?"

"Chief Garner and I need to talk to you," Travers said.

"In private," Garner cut in. "And not on the phone. We're a minute away."

"Okay," Cushing said yawning.

He found his tablet next to his phone and brought up the house security app and opened the gate with it. After he went in and took a leak and came back to his room, he saw Travers's car pulling in on the screen.

Thirty seconds later, he was downstairs at the front door in his stockinged feet and silk robe.

Opening the door, he was startled as Travers bumped into him hard.

Cushing almost fell himself as Travers crashed down, sprawling face-first onto the foyer.

Chief Garner followed quickly. Like Travers, he came in off-balance and fell down hard into the foyer on his belly with a woosh of outrushed breath.

Cushing had just registered that they were both handcuffed behind their backs when he saw the broad-shouldered man suddenly standing there, filling the open doorway.

He was in his forties, very fit and stocky. His pale face was square-jawed and his hard unsmiling blue eyes had the least amount of fear in them that Cushing had ever seen on anyone.

Cushing felt his heart rate suddenly kick up several notches as he noticed the man was holding a gun. Then Cushing's breath caught as he raised it.

"Move back," the man said.

A woman appeared behind him as Cushing followed orders.

It was the New York investigator, Colleen Doherty.

"Hands behind your back," the man said as Cushing was shoved against the wall.

"Good morning, President Cushing," Colleen Doherty said as Cushing felt cuffs bite into his wrists.

"I'm so sorry I didn't get a chance to speak to you yesterday morning," she said. "My name is Colleen Doherty and I'm an investigator representing Emilio Ramos. We need to review a few things with you if that's not too much trouble."

81

Martin Cushing's book-lined home office was the size of a public library branch. There were large oil paintings on the walls. Each had a brass plaque beneath it as if this were a museum.

"Sit on the couch," I said to the president as I dragged Travers and then Garner in behind him.

"Please help me," Travers said as I dumped him in the corner beside a comfy reading chair. "My knee! Please!"

I smiled down at him.

"Think glass half-full, dude," I said. "You still have one knee left. You could have none and in fact—will—if you don't shut up."

My eyes went to Cushing's vanity wall.

My eyes stayed on the photo of Jodi for a long minute.

I'm sorry, I thought.

Then I looked back at Cushing sitting there wide-eyed.

"This is Jodi's daughter?" I said, taking down a framed picture of him dancing with a blonde waif of a bride.

"Yes."

"Just the one kid?" I said.

"Yes."

"How do you like that?" I said. "Just like Emilio Ramos."

Cushing's breath started to come out in little gasps. He seemed to try to swallow but he was having trouble.

Instead of putting the picture back, I placed the picture down on Cushing's desk. Then I took down his University of Virginia law school diploma and placed it on top of the wedding picture. A photo of Cushing hoisted up by the Beckford Redhawks came down next to be stacked neatly on top of that.

"What are you doing?" Cushing said.

"Prepping for the estate sale," I said, glancing at him. "Lord knows your poor stepdaughter will have enough to do with the probate and everything else."

President Cushing started to weep then.

"Now, now, Mike," Colleen said as she sat in Cushing's tufted leather throne of an office chair that she had rolled out from behind his desk.

"We're just going to have a talk, President Cushing," she said. "Nothing to worry about provided you just tell the truth. It's time to come clean now that all of the, um, distractions are out of the way. If you could check your recollections and really try to start to build a picture for us about what exactly happened on the night of Olivia Ramos's death."

"I didn't do it. It wasn't me. It was Frank Stone," Cushing said.

"Go on."

"He was here that night. He came up from New York. He runs one of those mega hedge funds. He manages Beckford's thirty-four-billion-dollar endowment. I work for him. He got me this job."

"What do you mean that you work for *him*?" I said.

"It's complicated. It's easier to show you," Cushing said.

"Show me?"

"What I really do. What my real job is for Frank Stone. That bookshelf behind you is false. Press the paneling in until you hear a click."

82

I fiddled with it. When I pushed in, what sounded like a latch gave way and the bookcase swung out on an unseen hinge.

Behind it was a steel door with a lock plate.

"The key is in my desk," Cushing said.

I went and found the key.

"You first, moron," I said, pulling Cushing to his feet.

The small room I unlocked was dark except for the light that came from several computer monitors on a desk. It was cold. Powerfully air-conditioned.

Then I saw why. Along the back wall were rows of computer servers on a rack. There were over a dozen of them.

I looked back at the screens on the desk. The monitors were huge, the size of televisions. On each were sixteen different screens in a grid.

They were surveillance cameras, I realized.

"No," I said in horror as I saw what was on them.

Because they didn't show hallways or common areas.

But rather, bedrooms and bathrooms and showers.

They were Peeping Tom surveillance cameras of students themselves in their rooms.

"Yes," he whispered. "This is it. This is my job."

"You have hidden cameras?" Colleen said. "You watch…the students? The kids?"

On one of the monitors, a girl turned in her sleep under a comforter.

The screens unnerved me. A real urge to start shooting them flared up. They made me feel filthy for just being there.

I turned to President Cushing.

And the screens weren't the only thing I wanted to shoot.

"You scumbag," I said, putting the barrel of the Glock to Cushing's head. "You filthy disgusting scumbag."

"The parents send their kids here," Colleen said. "And this is what you do? You watch them? You record them?"

"Do you know what Beckford College is?" Cushing said. "Its significance in the scheme of things?"

"No, please enlighten us," I said as I sat Cushing down at the desk and I shifted the barrel to between his eyes.

"Beckford is known among the very wealthiest of elite Americans as a minor Ivy. It is a place that the Park Avenue rich send their black sheep who like to party. My job—my real job—is to gather information on these sons and daughters of the rich in compromising positions."

"Record them?"

"Yes. Every inch of the students' dorms is covered with the latest in pin camera tech. We capture everything. Everything they say. Everything they do. The sex, the drugs, all of it."

"To get your rocks off," I said.

"For blackmail," Colleen said.

Cushing nodded.

"Precisely. Leverage. These children are from some of the richest families on earth. Stone and his people then use this blackmail on a multinational, global wealth–level industrial scale. For insider trading. Political favors.

"The night of Olivia's death, Frank had come up to collect some evidence on a Japanese student who is the son of the prime minister. He had raped a passed-out girl and Frank wanted to use the video right away."

"He would collect the blackmail himself?" Colleen said.

"Yes. All of this is CCTV. A hardwired non-internet system. Otherwise, it would get hacked. But it's not just blackmail. We bring in honey traps. Provide drugs. That's Travers's specialty," Cushing said, nodding at the security director.

No honor among thieves here, I noted.

"It starts, of course, with the admissions department. These students willingly hand over all sorts of personal information that proves invaluable to us once they arrive on campus. Not to mention the medical staff, the advisors, certain professors and resident assistants. We all work together to groom these kids for whatever Frank says. We have jackets on all of them."

"You deserve to die, you know that?" I said, digging the Glock into his cheek. "You should be thrown into a volcano. All of you."

"Well, if you want to do that, you better get some tour busses," Cushing said, "because it's not just us. Do you think we are the only school that does this? Frank is on the board of half of the Ivy League schools in New England and there are other Franks."

"You're going to pay for this," I said.

"I know," he said quietly.

When he began to whimper again, I felt at his dry cheeks.

"No tears. See, Colleen?" I said. "How do you like that. He makes the sounds but his cheeks are dry as a bone."

83

"What happened to Olivia?" said Colleen.

"Olivia worked for the school newspaper," Cushing said. "I found myself in a tight spot after having attended that fundraiser down in Greenwich. The night Olivia died she saw Frank's car drive onto campus. Olivia thought if she got a picture of his car that she could bust me again for going back on my word and finally get me fired."

"Then what?" Colleen said.

"Frank's people thought it was something much more serious so they chased Olivia. She had actually swum across the river and when they caught her, she kicked one of the security men in the nuts. She wouldn't say who she was or what she was doing so they tuned her up. Broke her nose, her cheekbone, several of her ribs."

"What? They beat her? Some little girl?" I said.

"You must understand," Cushing tried. "Frank Stone does not mess around. He does business in several sketchy countries with some very dangerous people. They thought she was an industrial spy or maybe an assassin. It wasn't until after they had dealt with her that they learned that she was a student coming after me. We didn't know what the hell to do after that since she needed to go to a hospital. All we knew is that she couldn't reveal what had happened. Frank himself was here! So, we looked into her background, her broken family, and concocted the story that she died of an overdose."

"What did she really die of when they put her in the SUV?" I said.

Cushing stared down at the desk.

"Nothing," Cushing said.

"Nothing?" Colleen said.

"Nothing," Cushing said again very quietly.

"Olivia Ramos is still alive."

84

We stared at him.

"Frank took her that night. He took her with him in the Rolls when he left."

"Took her?" I said.

"Yes. We faked all the rest of it. We insisted on covering the cost of the funeral and convinced the mother to agree to cremation. There was no cremation. Frank owns the funeral home director. He owns everyone. Frank isn't like other people. He's in a different world."

"Where did he take Olivia?" Colleen said.

"She's with Frank on his boat. For the last year. He has a room below deck beside the engine where he keeps her, shares her with guests."

"I think I'm going to throw up," Colleen said.

"You're sure she's still alive?" I said.

He nodded.

"Yes. But he's actually leaving tomorrow with her out of

Montauk for a transatlantic trip. He's going to sell her in France. He's done it before. Frank likes to check out the talent. He watches and picks the ones he wants."

"Slavery?" Colleen said. "This piece of shit has brought back literal slavery?"

"No," Cushing said. "Frank didn't have to bring it back. In Frank's world, it never ended."

"How do you contact Frank? From the SAT phone I took off you?" I said.

"Yes. He's the only contact in it."

"One last question," I said.

"Yes?" Cushing said.

"What's the name of Frank's boat?"

"It's called the *Lampas*," Cushing said as we heard something from the doorway behind us.

Instead of turning, I immediately shoved Colleen into the corner on the other side of the desk with a stiff arm. I was dropping myself down flat as I heard the shot and I felt and heard the bullet crack the sound barrier by my ear.

Over the back of the chair that Cushing was sitting on, I saw Garner, still cuffed, on his feet now by the doorway, bent over. I noted that Travers was next to him, also on his feet and still cuffed, trying to support the chief with a shoulder.

That's when a second shot came from a gun that Garner clutched in his handcuffed hand. He was shooting from behind his back.

Before he could fire again, I sent Cushing in the rolling chair at the doorway with a shove as I rose to one knee.

Then Garner fired again just as I began emptying the Glock 17.

I used all seventeen in what felt like an eyeblink and when I was done, what was left of Garner and Travers wasn't pretty.

As I stepped forward, I saw that Cushing had fallen out of the chair. Garner's third wild shot had made a small neat hole right between the president's eyes.

"Colleen!" I called out.

"I'm fine! I'm fine!" she said behind me.

"Thank goodness," I said.

85

When Shaw awoke from his catnap, the Sikorski was in a hover.

Out the port window, Shaw could see the early bird fishermen on the Star Island dock stopped in their tracks, watching as they came in for the landing on the boat of Wall Street titan Frank Stone.

Of course, they were. Under the landing gear was a two-hundred-foot battleship gray yacht with three decks and all black windows that looked like something out of a spy movie.

Shaw had been in Manhattan about to head home when Stone called Control and said he wanted a personal debrief out here in Montauk.

And with pockets like this guy had, Shaw thought as they descended toward the second deck of his mega yacht, what Frank wanted, Frank got.

As he got off the bird, some knockout brunette came out of the lower pilothouse and led him inside and sat him in a luxury hotel–like stateroom. She told him he needed to cool his heels for a bit and offered him a menu, an actual menu like he was at a four-star restaurant.

He'd packed in some French toast and a quart of OJ and had actually fallen asleep when Frank's assistant woke him a few minutes later. He was led below deck to an even more opulent living room space and then Frank himself came marching in wearing jeans and an unbuttoned shirt.

Shaw had to bite his cheek from bursting into laughter at the entrance of Little Frank.

Even with the leg breaking, grow-four-inches billionaire thing, he was barely five foot nine.

He'd had a trainer to help him force some muscle tone onto his scrawny ass and now he wanted one and all to take in his teeny-weeny muscles.

Truly it was funny. He basically paid some guy to do push-ups for him and now he thought he was Genghis Khan.

What did he even want? Shaw thought, yawning from where he was sitting on a white couch. To chew his ass? Motivate him or something? Punish him?

Like his boss, Vance—and all rich guys—Frank had the blind spot of thinking money could buy you anything you wanted. What old Frank didn't realize was that there were a lot of different kinds of dudes out there in the world. Some of them were out of their freaking minds. Like this bomb squad cop, for instance. The guy drove around with freaking Semtex in the trunk of his car? You think you were gonna bribe this guy?

Bribe gravity sooner. Or time, Shaw thought.

"What the hell happened?" Frank said in greeting.

Shaw yawned again and was just about to go over it when the assistant showed back up with a SAT phone.

"Who is it?" Frank said.

"President Cushing, sir."

"Excellent. This concerns him. Just put him on speaker phone," he said, gesturing for the young woman to leave.

"Hello," said a cheery voice.

Shaw squinted.

It was a vaguely familiar cheery voice.

"Marty?"

"No, this isn't Marty, Frank. This is the guy who has Marty's phone."

Shaw, exhausted, suddenly started laughing.

"It's him," Shaw said brightly.

This guy really was good! Shaw thought.

"Him? Him who?"

"I'm the guy with the video, Frank. I'm the guy you couldn't kill. Try to keep up. And listen up. I've seen your little room in Marty's house. Your little setup. In fact, I'm looking at it right now."

"I don't know what you're talking about," Frank said.

"I have all the servers. Your blackmail is now my blackmail. But good news, Frank. I'm willing to cut a deal. We get Olivia back, you get the blackmail back. I hear you like boats. As it happens, me, too. Let's meet this afternoon somewhere discreet and do the exchange. Put your captain on and I'll give him the coordinates."

86

After I spoke to the captain, I hung up the SAT phone and lifted the binoculars up off the picnic table, pointing them across Lake Montauk.

You almost didn't need the binoculars.

Frank Stone's boat, the *Lampas*, was easily the largest in the marina.

"How did it go?" Colleen, who was sitting beside me, said.

It was a little after nine in the morning now. After leaving the carnage of Cushing's house, we had double-timed it here to Long Island in my truck. It had taken Colleen and me an hour to get to the ferry in Bridgeport, Connecticut, where we'd just caught the 6 a.m. one to Port Jefferson, New York. After an hour's crossing and another hour-and-a-half drive, we'd made it out here to Montauk.

Now we were sitting at a picnic table at a closed shoreline seafood restaurant near the Montauk Airport staring across Lake Montauk where Frank Stone's massive yacht was docked.

Just out of the water, I was still in my neoprene diving suit. My tanks and gear were already back in the truck bed.

It was all set.

Everything was ready to go.

There was a reason why I had sped here as fast as humanly possible.

I needed to be done by the time I made the call.

"I said, how did it go?" Colleen said again.

I relifted the binocs and looked at the yacht. Then I looked at the tinge of clouds out over the Atlantic to my left. It was a beautiful, cool, sunny morning.

"The water was darker than I expected but other than that, it went like clockwork as they say. It's all set," I said.

"We're doing this? Really?" Colleen said.

I thought about Jodi dead in that tunnel. I thought about Scotty and Daisy.

Then I thought about Olivia, across the water down in the bowels of that demonically evil billionaire's ship.

"Really," I said.

"You're sure?" Colleen said.

"I'm positive," I said. "It's the only play. And since that's the case, Colleen, this is the part I think you should skedaddle for. You don't need to get involved in this. When I'm done, I'll bring Olivia to you."

"Leave now? With Olivia right there? There is zero chance of me leaving, Mike. Zero."

I smiled at her.

At her fired-up angel eyes.

Who needs coffee, I thought.

"Okay, then. If that's your final say," I said as I stood and headed to the truck for a towel.

87

Shaw was enjoying the sea and sun from the lower deck of Frank's yacht at the appointed spot forty miles north of Montauk.

It was an almost cloudless day and, out beyond the rail where he was sitting under the canopy of the upper deck, the Atlantic in every direction was a striking and sparkling dark teal color.

The massive boat rocked up and down smooth as butter even in the heavy seesaw waves. Shaw wasn't really the nautical type, but even he thought the scene and the craft were quite impressive.

"Not a bad life, this yacht stuff," Shaw called back to Olivia.

Olivia was sitting behind him at an outdoor table with her hands cuffed behind her. She was staring off into space as if he had said nothing. She hadn't said anything since they'd been re-acquainted below in the broom closet–like room where she was being kept beside the engines. Even after Shaw was nice enough to take off her duct tape.

"You know, if you had just told me you were a student straight off when I pulled you out of the river, none of this would have happened."

She said nothing.

"So, it's your fault not mine."

More silence from the little bitch.

He looked out at the water again and thought of this crazy cop on his way. There was no land in sight.

Boy had a pair on him, he'd give him that, he thought.

A wind from the southeast rattled the tails of Shaw's shirt as he lifted his binoculars. He scanned the western horizon. Above it, long rags of clouds were moving north. Just as he finished his 360, he saw something small on the water to the east, a red speck.

"Hey, I see something. You seeing this?" he called out.

"Yes, we see it," called one of the new mercenaries in a British accent, standing at the pilothouse deck rail right above him.

Besides himself and Olivia on the vessel was a contingent of five very large armed-to-the-teeth fellows who had been helicoptered in.

They were Vance's newest hires. All Brits, all former SAS to a man.

Frank had skedaddled on their arriving helicopter.

He had other matters to attend to, he had said.

"Looks like a speedboat," the Brit above him, who the others called Captain Charles, called down. "Writing on the prow is *A... M...*"

"Who gives a shit," Shaw said. "That's him. How many on the boat?"

"Just one, it looks like. A man on the flying bridge. A white man."

"Are you sure about that?"

"Positive," Captain Charles said. "Unless he's in white face or something."

"No, you moron. I mean that he's alone."

"Yes. Just the one."

Shaw thought about that.

340

"Make sure. This guy is no joke, Captain Charles."

Captain Charles was actually no joke either. He was about six foot four or five and had to tip the scales at about three hundred pounds, most of it thick muscle. Many black Cockney-accented Londoners were laid-back, but he seemed quite the opposite.

"Thanks for the tip," Captain Charles said.

88

The powerboat I rented out of East Hampton was a 10K a day Deep Impact 399 center console that could truly haul.

But compared to the high-tech-looking super yacht I full throttled toward, it was like a goldfish approaching a whale.

Frank's boat was one heck of a ship. Dark gray steel hull, three decks, a front bow high and sharp as the business end of a cleaver. It had an industrial, almost military, vibe to it like it could break ice or maybe even shell a harbor. It had to be almost two hundred feet.

With a lift of my binoculars, I counted four large mercenaries on the second pilothouse deck and then a fifth. Two of them were pointing binoculars right back in my direction.

Then I saw another guy standing along the back rail of the bottom deck in the rear part of the yacht known as the "sole." A tall guy who gave me a wave. He seemed to be pointing binoculars back at me as well.

It was the drill sergeant mercenary I'd spoken to. I'd bet money on it. Dude looked like a Green Beret.

I didn't wave back. In the shadow of the second deck behind him, I could see a young woman sitting at an outdoor table. I looked at her arms pulled back behind her. Probably cuffed, but not to anything that I could see.

I looked at her face. It was Olivia. She seemed freaked out, of course, but healthy, alert, unharmed. She also didn't look drugged or anything as far as I could tell.

I took a deep breath and checked my watch.

"Good," I said to myself. "Good."

As I motored in to around fifty yards, two of the four men on the top deck lifted long guns to their shoulders. The fifth one, a tall muscled bull of a black dude, lifted a bullhorn.

"STAY WHERE YOU ARE! POWER DOWN YOUR ENGINE AND DROP ANCHOR OR BE SHOT!" he yelled.

I nodded with enthusiasm as I immediately dialed back on the throttle.

They'd already brought the yacht in bumper tight by the time my anchor finished dropping. Standing on my main deck, I stared across at a large heartless-looking dude on the other side of his port gunwale.

Balding and pale, the guy had a slight resemblance to the '80s singer Phil Collins. But he didn't look like he was in the mood to sing a catchy love song. He was pointing a Benelli twelve-gauge tactical shotgun at my chest.

"Don't shoot," I said to the man with a wide smile. "I come in peace."

Two more pale mercenaries appeared. They helped me over both gunwales, none too gently.

As I was deposited safely on board the beautiful yacht, the gigantic black dude arrived.

"Who else is on your boat?" he said.

His British accent surprised me.

"Nobody. Just me."

"You better hope so," he said, shoving me up against the wall.

The wide, smiling, tall Green Beret dude appeared to the left at the end of the starboard beam aisle as I was thoroughly frisked.

I smiled back in the soft gust of the breeze as I was led to the stern deck.

As I came into the sole, I glanced at Olivia in the shadow under the deck overhang. Her face was blank as she glanced back at me.

I quickly scanned the deck. To the left of the banquette that Olivia was sitting on was a set of stairs that led up to the pilot-house deck, and on her right was the closed door to the interior cabin.

"Noon on the button," Shaw said as I stepped across the teak. "I like punctuality in a man."

As we sat, I noticed the yacht moving away from my rental. You could barely hear the engines. It motored over about fifty yards to the north and then I heard the faint engines go to idle again.

What a boat, I thought again.

"Would you please give us some privacy?" the Green Beret said to the black Brit mercenary, who was still standing there, staring at me like he wanted to murder me.

"Don't worry, Mr. Shaw. I won't go too far," the big Brit said.

89

"Mr. Shaw, is it? Where do you get your help, Mr. Shaw?" I said as the large man and his two lackeys walked back up the aisle toward the bow. "There isn't one I've met so far that I've liked."

"Beats me," Shaw said. "I just work here."

"Where's Frank?" I said.

"He had other business to attend to."

"Cowards always do," I said.

Shaw smiled.

I looked around the beautifully appointed craft. It had to have a beam of what? Forty feet? I thought. There had to be multiple thousands of square feet of interior cabin. Half a dozen staterooms below deck. It was like a floating mansion.

"Look at the three of us," Shaw said. "Is there anything better than enjoying a day out on the water?"

"Not in my book," I said.

"What do you think, Olivia? Having fun?"

The college girl said nothing.

"She doesn't talk much," Shaw said. "Just like her old man. The silent type."

Olivia looked at him.

"Oh, wait," Shaw said. "Did I forget to tell you? I killed your father."

Even my eyes went wide at that one. He'd killed her dad? Colleen's client who'd been in jail?

"Bullshit," I said.

"'Fraid not," Shaw said. "I strangled him at his shit box in Washington Heights. No client no case, right?"

Olivia started to shake. Silent tears started to pour down her cheeks.

"Look, she even cries quiet," Shaw said. "Remarkable."

He looked back at me.

"So, what are we doing here?" he said.

I took out a thumb drive, flicked it across the table.

Shaw took out a tablet and stuck it in, hit some buttons. He watched Jodi's video twice.

I looked at the sociopath's face for some emotion as he viewed. There was nothing at all.

"You weren't kidding. That's some damning tape there," Shaw finally said after he was done.

He laid the tablet down on the highly varnished outdoor table between them.

"But where's the rest? The blackmail from the college."

I tossed him the padlock key.

"All the servers are in a storage locker in East Hampton. Address and locker number is on the fob."

"Right on the fob. Gee, thoughtful. Thanks," Shaw said with a chuckle. "But you have other copies of this footage, right?"

He began tapping the table beside the tablet with a finger.

I smiled. There was a sudden grayish tint in the air as a cloud slipped over the sun. I kept smiling.

"Of course, I do. But only for insurance. Once you let us go, you won't have to worry about it."

"I have to disagree there," Shaw said. "What's to stop you from sending it out when you leave here with her?"

"The knowledge that guys like you with your now almost complete global surveillance grid will never stop hunting us down," I said.

"What's to stop us from doing that anyway?"

I shrugged.

"Why bother if you get what you need. Even if we went to the press with the footage, they wouldn't even show it. You guys got that covered, too."

Shaw drummed his fingers on the tabletop.

"You killed my guys."

"How many people did you kill?" I said. "And you destroyed a town."

Shaw squinted, considering what I was saying. Then he brought a small Glock out of his pant's pocket as he stood, pointing the gun at my forehead.

"You can't be this stupid," I said, looking at him with genuine surprise.

Shaw laughed.

"You shouldn't have killed my buddies. They were like sons to me."

"Were they? Wow, that's touching," I said, checking my watch as I leaned back. "Don't make me laugh. As if you ever cared about anyone but yourself your whole life."

Shaw laughed again.

"You've got balls, I'll give you that," he said. "Ice cubes of extra-large size. I promise I'll use them ethically, for chum, when I go fishing later for swords when Frank helicopters back."

I shook my head as I checked my watch again.

"You're a real piece of work, Shaw. It's not your fault. You're human, I guess. You don't learn. Some people just can't."

"What do you mean?"

I checked my watch again.

"If you've got some place to be," Shaw said, "you probably should call ahead because, believe me, your plans have changed."

"Shaw, I told you I was a bomb squad guy, right? Well, before that I was a SEAL. You know the *navy* SEALs?"

"And?" he said.

"What do SEALs do, Shaw?"

"Cowboy around like obnoxious jackasses? Die young?"

"Besides that, we do underwater demolition, Shaw," I said.

I watched as a puzzled expression formed on his face.

"What if I told you," I said, "that when I called Frank Stone, it was from behind this boat, after I was done."

"Done?"

"You'll see. Any second now. It's just about time," I said with a laugh as I looked over at Olivia and smiled.

"Time?" he said.

I leaned over casually and hooked my hand in under Olivia's left arm where it was handcuffed behind her.

"Time for you and time for me," I said as I lifted my wrist and watched the second hand on my watch finally land with a deafening blast.

90

As the center of the ship's hull suddenly exploded, I felt an almost pleasant carnival ride sensation as Olivia and I and the table were flung upward by the blast wave that shuddered through the deck.

In the detonation's ear-ringing aftermath, I found myself and Olivia standing by the second deck stairs, getting rained on by the deluge of falling seawater that had been blown skyward.

When I turned, I saw Shaw was down on his ass in the port corner of the sole, trying to move the heavy table that was now flipped over on top of him.

Then I was moving, pulling Olivia by the arm up the wet stairs to the pilothouse deck.

The first thing I saw at the top of the stairs was that the teak floor of the second deck was littered with shattered glass and splintered wood. The second was that the Phil Collins look-alike was in the pilothouse doorway on all fours moaning.

Ignoring the dropped shotgun on the deck to the man's right,

I grabbed the man by the back of his belt and the back of his shirt and heaved him to his feet and threw him over the starboard rail.

I had lifted the shotgun and had just turned toward the stairs as the gigantic black dude appeared at the top of them. The big man very wisely dropped out of sight as I blew a gaping hole through the stairwell side gunwale where his face had just been.

"What now?" Olivia yelled.

I dropped the shotgun and tore off my right Converse low top and ripped free the handcuff key I'd taped to the bottom of my foot. I unlocked Olivia's handcuffs and dropped them clattering to the deck.

"This boat's going down. Jump, Olivia!" I yelled as I helped her over the starboard rail into the water.

I was up on the rail myself about to jump in after her when there was a tremendous groan of complaining metal and the sinking boat suddenly rocked back hard to port.

I yelled as I lost my balance and fell skidding across the tilted teak deck on my back like a shuffleboard puck.

The pain that exploded through the back of my skull as I suddenly came to an abrupt stop was incredible. I'd bashed the ever-living shit out of the back of my head against one of the steel posts of the port side rail, I realized groggily.

Sitting there stunned with my ears ringing, I could feel the rocking ship continuing to sink.

I looked forward as the blast-rocked boat teetered from side to side. Alarms were going off everywhere in the pilothouse, and to the port side of the vessel rose thick black smoke.

Holy shit, I thought as I noticed that the rolling deck was already descending. With its hull thoroughly blown to smithereens, I could feel the several million-pound steel vessel lowering slowly and steadily into the Atlantic like a coffin into a grave.

As I sat there blinking stupidly around me, one part of me knew how incredibly important it was for me to get the hell on the move. But another part of me was saying in my head like a calm voice, *No, just a second. Just give it a second. Catch your breath. Catch your breath.*

I was still unwisely listening to the deadly calming voice when I noticed some movement to my right.

I looked up and sat blinking amazed.

Shaw, wild-eyed, now stood at the top of the listing deck steps beside me.

Then he was kneeling down, straddling me and wrapping his big meaty hands around my throat.

91

"Die, die, die!" Shaw chanted through clenched teeth as he throttled me with surprising strength.

My throat burned as my eyes bulged. From my training, I knew there was a grappling trick to break an opponent's grip while being strangled. But with my concussion reeling through my already half-shut-off mind and 270 crushing pounds sitting on my chest, I couldn't quite remember it.

After a moment I began to gray out.

No, no, no. Not like this, I thought as I began to flail with my hands out to my sides to maybe push off the deck or the rail.

When my left hand found the thin curve of cold hard metal on the wood of the deck by my left leg, at first, I didn't know what it was.

Then my eyes lit up.

Water was coming in over the sinking yacht's rail onto my back as I reached up and clicked Olivia's dropped handcuff cinch tight around Shaw's left wrist.

The cold sea was suddenly there rolling over the rail, rolling over the deck, rolling over the both of us.

Then I slid to my right and clicked the other end of the cuff to the sinking ship's steel rail.

I snorted stinging salt water down the back of my already gagging throat as the sea closed over my face.

As we both became completely submerged a second later, I felt Shaw's grip on my neck slip.

I finally managed to snake my right hand up in between Shaw's forearms and I felt the grip loosen some more as I hammer-punched Shaw once and then twice in the chest.

It was only when I stiff-armed the bastard hard in the soft of his throat with the edge of my palm that he finally let go of me completely.

Then I was sliding out from underneath him, moving away to my left.

I quickly found the deck rail and had just put my foot on the top of it to kick myself free of the sinking vessel when I felt something seize my ankle.

I looked down.

With one outstretched hand cuffed to the rail of the huge sinking ship and the other outstretched one clutched onto my ankle, Shaw looked like a man playing an extremely desperate game of electricity tag.

My eyes narrowed as I brought up my free leg hard and aimed it and then I brought it down even harder.

I felt Shaw's grip break simultaneously with his nose as I smashed my heel into his smug face with everything I had.

Finally free, I looked up toward the surface now twenty feet above me and began to breast-stroke.

Even though my lungs were bursting, just as I was about to break the surface, I turned and looked down into the water one final time.

In all my life, I would never forget that ghostly image of Shaw and the now completely submerged multimillion-dollar steel yacht he was handcuffed to sliding away slowly, deeper and deeper down into the bottomless Atlantic.

It looked surreal, I thought, otherworldly.

Especially Shaw.

Because in that last moment, the mercenary no longer appeared to be a drowning psycho killer.

Instead, he suddenly seemed to be a legendary captain from a children's story, a happy, intrepid, magical nautical adventurer, frantically bon voyaging as he set underwater sail toward new lands twenty thousand leagues under the sea.

92

After I returned the powerboat to the dock in East Hampton where Colleen was waiting, the three of us headed to an Airbnb I had rented in Bay Shore.

Olivia was in no condition to do much of anything, so we just tried to make her feel as comfortable as possible at the house. She did manage a small smile when Colleen showed her the new clothes we had bought for her.

There was no way to imagine the hell she had been through. Beaten, kidnapped, trafficked. Victims of this abuse were no different than veterans with PTSD. It would be years before she felt like herself if she was lucky.

It was around six when we finally got back to the city in my pickup. We were going to reunite Olivia with her mother at her place in the Bronx. Which was going to be a challenge to say the least as the woman, like the rest of us, had thought Olivia had been dead for the last year.

As we came into the Bronx over the Whitestone Bridge, I

looked out at Manhattan's famous skyline to my left, lit up in an orange sunset haze. Then I looked back at Olivia to see that she was crying.

"Olivia, listen," Colleen said. "The stuff you've been through has nothing to do with you. It was done *to* you. You're innocent. It's the men who hurt you who are bad. Not you."

Olivia looked at me in the mirror.

"But my poor father," she said. "I got my father killed."

"No, no, no," I said. "You've got it all wrong, Olivia. It's the other way around. Your dad died to save you. Your dad was the one who led us to you. He started this whole thing."

"What?" she said. "What do you mean?"

"Mike's right," Colleen said to her. "The school and that bastard, Frank Stone, tried to pay your father off to leave it alone. They offered him half a million dollars to go away. He wouldn't do it. He didn't care about the money. He wasn't going to stop until he got answers.

"If it wasn't for your dad," Colleen said, "I wouldn't have been up here investigating and we would never have found you. He was the one, Olivia. Your dad saved you. It was your dad."

"It was?" Olivia said, rubbing at her eyes.

"Olivia, I'm a dad," I said. "Do you know how happy your father is right now that you made it out? He succeeded. He won."

"Exactly," Colleen said. "He beat these bastards. He never gave up hope. Now you get to live your life. I know it's hard and things are going to hurt for a long time, but you need to try to be happy. It's what your dad wanted. The only thing he wanted for you."

We got on the Cross Bronx Expressway and took it to the Major Deegan north and got off at the exit for Fordham Road. The apartment where Olivia lived with her mom was on a hilly street called Loring Place North.

"Right here," she said, pointing at an old brick walk-up with a rusting fire escape.

I pulled in at the hydrant in front and Colleen got out with Olivia to ring the buzzer. They rang a few times and nothing happened so they headed back to the truck. Just then a man came out and stood in the building's garbage way next to the front door. It was an older Spanish guy in a sheepskin-lined denim jacket. Olivia seemed to recognize him.

"That's my mom's super, Ralph. I'll ask him if he's seen my mom," Olivia said.

I looked down Loring as Colleen and I waited in the truck. It gave a nice view of a park on the other side of Fordham Road.

"I know this area," I said to Colleen. "Tolentine is around here, right? I went to summer school there after freshman year of high school. At the lunch break, we—er I mean some of the bad kids—used to sneak bodega beers in that park."

"The bad kids, huh?" Colleen said, looking at me. "You have to watch out for those bad kids."

Olivia walked back over and got into the truck.

"He says she's not here. She's at St. Nicholas of Tolentine Church. It's just around the corner."

"Mike knows where it is," Colleen said as I put it in Drive.

"Really? How?" Olivia said.

"He had to go to confession there once, right, Mike?" Colleen said, smiling.

We were at the corner about to make the turn when it happened.

Olivia leaped out the back door.

On the corner there was a laundromat and in front of it was a short black-haired woman with blue eye shadow. She almost fell down as Olivia all but tackled her. She was holding a bag of groceries but as we watched, she dropped them as she pulled Olivia to her.

"You think she's going to be okay?" Colleen said as the mom and daughter wept together in front of the laundromat.

"I don't know," I said. "But we got her home."

EPILOGUE

NO PLACE LIKE HOME

93

My burner phone rang when Colleen had just headed off to the ladies'.

"Dad! There you are," my son said. "I've been calling and calling. It kept kicking into your voice mail."

"Oh, now you want to call me, huh?" I said, smiling. "How's that for a switch. What about the time zones, son?"

"Very funny," Declan said. "How are you? How's the fishing?"

"Oh, it's okay, I suppose," I said as I saw Colleen heading back. "Pretty boring. Just fishing, you know."

"*Just* fishing? Are you feeling okay, Dad? You have a fever or something? How come you haven't called?"

"Son, I love you," I said as Colleen finally made it back to her barstool beside me. "But I have to hang up now."

Colleen and I both turned to watch the bartender pop the champagne I had ordered.

It was well into the evening now and we were where I always

go when I send hundred-million-dollar yachts to the bottom of the ocean, the Landmark Tavern in the Hell's Kitchen neighborhood of Manhattan.

I pulled out the barstool for Colleen.

"What a gentleman you are," she said.

"But of course," I said.

Now that everything was squared away, it was finally time for Colleen and me to have our date. I had chosen the Landmark as I had celebrated many a case closed in the famous Irish hangout when I was a cop. It was dark, the food was great, the beer was cold and The Pogues were serenading down from the former speakeasy's tin ceiling.

If this wasn't the ultimate place to trip the light fantastic on the streets of old Irish New York, what was?

Shaw didn't know what he was missing, I thought as I handed Colleen her glass of Dom Pérignon. It beat Davy Jones's locker. That was for sure.

"To Jodi," I said, clinking my glass to hers.

"To Jodi," Colleen said.

I got a text then. It was a picture.

A cute, little, smiling three-year-old in a pink Red Sox cap. I showed it to Colleen.

"Mathias's daughter!" she said.

I texted back.

No one messes with the Iron Norwegian!

#followthefrogman he texted back.

"Speaking of my frogmanning skills," I said. "It was a flawless demo, wasn't it? That ship was a couple of million pounds. I wasn't sure how long it would take to sink, but when that RDX charge I planted on her hull went off she went down like an oversugared toddler at naptime, didn't she?"

"Where the hell did you get this, um, RDX, if you don't mind me asking?"

"From my truck, of course."

"Oh, naturally. Beside the spare tire, I bet. How do you think this guy Stone is going to take you sinking his boat?" Colleen said.

"Colleen, I was a SEAL and a cop for too many years to count. I've banged heads with so many dangerous dirtbags, I've honestly lost count. You think I'm going to lose sleep over some Wall Street child pimp?

"And this company, Vance Holdings? I doubt that they want to send any more mercenaries my way. They have to have life insurance up the ying-yang. I think they've had enough of their premiums going up. In fact, you know it's funny. The only one out of them all who showed any real cowboy grit was that Chief Garner."

"Garner?" Colleen said. "Why him?"

"He tried to take me out with his hands tied behind his back."

Colleen laughed.

"It didn't work out, but come on, give the man a ten for cockiness and confidence. He went down with style."

"You're, um... I'm struggling to come up with the word. An actual certified nutcase?"

I lifted my champagne and looked at it.

"It's not me that's gone crazy, Colleen. It's the world. Like all good cops and soldiers, I just adjust my tactics to the terrain."

"What will you do now?"

"I'm going to buy a new truck and then since it's getting colder, I'm probably going to head down south to do some fishing."

"I see," she said. "You know, Mike, after all this I was thinking of taking a leave of absence and getting out of the city for a little while myself."

"Is that right?" I said with a smile.

"Yes," she said.

"Have you ever thought of a road trip?" I said.

"I have actually."

"One that involves fishing and drinking beer?" I said.

"Yes, actually," Colleen said. "You wouldn't want to give this girl a ride, would you?"

I looked at her, at her angel eyes staring back into mine.

Then I stood as The Pogues were replaced by U2's "One." I held out my open arms to her.

"Colleen Doherty," I said.

"Yes, Michael Gannon," she said as she stood herself.

"May I have this dance?" I said.

★ ★ ★ ★ ★